MAX HELSING

AND THE BEAST OF BONE CREEK

Read all Curtis Jobling's series!

MAX HELSING

Max Helsing and the Thirteenth Curse

WEREWORLD

Rise of the Wolf
Rage of Lions
Shadow of the Hawk
Nest of Serpents
Storm of Sharks
War of the Werelords

MAX HELSING

AND THE BEAST OF BONE CREEK

CURTIS JOBLING

VIKING

VIKING
An imprint of Penguin Random House LLC
375 Hudson Street
New York, New York 10014

First published in the United States of America by Viking,
an imprint of Penguin Random House LLC, 2016

LIBRARY OF CONGRESS CATALOGING-IN-PUBLICATION DATA IS AVAILABLE
ISBN: 9780451474803

Printed in U.S.A.

1   3   5   7   9   10   8   6   4   2

Designed by Kate Renner   Set in Droid Serif Pro

For Andrew Eaves—furry cousin, fossil collector, and fellow cryptozoologist.

PROLOGUE

xxx

THE MERMAID OF THE MYSTIC RIVER

The fisherman sat on the end of the jetty, huddled beneath his blanket, the hulking behemoth of the Tobin Bridge straddling the night skyline at his back. With its green painted girders lit up, the cantilever crossing dominated this corner of Boston, towering over the rolling waters of the Mystic River. The blood, sweat, and toil of good and honest Massachusetts men had gone into the bridge's construction in the 1940s. If there was a greater piece of engineering, or more handsome man-made structure, Henry Fitzpatrick hadn't seen it. Fitz might have been biased, of course, as his father and uncles had helped build it.

He hunkered down in his deck chair, a rod on either side of him, both set upon their rests. The lines disappeared into the darkness, out onto the water, the fluorescent markers on the nylon quivering in the breeze. If there was a bite, the elderly angler would see it. He checked them over. The one on the left, fine. The one on the right, fine. His feet were up, resting on the cooler, a trio of empty brown beer bottles stacked neatly beside it. Beneath the deck chair, his bulldog slumbered, snoring to his heart's content.

"Fine company you are, Shamrock."

The sound of traffic passing over the Tobin Bridge was a gentle reminder to Fitz that he wasn't the only soul awake at that ungodly hour. Not so long ago, there would've been company for him, up and down the wharf, other night fishermen sharing the river. Those days were gone. Fitz was the only one who remained, the only one who hadn't been scared off.

He glanced up at the moon, full and white overhead. He'd been warned by the gang in the bar not to go, to head home to his wife, Maggie, but Fitz wouldn't hear it. Not that he was averse to spending time with Maggie, of course, but Fitz was at his happiest on the jetty, and everyone knew it, even Maggie. The lure of the river was in his blood, as it had been in his father's, and his father's before him. Fitz checked the lines. Left, fine. Right, fine.

The folk who lived around the docks, who'd worked there all their lives, were a fearful bunch. Gullible, in Fitz's opinion. Two poor saps had gone missing over the previous full moons, so naturally the superstitious said this was the mermaid's mischief at work, luring the men to a watery grave with her siren voice. The Mermaid of the Mystic River. Fitz chuckled. Utter hokum. The two men had simply had one too many ales and walked off the wharf to their watery graves. They wouldn't be the first fools to get washed away down the Mystic.

Fitz reached down and opened his cooler, removing a fresh bottle of beer. He cracked the cap off, flicking it into the tide, a dozen feet below. It spun through the air, reflecting the moonlight before it plopped into the waves. He tipped the bottle back, taking a hearty swig, his eyes glancing at the rods. The one on the left, fine. The one on the right, bowing, flexing, the fluorescent marker humming on the line.

He placed the bottle down carefully, reaching across to take the rod off its stand. He stood and braced his feet on the rough timbers of the jetty, hand gripping the reel. He'd been here for three hours and this was the first nibble of the night. It was almost as if, until now, the fish had been scared away. Striped bass was what he was after, and his stomach was rumbling already as he imagined one cooked in butter and lemon. What a treat that would be for tomorrow's dinner. He wound the reel in.

The bulldog was awake now, whimpering beneath the chair.

"What's the matter, Shamrock? Get out here, ya lazy mutt."

The dog didn't come, instead knocking the deck chair over as he backed away fearfully.

"C'mere, ya dumb dog," snapped Fitz, irked by Shamrock's sudden and unexpected cowardice. The bulldog scampered down the wharf, abandoning his master. The rod suddenly yanked hard, almost shooting out of Fitz's grasp. The angler was an old hand and a canny fisherman, though, and he quickly struck back, cranking the reel.

"Big fish, are ya? That's fine by Fitz. The more bass for my plate," he snarled, grinning as he wound in the line.

"You might want to let this one go."

The voice came from the shadows at his back. Fitz half turned, not wanting to take his eyes off the bowing rod and taut nylon. A boy was walking forward, some young punk who was clearly lost and more than a bit deluded if he thought he could tell old Fitz how to fish. His drainpipe jeans had seen better days, his Chucks were so dirty they could've walked away by themselves, and if Fitz wasn't mistaken, he was carrying a lady's handbag across his shoulder.

"Who the hell are you?"

"Me?" said the kid in the bomber jacket and ratty jeans. "I'm your new best friend."

MAX HELSING WATCHED AS THE OLD MAN CONTINUED to wind in his catch, struggling and straining. The fisherman wasn't listening to the boy's sage words of advice. This was nothing new. Folk of most ages seemed more than ready to disregard what the thirteen-year-old had to say. He was obviously kicking off the wrong vibe, one that said pimply teenager as opposed to kick-ass monster hunter. The bulldog had the right idea. The hound was probably downtown by now.

As he leaned over the wharf edge and took a peek at the

choppy waters below, the battling old man raised an eyebrow at him. The fishing line was vertical now, pointed straight down, as it cut one way and then the other through the water.

"Okay, I'm no fisherman, but I *do* know you're fishing for bass. And I also know bass are about . . . yea big." Max made the shape with his hands. "I don't think you've got a bass on the end of your line, dude."

"Like I said, who the hell are you?"

Max was rummaging around inside his messenger bag. "That's not important, but what *is* important—"

"Is that a purse you're carrying?"

"Purse? Really? I like to think of it as my manbag." Max shook his head and pulled his hand out of the messenger bag. "What I was *trying* to tell you before you so rudely interrupted was that you might wanna stick these in your ears."

He held out a pair of wax earplugs, placing them atop the cooler.

"Will it mean I don't hear your voice?" grunted the man, wincing as he cranked hard on the reel.

"Probably, but more important, it'll save your life."

The man's laugh was sarcastic. "Get lost, ya little jerk. A man's at work here."

Max sighed with regret and popped his own plugs into his ears. "Ditto."

He leaned back over the side just as the "catch" emerged from the briny water. Max had been following this story from a distance for three months now. Local legend had always said there was a mermaid in the Mystic River. There was some truth to the story, of course, but this was no mermaid. It was a selkie, an ancient creature that had followed the Irish immigrants across the Atlantic centuries ago. Romantic folklore told that they looked like seals beneath the waves, but when they emerged from the water, they transformed into enchanting humans. The truth was far more grim. This particular selkie had been putting in appearances every three decades, regular as clockwork, rising for three full moons to feed before vanishing back into the deep. If it failed to feed on each of these nights, it would starve. It seemed to Max that a selkie's life was a bit of a cursed existence. Though Max felt sympathy for it, he wasn't eager for any more humans to be slaughtered. Tonight was Max's last chance to send the selkie packing.

The creature that emerged from the Mystic bucked and writhed on the end of the line as the fisherman continued to winch it in. It was never going to win a beauty pageant. Its head was bald with bumpy ridges, a pair of large pale eyes glowing like head lamps. The monster's mouth was wide and drooping, like that of a grouper, with jagged needle teeth jutting out from all angles. Max could see its throat flexing, wobbling, as a frog's might when it croaks. The beast was singing, Max realized, and he was relieved to be wearing his plugs—the song of the selkie was its principal weapon, and the way it bewitched sailors and fishermen.

SELKIE

AKA: selchie, Finwife, mermaid, siren

ORIGIN: Scotland, Ireland, Orkney, Shetland, and Faroe Isles

STRENGTHS: Great speed and agility in water, bewitching song.

WEAKNESSES: Prolonged exposure to air, low intelligence.

HABITAT: Predominantly the coastal waters of the Irish and North Seas, and east Atlantic Ocean.

The selkie of romantic legend spends its time at sea in the form of a seal, transforming into a human when on land. In fact, this carnivorous beast spends most of its life feeding upon fish and seabirds, but once every three decades, by the light of the full moon, will seek out man to feast upon. Only the flesh of humans gives the selkie its preternaturally long life-span—failure to dine in this manner will grant it a lingering, painful death by starvation. BEWARE the Song of the Selkie, for this is its greatest weapon!
— Erik Van Helsing, February 27th, 1852

PHYSICAL TRAITS

1. <u>Extremely Large Eyes</u>—Adapted for seeing in darkness.

2. <u>Saberteeth</u>—These curved teeth prevent captured meals from escaping.

3. <u>Song of the Selkie</u>—The selkie's musical song can enchant its victims, this thrall effectively convincing prospective meals that the selkie is a beautiful object of attraction rather than a hideous aquatic killer.

—Esme Van Helsing, November 1st, 1864

"The Mermaid of the Mystic River"

Reports local to Boston, Massachusetts, of a vengeful selkie having followed Irish families across the Atlantic. Two sets of abductions, thirty years apart, suggest there may be some truth in this. To Be Investigated.

—Algernon Van Helsing, June 22nd, 1935

RE: Mystic River
It's on the <u>TO-DO LIST</u>! Take earplugs to combat the power of the selkie's song—it can't be worse than Jed's snoring!

MAX HELSING

Oct 11th, 2014

Two humanoid arms ended with webbed hands and taloned fingers, while its lower torso was that of a serpentine fish, ending in a great tail that twisted and thrashed at the water. Its flesh had the pale greenish-gray pallor of a corpse that had been found after floating in the sea for days. The hook wasn't in the monster's mouth, of course; it was clenched in one of those grotesque hands, the line wrapped around its puckered forearm intentionally. It had meant to be caught. It wanted the man to haul it ashore. It needed the man's assistance if it was meant to feed.

"Okay, fishsticks," said Max, waving at the selkie from above as the fisherman reeled it in, ever higher. "Here's how it has to be. I'm afraid you're done snacking from the Boston All-You-Can-Eat Human Buffet. The restaurant is now closed. I'm giving you one chance to turn tail and disappear back to Atlantis, or wherever the heck it is you've come from."

Although the monster was warbling its hideous ballad, its eyes narrowed when it spied Max, its teeth gnashing as it rose closer to the wharf.

"Guess that's a no on the skedaddling, then?" said Max, straightening up and turning to the man. He was about to ask for help, but quickly realized it was futile. Twin rivulets of blood dribbled from the old angler's ears, while his eyes were pale and glassy, utterly entranced. Max shook him violently, trying to dislodge the rod from the fisherman's hands, but it was hopeless. The boy flipped open his messenger bag's flap, rooting inside for a knife to cut the line. Without that connection, the beast couldn't rise the twelve feet out of the river to feed. It would be doomed to go without, and would (hopefully) starve. Just as Max's hand closed around his pocketknife, he felt teeth clamp around his ankle. He cried out, looking down, expecting to find the selkie feasting on his foot. Instead, he found the little bulldog, returned to defend his put-upon master from Max. As the fisherman continued winding the monster in, the dog snarled, worrying the boy's drainpipe jeans, which ripped and frayed. Having Eightball, Max's own dog, with him right now would have been helpful—especially since he was a hellhound—but Max was alone on this one.

He shook off the dog, who bounced away then came straight back. This time he leaped, jaws snapping around the messenger bag and dragging it down to the ground. The knife went loose inside the satchel as Max hit the deck, the strap came free, and the bulldog danced away with the bag in his mouth.

"Crapsacks!" shouted Max, as the selkie's head appeared over the side of the wharf, its webbed, clawed fingers now gripping the timbers as it let go of the hook and the line.

Max scrambled forward to the empty beer bottles. One, two, three; they whipped through the air, striking the selkie in the head and splitting the ghoulish flesh. The injuries hardly spoiled the creature's good looks. It reached out, grabbing Max's foot and biting down hard. Its needle teeth punctured the tread of his Chucks.

"What *is* it with my *feet*?" he screeched, booting the river monster in the face.

The boy's hands went into the cooler, grabbing full bottles of beer now and sending them at the selkie. The creature ignored the barrage, crawling ever closer, claws digging into the decking. The cooler lid was the next thing to hit the beast, buckling as Max smashed it over the selkie's ridged, knuckled skull. Its mouth opened wide as it wailed in agony. Max could feel one of his earplugs coming loose. He jammed the cooler lid into its open jaws and then snatched up the loose coils of fishing line. He rolled over the monster, wrapping the line about the creature's neck in quick succession, three times in all. He yanked back hard.

The selkie shrieked and gurgled, big white eyes swelling wide like they might pop. Max cried out as he pulled with all his might, feeling the strong nylon cord cut into the flesh of his hands and fingers. The selkie's great fish tail flapped and slapped, striking the timber jetty as it gasped in vain for breath. One last cry from Max as the line reached breaking point, and there was a wet ripping sound, like piano wire going through an overripe cucumber. He felt the cord give as it sliced through the monster's neck. The selkie's head rolled away, the white light ebbing in those dreadful eyes as its black blood washed across the wharf.

The fisherman came to suddenly, shaking his head,

looking down in horror at the monstrosity from the deep that lay at his feet and the boy from Gallows Hill Middle School lying across its decapitated corpse. His bulldog trotted up and began to lap at the pool of oily fish blood.

"Bass is off the menu, I'm afraid, sir," said Max, anchoring his chewed-up Chucks on the dock as he clambered to his feet.

"Have you ever tried sushi?"

ONE

xxx

DON'T FORGET YOUR TOOTHBRUSH

"Are you sure you have everything?" Jed asked for the hundredth time.

"Yes," lied Max as he dashed past the old-timer in his La-Z-Boy. "I'm not some dingbat, you know?"

Of course, Max had left everything until the last minute. The selkie gig on the Mystic River had been a welcome distraction from Jed's never-ending nagging. Now, on the morning of departure, he was breathing down Max's neck (from the comfort of his recliner). Max slipped into his bedroom, out of the old man's line of sight.

"Eightball!"

It was bad enough that the hellhound was on Max's bed—his bedroom was a strictly no-go zone for the demonic pooch due to the sulfurous gases that emanated from his behind. The rotund puppy's head was buried within Max's backpack, merrily rooting through whatever the teenager had already packed. Max knew instantly what his puppy was after.

"Get outta there," Max growled, giving Eightball's shiny black bottom a playful but firm smack. The dog's head emerged, the contents of Max's emergency Twinkie stash smeared across his slobbering chops. With a clap of hands, the cream-splattered dog was bouncing off the bed and departing the room. Jed didn't even try to hide his laughter. Max shook his head, returning his belongings to the bag. It was bulging by the time he'd finished. Hefting it across one shoulder, he tramped back into the living room.

"Sweet spawn of Shug, what have you got in there, boy?" exclaimed Jed, rising half out of his chair as Max passed back by. "The kitchen sink?"

"You always said I should be prepared," said Max, slamming his backpack down onto the kitchenette counter.

"Yeah, prepared for all eventualities. Not the Armageddon."

"Sometimes, that's the same thing."

Jed pulled out his pocket watch and flipped it open. "You'd better shake a tail feather. You need a ride to school?"

"No, Syd's mom is picking me up. The bus doesn't leave until eight."

Max flipped open the kitchen cupboards, on one last raid for essential provisions. The five major food groups were covered: Cheetos, Hershey bars, gummy worms, Mountain Dew, and Combos. He crammed them into the top of the backpack and pulled the drawstring tight. All the while

Eightball sat at his feet, stumpy tail thwacking the ground as if he might earn another treat. His goggle eyes blinked imploringly, one facing Boston, the other Salem.

"You've blown it, dude," said Max, patting the pooch on the head and deftly dodging a lick in the process. "You want food, go to Jed. If you're *really* unlucky, you'll get some homemade clam chowder."

Jed rose from his chair and stretched, before limping across to the bookshelf. His hands flitted across the spines of the books as he peeked over the rims of his half-moon spectacles. His fingertips stopped as he found what he was looking for.

"Whatcha got there?" asked Max. *"Rheingard's Daemon Guide? Tales of the Undercity?"*

Jed tossed the pamphlet onto the counter.

Max peered at it suspiciously. *"Things to See & Do in the White Mountains?* Hardly *Goblin Slaying 101,* is it?"

"That part of New Hampshire's something else. You should read that and get to know the place before you get there. Real scenic. It was always a popular place for courting couples. Spent some time up there in my youth."

Max whistled as he flicked through the brochure before shoving it into a side pocket on his pack. "Hard to imagine."

"Me courting?"

"You being young."

Jed let that one go. "It's a magical place. You've got canoeing, rafting, swimming, hiking, climbing, waterfalls . . ."

Max stepped over Eightball and opened the closet door,

reaching past brooms, mops, and a brutal-looking morning star to get to his bomber jacket. "Do they pay you commission straight into your bank account, or do you get a brown envelope once a month?"

"I hope you're taking a slicker as well? That old jacket won't suffice if the heavens open. It can rain like nowhere else up there."

"I thought you said it was a magical place?" Max replied, donning the bomber and then lifting the pack onto his back. He clicked the belt around his waist. "You're not selling this to me."

"Compass? Hiking boots?"

"Packed."

"Flashlight?"

"Can I take yours?"

"Think again, kiddo. That was a gift from a very special lady. Crucifix, stakes, and wolfsbane?"

"This is a school trip, Jed."

"Regardless, you know what kind of world it is out there. There's the world the norms inhabit; then there's the one below the surface, the one that we must walk in. Just because you're out in the wilderness on an Outward Bound trip, that don't make things any less dangerous."

"I'm heading to New Hampshire. It's hardly Alaska."

"The White Mountains are mighty pretty; just stay on your toes. Don't relax *too* much. Monsters are everywhere, remember?"

Of course, Max never left home without having his

monster-hunting gear with him, but he'd been looking forward to this chance to get away from the day job. He picked up his cell phone and popped it into his pocket.

"You sure you wanna take your phone? What did Whedon say: 'They're antisocial and prevent you from enjoying the Great Outdoors to their fullest'? Aren't they banned on this trip?"

"For norm kids, sure." Max grinned. "Hey, are *you* going to be okay while I'm gone? You have everything you need?"

Jed raised himself to his full height and looked Max dead in the eye. "I've taken care of Helsing House for over forty years. I've raised both you *and* your father, all beneath this roof. I've fixed every broken window, leaking faucet, and faulty floorboard. I've seen families come and go— human *and* monstrous—and I've never once fallen short in my responsibilities. What I *don't* need is a jumped-up, wise-ass kid treating me like some doddering old fool. You hear me, son?"

"Winding you up is *way* too easy." Max chuckled as Jed growled. The boy snatched up his trusty messenger bag before disappearing out the apartment door. "I'll see you in a week!"

Max's descent through the four stories of Helsing House was less graceful than usual. His trademark banister hurdles were replaced by a clumsy pinball as his top-heavy backpack threatened to send him sprawling. He careened around the second floor landing and straight into Mr. Holloman with a *clang*. The silent giant caught Max by the backpack straps before he went head over heels down the next flight of stairs.

"Thanks, Mr. Holloman," said Max, as the iron golem brushed him off.

The door to 2C flew open down the hall, and ten-year-old monster-hunting disciple Wing Liu exploded from his apartment. The homeschooler scampered along the landing, his Chuck Taylors squeaking as he skidded to a halt beside Max and the golem. Wing raised a fist, and Max met it with his own.

"What's happening, Max? Whatcha got in the backpack? You on a job? Can I help? Lemme get my gear—"

"Whoa," said Max. "Hang on, buddy. No, I'm not working, and I don't need help. And what d'you mean, your gear?"

Wing grinned. "I've been putting my own monster-hunting kit together. Mainly it's just lots of bulbs of garlic, but it's a start."

Max laughed. "Your mom'll kill you if you've been raiding her pantry. Also, it's only vampires that freak out at garlic. Apart from suckers, most monsters like it as much as you or I."

"I hear you. Mix things up a bit with coriander and cayenne pepper."

"Go crazy," said Max with a grin.

Ever since he'd found out about Max's true calling, Wing had grown obsessed with monster hunting. Not only was he keeping his eagle eyes peeled for any monstrous happenings across the United States via the magic of the

Internet, he was also helping Jed rearrange his extensive library upstairs. As well as alphabetizing the various monster manuals, spell books, and other arcane tomes the Van Helsings had gathered over the centuries, he was uploading those works onto his laptop, which he'd renamed *The Beholder* in homage to some monster or another. On top of all of this, he'd even started dressing like Max. He'd talked his mom into his own pair of Chuck Taylors, and could be seen sporting a bomber jacket on even the hottest of days.

"So where *are* you going?" asked the ten-year-old.

"School trip for the week," said Max, squeezing past the silent Mr. Holloman as he went to descend the last flight. "Camping in the White Mountains in New Hampshire."

"Oooh, great place for cryptid spotting," said Wing excitedly. "Two weeks back there was a flying reptile photographed north of Dover, and there's been an increase in big wolf sightings over the last twelve months. Twice the size of regular ones. Don't know what that is—could be a *waheela* or maybe a lycanthrope, but it's gotta be worth—"

"Gotta go," said Max, speaking over the younger boy.

"Bring me back a souvenir?"

"Take Eightball for his daily walk and I'll grab you a fridge magnet."

Wing grinned. "Epic!"

The ringing of Wing's fist bump with Mr. Holloman followed Max downstairs, as did his pained yelps. Then he was out of the front door of Helsing House, bouncing down the steps and marching down the drive. Syd waited at the gate, her mom's dusty old Chevy idling behind her. She smiled and Max waved back as the sun shone overhead. Even with a pack on his back, there was a spring in his stride that hadn't been there before, an excitement building in his belly that if he didn't know better he'd have put down to a bad burrito.

"So this is what going on vacation feels like." He grinned, kicking up gravel as he approached his friend. "I could get used to this."

TWO

WELCOME TO BONE CREEK

It was around midday, and the boards of the covered bridge clattered as the old school bus rattled across it and emerged out the other side into brilliant sunlight. Max peered out the window, watching the river rush by beside the road, all rocks and churning white water as it funneled through the gorge. Mrs. Loomis, school nurse and occasional bus driver, ground the gears as the incline grew steeper, the bus struggling to deal with the mountainous road. Ahead, the forest began to thin as vegetation was replaced by neat hedges and outbuildings, barns and farmhouses popping into view. The students of Gallows Hill Middle School cheered in unison as they passed a carved wooden sign at the side of the road, confirming they'd reached their destination. The words were gouged out of an enormous piece of red timber: WELCOME TO BONE CREEK. ENJOY YOUR STAY!

There seemed to be only the one main road running

through the town, reminding Max of frontier settlements from those old Western movies that Jed loved to watch. He did a double take as he spied a horse tied up outside a bar that boasted a SALOON sign over the door. Most of the buildings were wooden, although the more important ones—police station, bank, and town hall—were all built from stone. Every wall, stoop, and walkway was decorated with window boxes and hanging baskets that bloomed with vibrant spring wild flowers. The old yellow bus pulled over outside the general store, the hydraulics groaning with relief as Mrs. Loomis turned off the engine. Instantly, the gentle sound of folk music rolled in through the open windows of the bus, emanating from the store. Max smiled to himself. He really was a world away from Gallows Hill. As one-horse towns went, there seemed few prettier than Bone Creek.

"Heads up," said Principal Whedon, rising as two teachers remained seated on either side of him. Knowing they'd had to endure Whedon's company for the last few hours, Max imagined Mr. Mayhew and Ms. Golden were both having second thoughts about having volunteered for this particular trip.

The principal clapped his hands. "Your attention! Since Mrs. Loomis has made such good time, you have ten minutes to explore, folks."

"Good time?" whispered Syd beside Max. "For a while there I thought she'd made time go in reverse. I've never been on such a long journey!"

The diminutive principal clapped his hands again, demanding their continued attention. "I don't want to see anyone buying contraband here. Put your hand down, Levin; you know *exactly* what I mean by contraband. You may be away from school, but that doesn't give you permission to violate the rules. My word is law, just like in Gallows Hill. Am I making myself clear?"

"Yes, sir," the children all murmured.

"Good. Ten minutes, then I want you back on the bus." He stood, looking at them, mustache bristling. "Go!"

Whedon stood aside as the twenty students piled off the bus. Those with smaller bladders ran ahead into the store, seeking out the restroom, while the remainder took a moment to stretch.

"Man," said Syd, arching her stiff back. "I hope the cabins are comfier than the bus. My back is wrecked."

"I bet there'll be a Jacuzzi to help with that."

Syd gave Max the side-eye. "You've never been camping before, have you?"

"We're staying in lodges, Syd. You know—high ceiling, stone fireplace, big moose head over the mantel."

She clapped a hand on his back. "You have so much to learn, my poor little town mouse."

Max laughed. "Syd, this is my first-*ever* vacation," he said. "I don't care if I have to sleep in a hole in the ground: it'll rock."

"First-*ever* vacation?" Kenny Boyle's face, framed with carrot-colored hair, suddenly appeared between them from behind, forcing the pair apart.

The eighth grader laughed. "You have got to be kidding me. You hearing this?" he shouted to his nearby buddies. "This is Helsing's first-ever vacation! How pathetic is that?"

Jeers erupted from Boyle's two accompanying minions, Ripley and Shipley. The fact their names rhymed was the only amusing thing about the pair. Ripley was a squat, heavyset unit who was making waves on the school wrestling team. What Shipley lacked in muscle he made up for in smiles, a permanent grin fixed to his thin face as he nodded along enthusiastically to all of Boyle's crummy comments. The bully turned back to Syd.

"Perez, what are you doing hanging with this clown when you could be with me?"

Syd smiled and patted Max's shoulder. "I've got all the clown I can handle here, thanks, Boyle. You'd probably push me over the edge."

Boyle grunted, unsure whether to be flattered or insulted. Max wanted to assure him it was the latter, but decided to remain silent, staring ahead and hoping the bully would leave it at that. Boyle brought his eyes back to Max.

"Gonna let your woman do the talking for you, huh?" He punched Max hard in the shoulder. "Man, you're such a loser, Helsing. Holler when you're bored of him, Perez."

"Don't hold your breath," muttered Syd as the bully caught up with Ripley and Shipley. "God, he's the worst, isn't he? You okay?"

Of all the kids who could've come on this trip, there was one name Max had prayed wouldn't be on the attendance list: Kenny Boyle. The eighth grader's mop of unruly crimson hair bounced as he and his gang entered the store. A chorus of laughter followed each lame joke. When you were the son of the chief of police, and a head taller than all the other kids in school, you commanded a certain kind of respect from your classmates. A kind of respect Max—and Syd, for that matter—had always refused to give.

"Don't worry, Syd. Like I said, I'm determined to have a good time, regardless of that crapweasel's presence."

Max and Syd made their way onto the shop's long porch. On the right side of the veranda stood what looked like an enormous carved figure of a bear up on its haunches, a rocking chair positioned beside it. The entire deck was loaded with all kinds of goods, mostly camping supplies. There were tin buckets and twig brooms, bags of chopped logs and baskets of kindling. An ancient-looking boat was suspended from the rafters, no longer water-worthy, its hide hull faded and threadbare.

A notice board was fixed to the wall on the left of the entrance, covered with ads and events for locals and tourists. Numerous business cards had been pinned to the cork, showing off apartments and vacation rentals, boat tours, and campsites. Private sales, services rendered, school fund-raisers, barn dances, hiking meets; Max cast his eyes over the ads, looking for anything out of the ordinary but finding nothing. No strange goings-on. No people going missing. No weird eruptions in the mountains with diabolical entities having been sighted, rising from the earth.

"Man, oh man," he said under his breath with a grin. "I can be a norm for a whole week."

The pair entered the store. They walked past tables of fishing tackle and rods, live bait, and landing nets. Shelves were overflowing with guidebooks and maps. Their schoolmates were already rifling through the various candy bars, soda cans, and bags of chips that had lured them in. The two friends passed between racks of canned goods and toiletries as they approached the counter. Max was so busy looking at the store's contents that he didn't see one of its customers coming the other way.

He collided with a toothless old man who carried a bulging brown paper bag in his scrawny arms. His dungarees had seen better days, while his leathery skin appeared to be fashioned entirely from California raisins. An enormous jar of pickles tumbled out of the top of the bag, but Max caught it before it hit the ground. Gingerly, he placed it back onto the old-timer's stash of provisions.

"Sorry, sir," said Max, stepping aside as the ancient fellow gave him a nod of appreciation, bushy white eyebrows flexing as he winked. The man's tobacco-stained gray whiskers twitched as he managed a smile and was on his way. Max was watching the man leave the store when he felt Syd's elbow jab him in the ribs.

"Looks like your vacation's over."

Two twentysomething backpackers stood at the register, but behind them was what could only be described as a wall of weird. Framed newspaper clippings and corny-looking monster masks jockeyed for position, while cuddly stuffed apes hung from plastic danglers in every spare space. A poorly executed painting of a hair-covered figure crossing a stream held pride of place in the center, its crude brush-strokes set off beautifully by its gaudy gold frame.

"Amazing, eh?" one of the backpackers said to Max in a thick Midwestern accent. He wore a big camera about his neck, and a pan, a pot, and two enamel mugs hung off the bottom of his backpack. "Bigfoot country, and we're right in the heart of it."

"Really?" said Max. "We hadn't heard."

"Oh ya," the guy's girlfriend chimed in. "They say there's bigfeet in these hills. Right, Frank?"

"Big*feet*?" said her boyfriend.

"Ya," said the girl. "How neat is that?"

Max smiled, put on his cheesiest grin, and gave her a thumbs-up. "Oh ya. Real neat!"

"You hoping to see one?" asked Syd, playing along with the couple's joke.

The man leaned in to Max and spoke in a whisper. "You know, there's no such thing, really."

"No?"

He laughed. "Pfft. No way! These little backwater towns survive on this kinda story pulling in out-of-towners like me and Sissy here. Bigfoot? Really? Did ya ever hear anything so preposterous? Betcha the town mayor wears a monkey suit once a year and gets his deputy to take a candid snap of him running across the creek!"

He mimed taking a rapid series of photos with his camera, his pans and mugs chiming against one another.

"Oh, Frank, be quiet, ya big goofball," said Sissy, giving him a smack on the arm and blushing. "The storekeeper'll hear ya!"

"Where you kids staying?" asked Frank.

"Some lodge on the creek, up in the woods," said Max.

"Oh, we're camping up by the river too."

"Hey, did you see the hillbilly?" said Sissy, excitement building in her voice.

"Hard to miss," said Max, as politely as he could manage.

"He was real quaint. Genuine hermit, lives up in the backwoods, so the storekeeper says. So neat."

"Look, if you're camping by the river, we may yet see you again," said Frank. "Be sure to say hi."

"We shall," said Syd.

"That'd be neat!" added Sissy. "Look out for the bigfeet!"

"Neat." Max nodded, still smiling, as the two backpackers left the store, clanging and waving as they went. Max turned to Syd. "Can you believe we've come all this way and there're monster shenanigans happening on our doorstep?"

"You don't know that. Could just be a stunt like Frank said, to pull in a few bucks for a sleepy little town."

Max spied a snow globe on the counter, the rough likeness of a bigfoot soldered into place inside. He gave it a shake and watched the globs of white descend over the plastic figurine.

"That'll be ten dollars, boy," said the storekeeper.

"I hadn't decided whether I was buying it," said Max.

"You touch it, you buy it," said the man, pointing to a sign beside the cash register.

"Wow, harsh," said Max, forking the cash out of his wallet. "You could teach Odious Crumb a thing or two."

"What's that, boy?" said the storekeeper, snatching the bill from Max.

"Pleasure doing business with you, sir," said Max, doffing an imaginary cap and turning to leave the store. He shoved the snow globe into his pocket. "Still, should make Wing happy. That takes care of my souvenir shopping."

Back on the porch Max heard the unmistakable chuckles of Ripley and Shipley from the right side of the veranda. Turning, he saw Boyle doodling on the wooden bear with a Sharpie.

"Your friend's disrespectful. Gonna get him in trouble."

Max and Syd turned and found the old-timer in the dungarees standing in the shadows beside the door, whiskers twitching as he worked his jaw. His bag of shopping sat on the porch at his feet, and he spat a blob of chewing tobacco into the ancient brass spittoon next to the veranda rail.

"He's no friend of mine," said Max.

"You kids staying on the river?"

Max nodded.

"I'm gonna say this once. Turn back."

"Back where?"

"Go home, wherever ya came from. The woods ain't safe."

"You live in the woods, though, don't you?"

"I know the woods. And more important . . . the woods know me."

Max's face was a mask of confusion.

"We're just here for the week on a school trip," said Syd.

"There's been bad things going on in the White Mountains lately. Real bad things."

"What bad things?" said Max, keen to hear more.

"Beware."

"Beware what?" said Max. "Trust me, whatever's out there, I'm not afraid of it. You'd be surprised at what doesn't scare me."

"Hmm," said the old-timer, spitting another glob of tobacco. "You'll be scared if the Beast of Bone Creek finds ya."

Max felt his flesh chill at the old man's warning. Ordinarily the idea of monstrous encounters or skirmishes with the paranormal got his blood pumping. But there was something about the old hermit's dark demeanor that told him this beast was seriously bad news.

"Is that your grandpa, Helsing?" asked Boyle from the end of the veranda, spying the conversation between Max, Syd, and the hermit.

Max ignored him, concentrating on the old man. "I'll be careful," he said, but for some reason the words rang hollow.

"You beware," said the backwoodsman, picking up his provisions.

"Enjoy your pickles," said Max as the hermit hobbled down the steps.

"Beware," the old-timer added again before setting off down the dusty road toward the edge of town.

"Grandpappy Helsing's really let himself go," said Boyle, his friends laughing at his cutting wit.

Max turned to the bully, and caught a better look at the carved figure. It wasn't a bear at all. It was a nine-foot wooden bigfoot, chiseled from a tree trunk. Max saw the Sharpie in Boyle's hand and spied the graffiti. His temper got the better of him, rising like a flash flood. He covered the distance in a heartbeat and snatched for the pen. The eighth grader held on tight, refusing to relinquish his grip on the Sharpie. Then Boyle was tumbling back, over the porch banister and out into the street. He let go of the pen, leaving it in Max's possession as he landed in the dust.

Max stared at the carved monster, the giant wooden hominid towering over him. Its arms were raised, fingers ending in chunky claws, its jaws revealing rows of crooked teeth. Its eyes had been painted blood-red, giving it a demonic and distinctly unfriendly appearance. Its long, shaggy torso was held up by squat, powerful legs, supported by enormous, broad feet. It may only have been carved in timber and an artist's impression, but it still conjured a shiver from Max.

"The woods know me," he whispered, repeating the hermit's words.

Max saw the graffiti up close now: *"Gallows Hill Posse Was Here."* He shook his head.

"Helsing!" bellowed Whedon. Max turned, finding the principal in the street, Boyle beside him, pointing at Max.

"See," said the bully. "Look what he did!"

"You vandal, Helsing!" Whedon screeched, black mustache quivering as he spied the graffiti and the pen in Max's hand.

"Ah," said Max, clipping the lid back onto the Sharpie. "I can explain everything."

Not that it would do him a lick of good.

THREE

xxx

LET'S GET CAMPING

A brief drive through the woods brought the school party to its journey's end, five miles north of town. The road stopped at a scratch of clearing, where an old camper van was already parked up. As Principal Whedon took in a lungful of fresh New Hampshire air, the other adults unloaded the bus. Backpacks donned, the kids set off after Whedon, who guided them down to the creek-side campsite. Mrs. Loomis and the other teachers brought up the rear, laden down with cases of food and drink. And Whedon's luggage, of course.

Max slapped a hand against his neck, splatting the insect that had just nipped his skin. He followed the principal but kept his eyes fixed on the forest. His nerves were on edge, and he couldn't decide whether to blame his surroundings or Whedon. Max had gotten an earful on the perils of teenage delinquency after the business with the permanent marker. Pointing out that Boyle was responsible had been hopeless. In Whedon's eyes, Boyle couldn't put a foot wrong, probably because his father was the chief of police in Gallows Hill and a man Whedon constantly tried to impress. Max had no such guardian angel.

"Get a move on, kids," Whedon called back, proceeding down a set of steps that descended the hillside. A series of short split logs had been embedded into the earth, providing campers with a crude staircase that led to the creek below. Max was halfway down the slope when he felt someone bang into him from behind, almost sending him flying. He somehow managed to keep his footing, while simultaneously snatching hold of the shorter figure who skittered past him. His fingers seized the backpack of Joe Benjamin, also known as JB, the bespectacled quiet kid who seemed to be the only person on the trip who was minus a buddy.

"You okay, JB?"

The kid in the glasses nodded as Max dusted him off.

"Quit cuddling him, Helsing, and get a move on!" shouted Boyle from behind.

It was clear to Max that the bully had shoved JB down the hill. Max helped the smaller boy steady himself.

"Just follow where I put my feet and you'll be fine."

At the bottom of the incline, the woods thinned out as the school group arrived at its final destination. Two totem poles supported a wooden sign that arched over the path, bearing the name of their home for the next week: BONE CREEK ADVENTURE CAMP. Boys and girls whooped as they passed beneath it, high-fiving, fist-bumping, and generally celebrating their arrival. The trees had been cut back throughout this area, affording visitors an unhindered view of the waters of Bone Creek as it cut through the forest. A pair of log cabins stood on the bank with a huge fire pit between them. A wooden jetty stretched out into the river, a diving board fixed to one end that would no doubt be getting some serious abuse in the coming days. An outhouse stood within the pines, promising spiders and bugs aplenty for any brave soul that chose to use it. Max caught sight of a third log cabin farther downriver, half-hidden by the trees, while upstream he spied a partially assembled white tent flapping in the breeze. Before he could investigate further, he heard a shrill whistle and the clapping of hands as a figure strode up the bank toward them and spoke.

"Welcome, oh welcome, boys and girls of Gallows Hill Middle School, to . . ." The man paused to give his best jazz hands. "Bone Creek Adventure Camp!"

The man was short—like, Principal Whedon short—with curly brown hair that sprouted out around a bald, pale summit. He scurried over excitedly, his goatee bobbing as he laughed. He wore a khaki shirt with a matching pair of shorts that were a touch on the tight side. A pair of shiny hiking boots completed the ensemble, with rosy red hiking socks rolled down around their tops. He strode straight up to the principal and took him by the hand.

"You must be Irwin!" he exclaimed.

"Principal Whedon," corrected the teacher with an embarrassed cough as the kids snickered.

The man winked in a dramatic conspiratorial fashion, giving Whedon a friendly nudge. *"Principal Whedon* it is. And I"—he pointed at a shiny brass name badge on his breast pocket—"am Gideon. I'll be your go-to guy while you're here in Bone Creek. I've got all kinds of fun activities for you boys and girls to get into. You are gonna have a *wild* time!"

He clapped his hands again, encouraging the schoolchildren to join in. Max couldn't help but get swept up in the tour guide's enthusiasm. He grinned as he clapped wildly, matching the man's high spirits and prompting a snort of laughter from Syd.

"Dork."

It was Boyle's voice, from the back of the group, low enough to be heard by Ripley, Shipley, and Max but not Gideon. Max couldn't tell who it was aimed at, himself or the exuberant host. If the camp coordinator heard it, he didn't react, continuing with his introduction.

"I live thataways," he said, pointing at the third cabin in the woods. "If you need any help at all during your stay, just holler and I'll come running."

To illustrate this information, Gideon mimed jogging on the spot. This prompted more giggles from Syd and Max.

"How happy is he?" whispered Syd. "If he walked around Boston with that smile on his face, they'd lock him up."

Gideon clapped his hands again.

"Okeydokey, here's what we're gonna do. Girls, you wanna be in the lodge on the right. Boys, you're bedding down on the left. Drop off your bags, grab a bunk, take a tinkle, and then I'll meet you back out here in fifteen minutes. I've got a whole mess of sandwiches and soda here for you to enjoy for lunch. Then I'll give you the full tour as we head to the first activity of the week: rappelling!" There was more clapping from their host accompanied by a muted response from the kids. "Let's get camping, campers!"

Max chuckled as he and Syd stomped over to the cabins, splitting when they reached the fire pit.

"Technically, this ain't camping," said Max, smacking a midge that had settled on his hand.

"What? You're suddenly the world's foremost expert on the great outdoors, city boy?" Syd laughed.

"Just saying. Unless we have to pee in a bucket, this ain't camping."

"I'll see you on the other side," said Syd, saluting Max as she peeled away toward the bunkhouse on the right.

The boys' cabin was a rustic affair, straight out of a Jack London novel. Steps led up to a deck that overlooked the creek, while an open doorway led into the lodge. An old oil lamp swung from the low ceiling, Max's head almost connecting with it as he entered the building. The main room was around fifteen feet square, with a large beaten-up wooden table at its center. The names of previous occupants were carved into the top. Benches surrounded the table, while a black iron wood-burning stove dominated the rear of the room. The three bedrooms were situated off a short corridor running from the back of the kitchen area. Max stumbled as his foot found the rotten end of a loose, creaking floorboard. The timber bowed, threatening to twang up and hit him on the butt, cartoon-style. He danced lightly off the treacherous wood.

"Just how old *is* this place? Did Davy Crockett vacation here?"

He was shoved aside by the other boys as they charged in, keen to grab bunks with their friends. By the time he and the last kid, JB, reached the corridor beyond the kitchen, the first two rooms were taken. Even Mr. Mayhew, the younger male teacher, had picked a cot.

"Sorry, Helsing," brayed Ripley from the top of one bunk. "All the best beds have been taken."

"Looks like you and Nerdnuts are in the cupboard!" added Shipley.

Cupboard wasn't wrong—Max knocked over a yard brush on his way through the third door, stepping over boxes, logs, and half-empty cans of paint thinner. Sure enough, the last of the three rooms was barely big enough to swing a gerbil in, let alone a cat. A narrow gap of perhaps two feet separated the pair of bunk beds, while a cobweb-covered window faced out into the woods at the rear of the lodge. One of the top bunks was out of action, its mattress missing, revealing splintered slats across the frame. There was also a peculiar, rotten smell that Max couldn't quite place. He wondered for a moment if it was perhaps coming from beneath the floorboards. Who knew what horrors lurked there?

"Bit of a fixer-upper, JB," said Max, as the smaller boy dropped his pack on the bed with the busted top bunk. Max threw his bags onto the bottom of the other and squeezed through to the window, stepping gingerly over an old tin bucket that seemed placed there purely as an obstacle.

Pulling the sleeve of his jacket over the palm of his hand, he gave the glass a wipe. The grime smeared away, giving him a clear view of the forest. He watched it for a moment as JB proceeded to empty the contents of his backpack over his blanket. Beyond the dirty pane he could see birds hopping across the forest floor all along the camp's edge. There was movement in the canopy overhead too, as the darting squirrels left shadows in their wake.

Max thought about the Beast of Bone Creek. He'd never seen a bigfoot, but that wasn't to say they weren't out there. He peered through the maze of trunks, looking deeper into the wild forest. He felt the hairs tingle up and down his neck, and goose bumps briefly played across his flesh. He'd often joked about his Helsey sense to Jed, an innate feeling he got when something wasn't quite right, when something supernatural was about to happen. Max was getting that vibe now as he stared into the woods. Something dreadful was coming.

"Move," snapped Whedon from behind, causing Max to jump and headbutt the window. He rebounded and fell back, clattering the bucket and causing it to roll onto its side. He turned, nursing his stubbed nose, amazed at how stealthy the principal could be. Whedon righted the bucket and tossed his pack onto the bunk above Max's, causing the teenager's heart to sink.

"Looks like I'm up top, Helsing, where I can keep an eye on you," said the principal, mustache twitching. "And try not to kick over the pee bucket again."

FOUR

xxx

A GUIDED TOUR

With their backpacks deposited and a picnic lunch tossed down their throats, the students were ready for all the thrills Bone Creek Adventure Camp could throw at them. Gideon gave them the tour of the grounds immediately surrounding the lodges, including the jetty that led out into the river. The water was crystal clear, and the tour guide pointed out the brown and rainbow trout that populated this stretch of the creek. A boat shed a little farther upstream housed kayaks, which the students would put to good use later in the week. There was a fire pit that could be enjoyed in the evening, with the assistance of a responsible adult. Whedon quickly let Gideon know that he'd been a Boy Scout in his youth, so getting a fire started would be no problem. He'd also taken the cell phones from any students who'd risked bringing theirs, insisting this was going to be a week with no interference from the outside world. Max, of course, had hidden his away, locked and on silent, before their arrival. He was in no hurry to ditch his cell, not when it was a lifeline to Jed.

Mrs. Loomis said her good-byes to the gang, remaining at the campsite to start preparing the evening meal for everyone. Then they were stepping along the bank, the tour guide leading the way, waving his long knobbed walking stick like some backwoods Jedi.

"So, Bone Creek gets its name from the veins of white zinc you can see in the rock," said Gideon. "Just one of many unusual varieties of ore and precious metal you'll find in these mountains. Anybody know the name of the indigenous group who hail from these hills?"

JB raised a trembling hand.

"Is it . . . is it the Pigwackets?"

Boyle's laugh caused some geese to take flight from the riverbank.

"That's not something to be laughed at, young man," said Gideon, the humor gone from his voice. "Very disrespectful."

He shook his head as a stunned Boyle muttered an apology, unaccustomed to being put in his place. The funny little tour guide was growing on Max by the minute.

"You were right, young man," he said, returning his attention to JB. Max gave the smaller kid a little fist bump as the tour guide continued.

"Members of the Pequawket community still live here. And indeed, the name is often pronounced *Pigwacket*." Gideon cast his walking stick across the slow-moving water. "The Saco

River was always home to the Pequawket, all the way up here into the mountains. See the boathouse over there?"

He pointed the stick toward a rickety wooden building that sat on the bank, supported by stilts as it stretched out into the river. Max imagined a flood could wash the run-down shack away.

"We have a historic Pequawket canoe in there. I'll show you later. *Please* nobody touch it, though; it's antique. Like my jokes. Bone Creek was especially important to the Pequawket, a key spiritual site. Upriver you'll find other ancient sites of great cultural significance. That's if you know where to look."

"Hey," said Syd, pointing ahead. "Aren't those the guys from the general store?"

A lush, grassy outcropping jutted into the river bend, with a twisted old cherry tree perched on the bank, its exposed roots trailing into the creek. The white tent Max had spotted earlier sat beneath its boughs, and sure enough, the two twentysomethings from the Midwest, Frank and Sissy, were seated on camping stools in front of it. A little gas stove roared away, a coffeepot balanced atop it. They waved when they recognized Max and Syd among the group as the school party drew nearer.

"Howdy, folks!" said Frank as the children filed by. Syd and Max stopped to chat.

"Looks like we're neighbors," said Syd. "We're staying in those cabins just downstream of here."

"Neat!" said Sissy, fingering a dainty gold crucifix on a chain around her throat. Max suspected many things in life were neat for Sissy.

"That's a pretty necklace," said Syd.

"Frank gave it to me," simpered Sissy, squeezing her partner on the bicep. "After he proposed when we got here!"

"You'll get your ring when we get home, honey," said Frank. "Just need to pry it out of Grammy Jean's hands first."

She gave him a playful punch as the kids all walked past.

"You lovebirds got your permit for camping?" asked a smiling Gideon, stopping beside them.

"Yes, sir," said Frank, about to reach back into the tent to fetch it.

"Oh, don't you worry," said Gideon with a wave of the hand. "I'll be back this way later; can check it then."

"Sure thing, mister," said Frank. "Say, Sissy and I heard all about the bigfoot. You don't believe in them, do you?"

"Well, what do *you* think?" said Gideon, keeping his voice low. "My livelihood depends on out-of-towners visiting this little piece o' wonderful, so I'm not about to start telling you bigfoot ain't real. I reckon nonbelievers will see nothing in these woods."

He was whispering now, and Sissy leaned close to catch every word.

"But those folk who still have a bit of imagination, and can believe in something magical or unexplained? Who knows? They *may* see things moving, out there in the wilderness, creeping through the trees and wading across the creek. Stalking ever nearer until . . . BOO!"

Sissy jumped, and she wasn't alone. Frank and Syd were both startled, and even Max's heart got a jolt. Gideon burst out laughing.

"Gracious me, you should see your faces," he said, clapping his bare thigh as they all breathed a sigh of relief. "I do love frightening the tourists. Get yourselves down to the campfire tonight, and we'll see if we can rustle up some more creepy tales. Whaddaya say?"

Frank looked to Sissy, who nodded eagerly. "Okeydokey," said Gideon as he set off again. "Bring your coffeepot!"

Max and Syd fell back in line, following their classmates upstream and leaving the two campers behind them.

"I can't believe he did that," said Syd, as the tour guide made his way back to the front of the procession. "I nearly had a heart attack. What an ass!"

Max grinned. "I like him. Maybe we can swap him for Whedon. Pull the old switcheroo and leave walrus face behind when we head home."

They walked on, the forest canopy hanging over them as they flanked the river to their left. Max felt something ping off the right side of his head. He turned in time to see a pinecone bounce to the ground nearby. He looked up, searching the low-hanging branches overhead, but they were bare of cones.

"What's the matter?" asked Syd.

"I just got hit by a pinecone," said Max, ruffling his hair where he'd been struck.

"Probably Boyle."

"Nope, he's up ahead. This came from the forest."

"A squirrel, then."

"Must've been a really angry squirrel, and with dead-eye aim, too."

Max kept his eyes on the forest from that moment on, the trail growing steeper as they followed the gorge and river. The slow-moving waters were replaced by rushing white rapids as the roar of Bone Creek grew. Rock faces rose all around them, leaving half the ravine in shade. The cliffs on their side of the river remained bathed in a warm glow, the rocks varying shades of white, gray, and beige.

"Can you hear that, boys and girls?" called Gideon as he led the way. "That's Battle Falls, up ahead. Over a hundred-foot plunge down into the Dead Pool, so called because it's a portal to hell."

"Really?" asked Boyle.

Gideon turned to Whedon and the other teachers before loudly saying, "What do you teach these kids at school?" That got big laughs. "It's actually called that because when it's in shadow, like now, the surface looks as black as oil. Lifeless. Not terribly welcoming. Still, doesn't stop the occasional brave, or suicidal, soul from diving into it from the top of the falls."

"For real?" asked Syd.

"Oh yes. Wouldn't catch me making that dive, though."

"Me neither," muttered Max to Syd.

"Chicken," said Syd, who'd dived for the school swim team.

"Until we grow gills and flippers, I'm staying out of the water wherever possible." Max spied something glittering along one of the sunlit cliffs. He pointed the sparkling rock face out to Syd. "See that? Quicksilver ore. I bet you this is gnome country."

"Do you see monsters everywhere?"

"I don't imagine them, if that's what you mean?"

"So there are gnomes up here and that's some magical vein of precious metal?"

Max grinned. "On second thought, looks more like pigeon poop catching the sunlight." When she punched his shoulder, he knew he deserved it. "Nah, I don't think there are any monsters up here. Apart from bigfoot, of course."

"You think there *is* a bigfoot up here?"

Max thought about it for a moment, looking back the way they'd come. The river was swallowed by the forest below, which spread out as far as the eye could see around them. The view took his breath away, and he could see how such things could bring a soul closer to something divine.

"Are there bigfoot out here? Probably. Are we going to meet any? Highly unlikely."

"How can you be sure?"

"Put it this way. The last thing you'd want to do if you were a Sasquatch is go anywhere near a bunch of humans."

"Why's that?" asked Syd as they continued their ascent along the cliff path.

"Think about it, Syd. Industry, pollution, and deforestation. Guns." When Max looked back to his friend, his smile was gone. "Humans are monsters."

FIVE

xxx

HERE BE (TINY) DRAGONS

After a half-hour rappelling tutorial from Gideon, the guide was convinced the students were ready for the real deal. He fitted them into their harnesses and handed out colorful, shiny helmets that were secured onto their heads. Those who weren't confident enough remained at the base of Little Crag with Whedon, Mr. Mayhew, and Ms. Golden, while Gideon led the more adventurous souls to the summit. This band of adventurers included Max and Syd, as well as Boyle and his sidekicks. Max was pleased to see JB come along.

The first two over the top were Syd and JB. Max heard his friend talking to JB all the way down, matching his speed as they rappelled their way to the bottom. This cliff was perhaps sixty feet high, but was still considered a beginner's descent by Gideon. The taller rock face for more advanced climbers was farther away, and once Boyle caught wind of this fact, he insisted that this be his route down.

"Better let me go solo," Boyle told Gideon. "I'm sure none of these chickens can handle the advanced cliff." The guide frowned.

Max's hand shot up before he could think better of it. "I'll take a crack at it."

Once the remaining kids had made their way to the base of the beginner's cliff, Gideon leaned over the edge.

"Mr. Whedon!" the tour guide called down. "I'm taking these last two students to High Crag, a little farther along that lower path. If you'd like to make your way around the cliff base a few hundred feet, you'll find the landing site."

"Very good," the principal called back, before adding an afterthought. "Be careful up there, Boyle!"

Boyle chuckled as he followed Gideon up the track, Max falling in behind the bully. They passed Battle Falls, seeing it spilling from the cliff tops and showering the Dead Pool far below. A great expanse of water gathered at the cliff's plateau, where many tributary streams met before surging from the cliff top. A pinecone bounced off the rocks at Max's feet, causing him to look up suddenly, scouring the forest where it hung over the rock face. To get hit by one cone was bad luck; two was mischief, without a doubt.

"Hey, Helsing," said Boyle, as they left the falls behind them. "I can think of a way you can get down the mountain real quick."

"Does it involve you pushing me off by any chance, Kenny?"

If the view from Little Crag was spectacular, then High Crag was nothing short of breathtaking. Even Boyle fell silent. With the sky clear and blue overhead, they could see for miles. Far below, Max spotted Bone Creek winding its way through the pine canopy, the water shining silver as it snaked toward the east. He could even see the lodges at the campsite, and the bright white smudge of the Midwesterners' tent on the riverbank.

At his back, the mountains rose ever higher, the trees at their summits replaced by cold, barren slopes. Even the air felt different, clear and pure. It was as close to heaven as Max had ever been, apart from his numerous run-ins with monstrous miscreants. He sensed something else, too: a spark of electricity, not dissimilar from what he felt when he encountered fairy folk. For a moment, he thought he could hear music playing, as the wind rushed through the pines.

"Now listen," said Gideon, content that the ropes were secure and the boys' harnesses and descending mechanisms were both functioning. "I don't need any tomfoolery on this descent, boys. This cliff is just shy of a hundred and fifty feet, from foot to summit. It hasn't been used for a while, as the kids I bring here tend to be gentler souls. You two appear to be made of sterner stuff, though."

Boyle's chest puffed out at this while Max shook his head.

"The route down is perfectly safe, but as it hasn't been used in a while, you may find a bit of moss here or there that could prove slippery underfoot. So be careful on your way down. Your harnesses are in tip-top condition—just remember to use your descenders like I showed you. Apply pressure to the descender and this applies friction to the rope and—bingo—you stop your descent."

"Yeah, I know," said Boyle impatiently. "I've *done* rappelling before. I go climbing in Montana every fall with my uncle Wilbur. He's climbed all over Europe."

"Okeydokey," said the tour guide, stepping back from the edge. "The mountain's all yours."

Max didn't have an uncle Wilbur who had climbed all over Europe, and Jed had never been able to afford to take him on vacations when he was growing up. He had, however, visited the Undercity, where he'd leaped across yawning, bottomless chasms, scurried up walls of splintered obsidian, and crawled through claustrophobic tunnels while being chased by flesh-hungry kobolds. How difficult could rappelling be?

He was first over the edge, easing up on the descender lever to allow the rope to run smoothly through it. But the rope raced through the mechanism, sending Max plummeting the first twenty feet in a free fall. His feet bounced off the rock face, the granite scuffing his knees before dropping away beneath him. Max yanked hard on the descender, his progress halting instantly as he twirled like a puppet on a string. With his heart in his mouth, he tried to right himself, wincing as he bounced off the wall of rock. Max took a moment to gather his wits before leaning out against the cliff once more. He maneuvered his body into a horizontal position at a right angle to the rock face. Tentatively, he eased up on the descender. Then he was moving again, the rope running steadily through his tackle and harness as he rappelled down the mountainside. He heard the shouts of his classmates and, looking down, spied their colorful helmets as they all waved at the sight of him. He couldn't make out Syd among them, but he'd recognize her whooping cheer anywhere.

Glancing up he saw Boyle above him, making easier work of the descent. The eighth grader's route was five feet to the right of Max's passage down the rock face. This was to ensure the rappellers stayed apart and didn't collide with each other. Max was doing a good enough job of colliding with himself, untangling the rope from around one leg. Boyle was clearly an experienced climber, and was catching up with him. The only way Max was going to win this contest would be by releasing his descender and falling the entire distance. It looked like Boyle was going to win this one.

Max was halfway down High Crag when he heard a chirruping sound close by. Anybody else might have dismissed it as a wild bird, perhaps a finch or warbler. But Max's ears were as well trained as his eyes when it came to spotting something supernatural. He looked to his right, trying to pinpoint where the sound was coming from.

Lying on a narrow ledge, basking in the late afternoon light, was what appeared to be a lizard, perhaps a foot long from head to tip of tail. Its scales shimmered, glaring golden in the sun's rays. The chirruping noise came with each

ROCK DRAKE

AKA: dragonette, cliff dragon

ORIGIN: Universal

STRENGTHS: Flight, camouflage, lightning speed, acidic breath weapon.

WEAKNESSES: Animal-level intelligence, fragile form.

HABITAT: Hill and mountain dwelling, especially cliffs.

The smallest of all the dragons (no more than two feet in length), the rock drake is a reclusive flying lizard that roosts in remote mountainous regions of every continent. Unlike its larger brethren, the rock drake doesn't possess the power of speech, or any spell-casting ability. However, its breath weapon can be deadly: a highly corrosive spray of acid that is capable of dissolving most nonmagical materials. Fortunately, they are more likely to run from interaction with humans than seek it out. —Erik Van Helsing, April 30th, 1860

PHYSICAL TRAITS

1. _Lightning speed_—Ungainly on land, rock drakes are swift and speedy in flight.

2. _Chameleon skin_—Able to camouflage itself, disappearing into its surroundings.

3. _Acid breath_—Projectile stream of liquid, predominantly used as a defense mechanism. AVOID surprising or angering a rock drake.

—Esme Van Helsing, September 9th, 1862

Thought we had one of these in the attic of Helsing House the other day. Turned out to be a pigeon with a nasty case of butt-squirts. MAN, I don't know <u>WHAT</u> it had been eating, but pigeon poop is lethal!
PS: You'd need to be a total <u>NUMBNUT</u> to stumble onto a rock drake. . . .

MAX HELSING May 8th, 2015

exhalation of breath, a sound of contentment not dissimilar to the purr of a slumbering cat. Most interesting to Max, though, was the gossamer-thin pair of wings that arched up from its back, wide apart and resting against the warm cliff face.

"Rock drake," Max whispered, unable to resist a grin.

Most of Max's life was spent either hunting down or rehoming monsters of varying shape, size, and flesh-eating persuasion, but the fanboy in him got a real kick whenever he encountered something new. Finding a creature as beautiful and rare as a rock drake in such an incredible setting was a big win. Max knew all there was to know about rock drakes via the *Monstrosi Bestiarum*, the "Who's Who" or "What's What" of all things monstrous. It was an ancient tome he took everywhere with him (it was in his bag back at the lodge presently), and had been handed down from one generation of Van Helsings to the next over many centuries.

"What are you doing here, little fella?" he whispered.

The rock drake didn't respond, its eyes still closed, its wings soaking up the sun's rays as a butterfly's might. Perhaps it hadn't heard him and was unaware of his approach. Max had always been fascinated by the more marvelous creatures that shared the world he lived in. Sure, there were ghoulish supernatural horrors like vampires, zombies, ghosts, and demons, but there were also the mythical beings of ancient folklore—dragons, sea serpents, mothmen, and thunderbirds. They weren't undead. Nor were they essentially magical, although they were often connected to the fey world. They were their own subspecies of creatures that already existed in Max's world—cryptids—split away from a shared genus. No doubt rock drakes were distant cousins of alligators, but he'd hate to do the science and connect *those* dots. Likewise, the bigfoot of local Bone Creek legend would no doubt be a much removed ancestor to Max. Well, Boyle, perhaps.

Boyle.

Max looked up and saw the older boy approaching, maybe a dozen feet above.

"Yo, Drogon," Max said to the tiny dragon. "Shift your booty!"

Still it slumbered, oblivious. If Boyle were to stumble upon the beast, a number of things could happen, none of which would be pleasant for anyone involved. The drake, startled, might attack Boyle. Teeth *and* a breath weapon could prove very bad for the police chief's son. Alternatively, Boyle's foot might find the creature. It was a delicate thing, and he doubted how well it might fare in a fight with the bully's heavy hiking boot. An encounter where boy wakes dragon and dragon flies away would be harmless for the dragon, but a world of trouble for Max. If Boyle were privy to the existence of monsters, that could prove disastrous for Max, his work, and the monsters he considered his friends.

Max inched to his left along the rock face before allowing momentum to swing him back the other way. Instantly, both lengths of ropes were in a tangle.

"Helsing!" shouted Boyle from a few feet above. "What are you doing, you freak?"

"Sorry, Kenny! Lost my footing!"

The ruckus was more than enough to wake the dragon.

Max was already mouthing the words to his cantrip, a simple calming spell he'd learned from Jed in his earliest studies. It was ineffective against any monster with a higher-than-animal intelligence, so Max was left praying it would work on the winged lizard. Ignoring the cussing bully overhead, Max hurried the ancient words out as the tiny dragon recoiled, ready to belch acid at him. Suddenly it stopped, calmed, and with a blink of its black eyes, it dropped off the ledge. Max watched it glide away, probably mistaken for a soaring hawk or some such bird by the gang below.

"You could've killed me, you nugget," grunted Boyle above, yanking Max's rope and sending him spinning clear.

"Are you all right, Boyle?" shouted Whedon below, as the bully continued on his way, cussing as he descended.

Max watched him go, bouncing off the rock face all the way, but paid little attention. He could live with being the bad guy if it kept the dragon safe and its existence secret.

Max hung there from the cliff face, contemplating a couple of conundrums. First, was there anything Max could possibly do to make Principal Whedon hate him more? And second—and most important—if a rock drake was alive and well and living in the wilds of Bone Creek, what other creatures inhabited this strange, secluded forest?

SIX

xxx

MISPLACED MONSTERS

"You've got to be kidding," said Syd, her voice an excited whisper by Max's ear.

He shifted uncomfortably on the log, dabbing more insect repellent onto his exposed skin. "I kid you not. I swear I've been bitten to death. I've encountered zombies with less taste for my flesh."

"Screw the mosquitoes," hissed Syd. "You saw an honest-to-goodness dragon?"

"You make it sound like something dwarves would be scared of. It was actually a rock drake." He held his hands apart to show the size of a pigeon. "About yea big."

The students all sat around the fire pit, toasting marshmallows in the flickering flames. The hour was late and it had been an exhausting day for all. Hard to believe they'd started the day in Gallows Hill as they now lounged beneath the stars. The evening meal hadn't gone entirely as planned.

Lighting the fire took twice as long as it should have. Principal Whedon had blamed a multitude of poor conditions for his failure to get it going, including damp wood, poor light, and hidden ground winds, whatever they were. Thankfully, Ms. Golden had stepped in and summoned up flames with a minimum of fuss. Chili was served, dinner was devoured, games were played, and then the marshmallows were unleashed.

"But still: *a dragon*!" said Syd. "Would you expect to find them up here?"

"I'd expect to find something like that in an area that was known for supernatural activity. As far as I knew, the White Mountains weren't that place."

"The White Mountains cover a big area. Maybe Bone Creek is the range's little corner of crazy?"

Syd was no norm. She'd had plenty of monstrous encounters with Max in recent times. There was little he could say that would cause her alarm. But he kept his voice low so the norms around them wouldn't lose their cool.

"If we were going to bump into anything on this trip, I was expecting a hairy hominid, not a rock drake. Certain cryptids are usually sighted in specific areas—"

"Cryptids?" said Syd.

"Misplaced beasts, strange creatures that get spotted all over the world by the public who invariably fail to grab any proof that they're real. Don't get me wrong, some of them are hooey, but many *do* exist: the Yeti, the Loch Ness

Monster, Ogopogo. The study of them is called cryptozoology. You should mention it to Wing when we get home. He'll send you to sleep with what he's learned about cryptids."

"So where would a rock drake normally be found?"

Max spied Boyle and his pals across the fire, the bully's freckled face twisted into a sneer as he watched them.

"That's just it," he whispered. "They're more common in areas of fey activity."

"Fairies?" said Syd, licking the last bit of marshmallow off her fingers. "Is Bone Creek a hotspot for fairy activity?"

"I don't have the answer. But Gideon might." He rose. "But first, I gotta take a leak."

"Too much information," said Syd, wrinkling her nose.

Max stalked around the campfire en route to the outdoor latrine on the edge of the woods. Whedon was keeping to himself, sitting on a deck chair away from the marshmallow-crazed crowd. He had a head lamp strapped to his forehead, which he was using to read by. He was quite clearly sulking after his emasculation at the expert fire-starting hands of the younger Ms. Golden. As Max passed Whedon, he felt the principal's eyes fixed upon him.

Through the trees he went, branches crunching underfoot until he reached the tiny wooden hut that passed for a bathroom. He opened the door and stepped inside, placing his flashlight on the edge of the rickety sink that was fixed to the wall. He locked the door behind him and used a boot to lift the lid. Max had faced all kinds of horrors on the job, but he still didn't relish getting surprised by a spider when his defenses—and pants—were down.

As he finished his business, Max suddenly became aware of the sound of twigs snapping outside the outhouse.

"If you're trying to scare me, Boyle," called Max, "you'll need to try a lot harder."

No reply. Zipping up, he flushed and turned to the sink. He ran the water, rinsing his fingers, before drying his hands on his jeans. As he turned the tap off, he heard another sound: nails along timber, scraping and scratching. Nails . . . or claws? Max felt a familiar shiver race up his spine. The outhouse trembled suddenly, as if a great force had seized and shaken it. Grabbing his flashlight, Max flicked the latch and kicked the door open, leaping out of the shack and spinning around.

Only trees and darkness surrounded him. A thin mist curled about his ankles. He peered around the back of the outhouse, searched the walls for telltale marks, even scoured the ground for footprints, but there was nothing.

"Get a grip, Helsing," he muttered, setting off back to the campsite. As he walked, he tried to convince himself that he'd imagined what had happened, but the feeling stayed with him: something was out there, watching him.

He found Gideon sitting with Frank and Sissy, enjoying a mug of coffee.

"Mr. Gideon?"

The tour guide looked up with a smile. "Oh, no, it's just Gideon. Max, isn't it?"

"Gideon tells us you rappelled down High Crag this afternoon. How neat was that?" asked Sissy, twirling her necklace around her forefinger.

"Rappelled is a bit of a stretch," Max said, smiling, before turning back to Gideon. "Could I talk with you?"

"Do you guys mind?"

"Go ahead," said Frank. "We'll keep the log warm for ya!"

The tour guide rose and walked with Max toward the riverbank, the enamel mug still steaming in his hands. Max noted that Whedon's eyes were following him. After the business on the rock face, Max had secured his position as Public Enemy Number One. Max and Gideon stepped out onto the jetty, where the sounds of Max's schoolmates were dampened by the babbling rush of the creek.

"I was wondering," Max began, "after our chat this afternoon: do *you* believe in bigfoot?"

The tour guide ran a hand through the wild nest of curly hair that encircled his bald head. "I've been up and down this creek more times than I've had hot dinners and I've never seen a Sasquatch. Only Ike Barnum knows these woods better than I do."

"Who's Barnum?"

"A hermit who lives in the forest close to the summit of Battle Falls. Backwoodsman."

"I think we met him when we arrived in town this afternoon. At the general store."

"That sounds about right. Old Ike comes down once every few months to grab essentials. Pickles, usually, and a tin o' tobacco. He was born in these mountains and he'll no doubt die here too."

Max nodded. "He said we needed to beware the Beast of Bone Creek."

"Barnum said that? Maybe he's gone a little stir-crazy, up there all alone. But if anyone's seen something, it's probably him."

"But do *you* believe there's a Beast of Bone Creek?"

"Between you and me," said Gideon, "maybe there is. I've heard things I can't explain up here, late at night. Strange sounds." He clapped his hands. "Barnum's right to tell you to be wary when you're out in the mountains; there're all kinds of things that can cause you harm. As for bigfoot, Max, I'd personally need a bit more evidence before I tied my flag to the 'squatch-mast!"

They strolled back to the camp, in time to find Frank and Sissy leading a rousing chorus of campfire songs. Max rejoined Syd on the log, while the tour guide started to conduct the sing-along. Everybody seemed to be having a most splendid time, except for Whedon.

"Okay, folks, let's call it a night!" shouted the principal over the singing. There was a collective chorus of *aaaaws* from the students, and even the couple from the Midwest shared their disappointment.

"Mr. Whedon," said Boyle, making his voice heard over the noise of his classmates. "Any chance I can call for a cab to get a hotel room in town? This place is a dump." He turned to Gideon. "No offense."

"None taken," replied the camp director, rolling his eyes.

"Kenny, you need to stay here with your classmates," said Whedon. "I promised your father I wouldn't let you out of my sight."

"Sucks to be me," muttered Boyle, sitting back down with Ripley and Shipley.

"You heard me, didn't you?" said Whedon to the others. "Bedtime. Let's go."

"Aw, really?" said Gideon, pulling a sad face and putting his hands on his hips. "C'mon, Principal Whedon, the boys and girls are having such a swell time. Can't you give them ten minutes more?"

Even in the dark, Max could see the color flushing Whedon's face.

"Rookie error from Gideon," whispered Max. "Mistaking Whedon for a real human being."

The beam from Whedon's head lamp passed over the musical mob. "Tomorrow we've got an early morning and a busy day of activities. You have two minutes to get yourselves into your bunkhouses. What are you waiting for?"

The children and teachers rose and trudged back to their lodges. The couple waved good night and set off back up the riverbank in the direction of their tent. Only Gideon was left behind by the fire pit, waving merrily to the departing school party while imparting one last cautionary pearl of wisdom.

"Good night! Sleep tight! Don't let the bedbugs bite!"

SEVEN

xxx

BEDBUGS

Max lay in his bed, staring up at the warped slats of wood that spanned the bunk above. Each time Whedon moved, the thin strips of timber groaned. If Max concentrated, he was sure he could hear the fibers splintering, ready to deposit the principal upon him at any moment. Then, of course, there were the noises. Scratching, murmuring, belching, and other less palatable sounds, all emanating from the mustachioed headmaster.

Max had witnessed some truly terrifying sights in his fledgling career as a monster hunter. Bloodsucking vampires topped the list, with flesh-eating zombies, shapeshifting lycanthropes, and tentacled schattenjägers all close behind. Few of these fiends matched the horror of Principal Whedon—dressed in vest and long johns—clambering up a bunk bed ladder inches from one's face.

He looked across at JB, fast asleep in the next bed. Max

craned his neck, trying to hear if any of the other guys were still awake. He heard nothing but a discordant chorus of snores drifting throughout the lodge. Pulling back the blanket from his bed, Max swung his feet onto the cold timber floorboards. He winced as he rose, trying not to cause a sound, though the bunk betrayed his every move. The frame moaned as he levered himself from his mattress, but for once Max's luck was with him. He stepped over the pee bucket—thankfully, thus far, unused—and across to the window.

Max wiped the misted glass with his forearm and looked out. The odd shaft of moonlight found its way through the pine trees, illuminating the bare earth of the campsite. Nothing moved. Max lingered a moment longer, watching the forest for any sign of life. The occasional light twinkled, floating through the darkness, the glow of a firefly, no doubt. He felt a shiver race across his flesh. Squinting into the dark forest, he had that uncanny feeling that something supernatural was staring back. Reaching into his pajama pocket, he pulled out his cell phone and punched the PIN. The display came up, glowing blue. He still had questions, and there was only one person who could help him: Jed.

What could Jed tell him of the Beast of Bone Creek? Of bigfoot sightings in New Hampshire? Better still, was he aware there were rock drakes and heaven knew what else living in the White Mountains? Max hit the compose button and started typing a text message.

Hey, Jed—

"I'll take that," said Whedon, reaching down from his bunk to snatch the cell from Max's hand. "Consider it confiscated." The principal slipped the phone under his covers. "You seem intent on pushing your luck at every opportunity, Helsing. Just like your father—until his luck ran out. What you need is some real discipline, the kind only professionals can give. You step out of line again, I'll take steps to make sure you get it."

"What, like suspending me?"

Whedon smirked. "And leave you to your own devices? Suspension only works when there's a parent at home to reinforce the lesson."

Max shook his head. Whedon wasn't making any sense. "What d'you mean? I've got Jed keeping me in line."

Whedon laughed humorlessly. "Cross me again and I'll report that old fool to social services. We'll have you whipped out of that dusty old house and put into foster care before you know it, with the state keeping an eye on you. How does that sound, Helsing?"

Whedon had no idea what was at stake. Max had a job to do, protecting the norms from the monsters, the fiends, the things that went bump in the dark. Jed was integral to that mission. Besides, the old boxer was the only family Max had left. There was no doubting Whedon could pull whatever strings he liked and ensure that Max was thrown into the system. His life with Jed would be over, as would his life as a monster hunter, and who knew what that meant for humanity?

"You and I have an understanding, young man?"

Max nodded.

"Back to bed, Helsing."

Max collapsed onto his mattress. Would Whedon carry through with those threats? Max couldn't risk finding out. The principal shifted about again overhead, the bed frame protesting with every movement and causing Max to wince. There was a short, sharp, high-pitched emission that could only have come from one place. Max rolled over and buried his face in his pillow.

This was going to be a horrible night.

SISSY PETERSON COULD NOT GET WARM.

"Frank," she whispered to her fiancé. "Are you still awake?"

He didn't reply, wrapped up in his sleeping bag beside her, toggle drawn tight beneath his chin. Typical. She hated being the last one awake. When she was a kid growing up in Fergus Falls, she and her sister had shared a bedroom. Invariably, her big sis would nod off first, leaving Sissy with only the darkness for company. She'd always had a wild imagination, and it didn't take much for her to see the shapes start to shift in the shadows. It was the same beast, every night, creeping toward her, glowing eyes, gnashing teeth, breath steaming as it approached. A loud cough and a kick to her sister's bed would be just enough to wake her sibling and disturb her from her slumber. Then it would be a race for Sissy to fall asleep.

Sissy smiled. Those kids from Boston seemed a neat bunch, as was the tour guide who'd made them feel welcome since arriving in Bone Creek. It was going to be a fun week if they kept crossing paths with that crowd.

The twig snap brought her out of her reverie instantly. She lay still, listening for further sounds. She and Frank often went camping, and were used to wildlife sharing their campsite with them. Chipmunks, porcupines, rabbits, and such. Those critters didn't tend to cause twigs to snap, though. Only a heavy footfall would do that.

"Frank," she whispered. "I think there's something out there."

No reply.

Sissy shook her head. This was like being a kid again. Her imagination was getting the better of her. She must have been hearing things. As she breathed a sigh of relief she heard another twig snap.

Crack!

A bigger one, perhaps a branch? What could break a branch? A coyote? Were there lynx in the White Mountains? A black bear, perhaps?

"Frank!" She was louder now, giving her fiancé a shove. He grunted, reluctantly stirring.

"Whassit, Sissy?"

"There's something *out there*," she said, pointing at the tent wall.

"Oh, c'mon, honey. You and your imagination. You're just dreaming or somethin'."

"I am *not*," she insisted, giving him another shove. "There's something outside the tent, moving around."

"Probably a raccoon."

"It is *not* a raccoon."

Frank struggled upright in his sleeping bag, looking like a man-size caterpillar as he peered at her.

"If it puts your mind at ease, I'll take a look," he said, smacking his lips, freeing one arm from the confines of his cocoon as he craned forward, doubling over.

"Be careful," Sissy whispered.

"Sure," said Frank with a smile as he grabbed the tent zip and drew it up. "Last thing I need is a smackdown with a squirrel." He gave her a wink and turned back to the tent flap, drawing it back.

One look outside was enough.

Frank let out a cry and dropped the flap back into place, his fingers fumbling frantically with the zipper. Sissy let out her own yelp of shock, grabbing Frank by the shoulders and shaking him.

"What is it, Frank? What's out there?"

Before he could reply, the foot of his sleeping bag was suddenly yanked out from under him, whipping his feet up, and causing him to fall back in the tent with a *thump*. He looked up at Sissy, one arm hanging out of his tightly bound cocoon, and gave her a look of abject fear. Slowly, something drew him down to the bottom of the tent toward the exit.

"Get me out of this thing!" he screeched, fingers fumbling for the toggle that kept him from emerging from the bag. Sissy reached for him, trying to help, her fingernails leaving scratches across his shaking hand.

From outside, there was a low growl.

"Please, god, no!" Frank screamed, as he was shaken furiously from side to side by his legs. Sissy's hands clutched at his freed arm as his face twisted into a mask of horror. Frank's cries rose higher as Sissy held on with all her might. Then with a vicious yank he was torn from her grasp and dragged, wailing, into the darkness.

His screams stopped suddenly, and Sissy found herself alone. Her panicked breathing changed to stifled sobs. Her hands found the flashlight beside Frank's bedroll, trembling as she picked it up. She tried hitting the switch once, twice, three times, her fingers numb with shock. On the fourth attempt the light burst into life, and Sissy cast it over the bottom of the tent, then aimed the beam at the gap in the flaps. She kept the flashlight trained on the thin sliver of darkness as if that might hold back the night, and whatever terrors lurked within it. She held up the crucifix that Frank had given her.

When the tent flap eventually peeled back, and the Beast of Bone Creek appeared, Sissy's own scream caught in her throat. The tiny crucifix slipped from her hand. All strength and sanity evaporated in that terrible moment, as a monster from her childhood, forged from nightmares, returned: breath steaming, teeth bared, eyes aglow with hunger.

EIGHT

xxx

MORNING IS BROKEN

Max had enjoyed better nights' sleeps. Truth be told, he'd had more enjoyable tooth extractions. Whedon's full repertoire of snores had been deployed over the course of the night, from gentle clucking through full-on buzz saw. Furthermore, his skin was alive with fresh insect bites. Whether they were flying, crawling, or flesh-eating insects was difficult to tell, but the Great Outdoors had certainly lost its appeal. Weary and aching, he'd fallen out of bed to a commotion in the lodge's main room, where raised voices ensured that nothing in Bone Creek remained asleep. The sight of Syd poking her head around the doorframe made him reach for his sleeping bag, drawing it over his boxer shorts in an attempt at dignity.

"What part of 'Boys' Dormitory' don't you understand?"

"Whatever, Helsing," she said, rolling her eyes and dismissing him with a wave of her hand. "Pull your pants on and make yourself decent. You need to get out there to hear this."

Hopping into his jeans, Max followed his friend into the lodge's communal room, where not only the boys were gathered, but also the girls. Whedon and Mr. Mayhew stood beside Gideon, blocking the exit. The tour guide was all smiles, trying to calm the growing clamor. Whedon was less compassionate.

"Keep it down! You need to cooperate. Listen to what Mr. Gideon has to say."

The little man smiled appreciatively at the principal's stern words before addressing the kids.

"There really is nothing to be alarmed about, children. This is just a routine investigation from the Bone Creek police. A minor case of missing persons is all. I'm sure they'll turn up safe and sound. In the meantime, I've got a full schedule of fun planned for us, starting with kayaking—"

"Who's missing?" shouted Ripley from the rear of the mob.

"Yeah, who are they looking for?" added Shipley beside him.

"Please, guys, don't worry yourselves," said Gideon. "We have good police in Bone Creek. They'll find our lost lovebirds, fear not."

"Lovebirds?" hissed Max to Syd. "Is he talking about Frank and Sissy?"

"Yeah. Seems they disappeared in the night. They've left

everything: their gear, their tent, even their backpacks."

"It's bigfoot," said JB quietly. "That's what everyone's saying."

Max could see the gossip flittering around the common room, could read the word upon the lips of his schoolmates. Max concentrated on what Gideon had to say over the flood of dumb questions.

"Boys and girls, I'm very confident that the police will locate Mr. Gunderson and Ms. Peterson. I promise you that nothing untoward has befallen our neighbors. There's every chance that they've set off early for a day's hiking."

"They left their boots, you said!" shouted Boyle, not letting the tour guide off the hook. "And all their clothes."

Gideon smiled and wagged a finger at the bully. "Then maybe they've gone for a bracing skinny-dip!"

"I ain't buying that," said Boyle. "I know how this stuff goes down, man. My dad's the chief of police in Gallows Hill. Crime fighting's in our blood."

Max barely stifled a snort of laughter. He turned to Syd. "Can you cover for me? I'm gonna go take a look."

"We're not allowed out, Max. We have to stay in here until we get the green light to leave. Whedon's barring the door."

"Please, Syd. This is me you're talking to. Just keep Whedon busy if he asks where I am."

"Busy?"

"Tell him I'm in the bathroom, suffering from an

assquake or something." He tiptoed back to his bunkroom, barefoot.

"Max," she hissed, but it was too late.

The paneled sash window provided little obstacle for Max, who pried it open and slid it silently up. He threw one leg out, then the other, lowering his torso through the gap until only his head and shoulders remained. He raised one hand, drawing the window back down as he clung on to the exterior sill, before allowing himself to drop onto the grass below. He landed deftly, rolling and coming up in a crouch.

Making a mad dash to the forest, Max quickly found cover in the tree line as he headed upriver toward where the couple from Minnesota had set up camp. An elderly police officer stood a short distance from the campsite, arms folded firmly across his chest. His glowering expression could've curdled milk, and his droopy white mustache gave him a look of abject misery. A second man, also wearing the uniform of the local police force, picked his way through the campsite. He was young, all vim and vigor as he stepped swiftly around the tent, snapping away with his camera. There had clearly been a ruckus; much of the missing pair's gear had been tossed around the area. Max was immediately drawn to the tent itself, which sagged to one side like a half-deflated football. The white material was torn and tattered, fluttering in the breeze.

"What do you think, Uncle Earl?" asked the younger man, as Max settled in a dense thicket of bushes within earshot.

"It's Sergeant Earl when we're working." The old-timer removed his hat and scratched the thin wispy hair of his scalp. "Don't rightly know what to think, Walt. Ain't no—"

"Bigfoot," said the young officer, interrupting before his uncle could reply. The older officer shot him a withering look.

"This ain't bigfoot," said Earl.

The youth looked up. "You don't think there's been an attack, then?"

"I never said that," said Earl. "But it ain't bigfoot—there ain't such a thing; didn't your momma never tell you that? Maybe it's a bear or somesuch." He stepped forward and crouched before the tent to point at the shredded cloth as it was caught by the breeze. He made a swiping motion with his hand, inches away from the canvas. "These look like claw marks to me. Distance between them tells me we're looking at a big one."

"Grizzly?"

"Did you *ever* pay attention in school, boy?" said Earl, shaking his head at his nephew's ignorance. "We don't get brown bears in the White Mountains, which would make this a freakishly big black bear."

"That usual?" asked a sheepish Walt. "A bear getting up close 'n' personal with folk?"

"Not really. They'll keep their distance normally, only coming into contact with humans if their habitat becomes threatened or unstable. The White Mountains is a big patch of wilderness. No need for them to be sniffing around here."

"What about wolves?"

"We don't get them up here, and that would be a bold or desperate wolf that chose to attack a couple of people. Besides which, the claw marks." Earl held the span of his hand over the ragged slashes again. "Nope, it's no wolf."

The young officer stood tall and whistled. "I swear, Uncle Earl, this has got the Beast of Bone Creek written all over it. It's bigfoot, is what it is."

"It is *not* bigfoot," repeated Earl, standing tall to tower over his nephew. "And you need to keep that flapping mouth shut, you hear? What we have here is missing persons. They're in these woods somewhere, and I—we—will find them. I've already put a call in to Nottingham: they're sending a scuba specialist out tomorrow to start trawling the river, but I'd hope this pair will have turned up by then. The *last* thing we need is rumor getting out that there's honest-to-goodness bigfoot activity in Bone Creek."

"But isn't that good for business, Uncle Earl? This should bring in more tourists, surely?"

"Tourists?" exclaimed the older man. "This news will guarantee us every loon, goon, and news crew from the surrounding states turning up to catch sight of something that's *not real*. That kind of exposure will get in the way of our search for this young couple. It's entirely unhelpful. We need to keep this low-key. Nothing alarmist. You understand?"

Walt shrugged. "Just sounds like bigfoot to me, is all," he mumbled.

Although he continued to eavesdrop on the conversation, Max was no longer watching the grown-ups. He was scanning the undergrowth where he was hidden, a peculiar yet familiar feeling creeping over him. Whatever had encountered the Minnesotans last night had lain in wait in this exact area, Max was sure of it. The foliage provided perfect cover from the campsite—he could hide there for hours and the officers would never find him, not unless they climbed into the thicket. The ground was cut up with animal tracks, small paw prints, hoof marks from a deer, the regular stuff one would expect to find in woodland—no enormous hominid footprints. There was, however, a faint musty odor in the air that caused Max's nostrils to flare. His head recoiled as his nose found its source.

Snagged upon a thorn was a tuft of rusty brown hair, about two inches in length. It was at head height with Max, confirming that whatever had been here, scoping out the campsite, had been big. He plucked the evidence from the bush, surprised to find the hair was wiry to the touch, coarse and fibrous. He gave it a second sniff, regretting it instantly. The musty odor, unmistakably bestial, caused him to gag. His gaze flicked back to the campsite at the sound of the deputy's excited voice.

"See! I told you! What's that if it ain't a Sasquatch print?"

Earl had joined the deputy, leaning over his shoulder. Max could see it from his hiding place, though, clear as day: an indentation in the hard, packed earth close by the tent.

Earl whistled. "That could be Mr. Gunderson's bare foot.

I swear, Walt, if you weren't my sister's son, I'd think about having you discharged from the force."

"Uncle Earl, look at it!" said the officer, exasperated. "It makes LeBron James's feet look like a dwarf's."

Earl was no longer listening to his nephew. He was focused on the bushes, stalking slowly in Max's direction, his eyes narrowed. Had he heard him? Max wasn't about to find out. Tucking the tuft of fur into the back pocket of his jeans, he started to retreat, keen to get back to the lodge before he was missed. By the time Earl found his little hidey-hole, Max was long gone.

NINE

xxx

"MESSING ABOUT IN BOATS"

The boathouse was a deathtrap. Every wall was stacked with canoes and boats, balanced precariously on top of one another. As the kids ran amok trying to pick the right kayak, Whedon had screeched and squawked like a constipated cockerel, quoting a hundred and one health and safety misdemeanors. Max had been particularly taken by the moth-eaten Pequawket kayak at the back of the shed, all peeling hide and frayed stitchwork. Gideon had pooh-poohed his request to use the antique boat—apparently, the last thing the camp coordinator wanted to do was fish a drowned schoolboy out of the creek.

As if the boathouse wasn't bad enough, then there was the water itself. While the girls showed restraint, trying to master the surging waters of Bone Creek, most of the boys wasted no time in charging, ramming, and capsizing their friends with piratical enthusiasm.

Max and Syd kept their distance from their more bois-
terous companions, having found a calmer stretch of water
in the river. Max was wrestling with his kayak and losing
the battle. Like rappelling, canoeing was a lot harder than
it first appeared, at least for Max. Syd was having no such
problems, circling him effortlessly while he fought with the
current. All the while, Max kept his eyes fixed on the riverbank, scanning the tree line. That feeling that he was being
watched, just like yesterday, hadn't gone away. If anything,
it was intensifying, making Max question whether he was
being paranoid. Was there a beast loose in Bone Creek? A
bigfoot? All evidence was pointing toward it. And why had it
abducted the campers? Were they even alive? Max winced,
his head spinning with unanswered questions. Whedon
was marching up and down the bank, shouting orders at
the children from the safety of dry land while Mr. Mayhew
and Ms. Golden joined them in the water.

"I don't like it," muttered Max.

"Your life preserver?" said Syd. "I think it suits you.
Brings out your eyes."

Of course, Max's floating device was bubblegum pink,
the result of being the last kid into the boathouse.

He mimed dying from laughter before replying. "Frank
and Sissy, funny girl."

"Me neither, but what can we do? We're here on a school
trip. You haven't got your monster-hunting hat on, Max."

"Syd, it's never *off*. I can't just stop being who I am. If
there's something monstrous going down, I'm there."

"Are you convinced this is monstrous?" she asked, keeping her voice low so the other kids couldn't hear the conversation, though there was little chance of that. There was too much shrieking going on as Boyle and his buddies splashed water all over the girls around the bend in the creek. Within the din, Max caught a high-pitched squeal; if those idiots had found a beaver or otter to torment, there'd be hell to pay. He let his kayak sidle up alongside Syd's, grabbing her paddle to stay upright.

"I might not have thought anything if I hadn't found that rock drake yesterday. That got me spooked. Then those two go missing—*and* a possible footprint? *And* the fur in the forest? Yeah, I reckon something bad's gone down, and I'd put my money on it being monstrous."

"Do *you* think it's bigfoot?"

"That tuft of fur I found could be Sasquatch. It was caught on the branches pretty high up, which would probably rule out a bear unless it was on its hind legs."

"What about the footprint?"

"Faint but large," replied Max. "Jed would probably be able to tell me what that fur comes from. He was a big-time hunter back in Grandpa's day, before the world wised up and realized it was a pretty pathetic pastime."

"Has Jed ever seen a bigfoot?"

"No idea. This is why I need to talk to him. But Whedon has my cell."

Syd allowed her kayak to drift into the middle of the stream toward the faster-flowing section of the creek.

"Gideon said we were all going to town after lunch for souvenir shopping. Maybe you can make a call then?"

"Sounds like a plan," said Max, following her into more challenging waters.

From upstream, the braying sounds of Boyle and his friends continued to make Max's skin crawl. Again, Max heard a high-pitched squeal. "You hearing that?" he asked with a wince.

"What?" asked Syd, but Max was already paddling clumsily upstream toward where the other kids were gathered.

He passed the girls, who had now firmly removed themselves from Boyle's shenanigans. Gideon was among them in his own kayak, after giving up remonstrating with their male counterparts. His overinflated life preserver looked like an enormous bosom that might explode at any moment. It made Max's pink vest look positively cool. The water frothed around Max, white and volatile, as the river cut its way through a narrow channel. Suddenly he was around the bend in the creek. Boyle was in his element, Ripley and Shipley keeping a safe distance as he repeatedly struck the water with his paddle.

"Hit it again!" shouted Ripley, waving his own paddle in his meaty hands.

"Go, Kenny!" whooped Shipley, ever the grinning cheerleader.

To the naked eye, it appeared as if Boyle had lost his mind and was simply thrashing the water in a fit of idiocy. Max knew better, though. He heard the squeals again, shrill and panicked, causing his stomach to churn. They were squeals of terror.

"That is one freaky-lookin' fish!" Boyle laughed.

He looked up just in time to see Max's kayak crash into him.

"Incoming!" yelled Max, deliberately too late, as he maneuvered himself between Boyle and whatever he was pulverizing in the water.

"Helsing!" cried Boyle, as the kayaks collided and his almost went over. Max managed to give the other boy a knock with his paddle, catching him across the temple.

"Oops, sorry, Boyle!" he shouted. "How do you drive these things again?"

His hapless kayak act took little effort, and was working. Max drew the attention of the other boys with his blunders while Boyle struggled to remain upright. Half submerged in the turbulent water, Max spied what Boyle had mistaken for a fish. Fairy glamour had a way of tricking the perception of those who were uninitiated, but Max saw it for what it was. Whereas Boyle saw a dying fish, Max saw a water nymph.

She was perhaps a foot in length, a perfectly formed miniature humanoid, her flesh shimmering with iridescent silver scales. She twisted and twitched in the current, gasping as if she were breathing her last. Max could see the discoloration along her right side, where Boyle's oar had damaged the skin, the scales flaking away from her body. Max remained between Boyle and the nymph, buying the fragile river spirit the time she needed to regain

NYMPH, WATER

VARIANTS: Naiad, Oceanid, Nereid

ORIGIN: Ancient Greece

STRENGTHS: Power to control bodies of water, save souls from drowning.

WEAKNESSES: Delicate constitution, tied to their water source.

HABITAT: Water nymphs can be found in various kinds of aquatic environments—the Naiad of rivers and streams, the Oceanid of the high seas, and the Nereid of the Mediterranean.

Historically and in classical literature, water nymphs have been recorded as being both helpful and mischievous to travelers. Not to be confused with sirens, mermaids, or selkies, the nymphs are highly intelligent and protective of the bodies of water to which they are guardians. They come in many shapes and forms, from the life-size humanoids of Europe to the smaller North American variety, often mistaken for silver fish—fairy glamour allows them to conceal their identity from the feebleminded.

—Erik Van Helsing, December 1st, 1855

PHYSICAL TRAITS

1. _Watercraft_—Ability to control the course of a body of water, albeit only briefly. This can include calming of turbulence, stemming tides, changing direction of flow, and even parting pools.

2. _The Nymph's Kiss_—The breath of a nymph can supposedly breathe life back into a drowned or drowning man.

—Esme Van Helsing, May 4th, 1864

Getting a sneaky smooch from a fairy sounds like fun, but drowning to test the theory doesn't seem worth it! Rumor has it there's one in the stream in HEMLOCK WOODS. Syd and I are gonna check it out. Fishing net and bucket should do the trick. . . .

MAX HELSING

June 14th, 2015

her senses. Her movements become stronger, more controlled, as she recovered from her shock. For the briefest, fleeting second, her eyes connected with Max's. Then she rolled in the crystal clear water and kicked away, darting toward the deeper waters in a flashing streak of silver. Max smiled, cherishing his small victory as the nymph vanished from view.

"Yo, Helsing."

"What, Boyle?" said Max with a weary sigh, turning about in his kayak to face his foe.

The paddle caught him straight across the temple. The kayak capsized, and Max went under. Three things occurred to him as he was deposited into the chill mountain waters of Bone Creek. First, he hated kayaking. Second, he hated Kenny Boyle even more. And third, he suddenly discovered a newfound appreciation for bubblegum-pink life preservers.

TEN

xxx

THE BOY AND THE BLOODSUCKER

Max stood naked in the boathouse, holding his towel open, and stared down. He could've fainted. There, high on his inner thigh, dangerously close to his unmentionables, was the biggest, most bloated leech he had ever seen. Its black flesh pulsed as it fed on him, firmly attached to his leg. Max took hold of its dark, moist body and pulled. The skin came with it, as the leech refused to let go of its tasty meal. Max placed a finger against his thigh beside where its jaws were locked on. He slid his nail along, pushing the creature aside and causing it to release him. His skin twanged back, spattering the floorboards of the boathouse with dark liquid as the leech squirmed in his grasp. He dropped it off the launch, the bloodsucker landing with a meaty *plop* back into the water it had come from.

"And I thought vampires were bad," Max muttered,

toweling himself dry. "Never thought I'd agree with Boyle, but I'm just about done with this dump."

He was buttoning his jeans when he noticed a movement through the cracks in the timber board walls of the boathouse. He froze where he was, turning his head to listen. Whatever was out there was doing its darndest to tread stealthily, and it was working. Was it the beast from the night before? Max looked around for anything he might use as a weapon. Only a twin-headed kayak paddle with bright red blades was close to hand. He snatched it from the rack and darted out the front of the boathouse.

Sprinting barefoot around the back of the shack, he leaped out, paddle raised like a nautical Sith Lord. Whatever had been there was gone, but Max spied the bushes moving up the slope. Max was off after it, dashing up the incline into the woods, eyes fixed on the moving undergrowth ahead.

Ducking beneath branches and bounding through bushes, Max powered on, in monster-hunting mode. He had no doubt he was chasing the Beast of Bone Creek at last. Leaping over roots and rocks, Max saw the branches and leaves rustling just ahead of him. He spied a dark shape darting left, trying to peel away from his path, but he cut it off, changing the angle of his sprint and diving left. He exploded through the undergrowth, paddle raised and scything down.

There was no bigfoot there. Instead, there was a grubby little man, no taller than Max's knee. The fellow looked up in shock as the paddle came down, leveled at his fur-covered head. Max twisted his arms at the last second, driving the makeshift staff into the earth just inches away. The man fell back, landing with a *thump* in the soil, as a breathless Max towered over him, chest slick with sweat. He pointed the paddle at the tiny man.

"Who are you?" he said, gasping. "And what have you done with the campers?"

"You going to kill me, Van Helsing? Is that it?"

The strange fellow dusted himself off and glowered at the boy. His weather-beaten skin was brown and leathery, and he carried a set of panpipes in his belt. His clothes were fashioned from patchwork animal skins—predominantly squirrel, from the looks of them—and adorned with birds' feathers. His ensemble was topped off by a rabbit pelt that he wore as a hat, tied beneath his chin by the paws, the bunny's ears sticking up as if it had just been surprised.

"How do you know my name, dwarf?" said Max.

The little man flicked dirt from the top of his panpipes with a tiny finger. He snarled, rising indignantly. "How dare you. I'm a brownie. Not that you'd give a flying fart, monster slayer!"

Max jabbed at the brownie with the paddle, sending his bottom back to earth with a bump.

"Stay put, short stuff," said Max. "I'm not done questioning you. Where are the two people who went missing last night? What've you done with them?"

The brownie placed the pipes to his lips and blew across

BROWNIE

AKA: domovoi, Jack o' the Bowl, gruagach, Heinzelmännchen

ORIGIN: Europe, widespread

STRENGTHS: Command of magic, stealth, great constitution.

WEAKNESSES: Oath-bound as guardian to particular place.

HABITAT: Guardians of homes, mills, woodland, hills—many have strong ties with nature.

These fairies are short of stature but large of heart, working alongside humans to mutual benefit (see: "The Elves and the Shoemaker"). The rising population of man has pushed the brownie to the far edges of civilization, where they claim stewardship over forest, field, and fen. Avoiding direct contact with humankind, brownies—like many fey folk—traveled to the New World with early settlers, finding new homes alongside indigenous magical creatures in America's wilderness.

The magical talents of brownies are rich and varied, encompassing all manner of arts and crafts, including music, song, and dance. This is the conduit for their enchantments.

—Erik Van Helsing, August 2nd, 1849

FIELD ACCOUNT—THE BANGOR BROWNIE

I was called to the wood mill of Mr. Archibald Hucknell of Boston, Maine, investigating a haunting that had led to anxious workmen. To my surprise, there was no restless spirit haunting this lumber yard. Instead I found a short, squat fellow, no higher than my knee, who had staked guardianship over the mill. It took all of my powers of persuasion to convince him that Mr. Hucknell had no need for his services. Crestfallen, the brownie's spirits soared when I found him a forest that would benefit from his protection. He remains there to this day.

—Esme Van Helsing, November 11th, 1868

In a splendid line from Thomas Keightley's seminal work, <u>The World Guide to Gnomes, Fairies, Elves, and Other Little People</u>, the brownie is described thus: "a personage of small stature, wrinkled visage, covered with short curly brown hair, and wearing a brown mantle and hood."

—Algernon Van Helsing, November 8th, 1942

I prefer CHOCOLATE CHIP COOKIES. Sorry. Couldn't resist.

MAX HELSING Nov 20th, 2014

them. Instantly Max swayed where he stood. He recognized the tune—he'd heard it before, atop High Crag before rappelling. The notes put him at ease and caused the fight to flood from his body. He was no longer so keen on smashing the paddle over the brownie's head. Sleep was a more promising proposition. He was even eyeing a nice bed of moss when his training kicked in.

Fairy enchantment: Jed's lessons had taught him how to react. The key was distraction, anything to take his mind off the music for the briefest of moments, but also to distract the spellcaster.

Max sang a line from his favorite Queen song—badly—the lyrics disrupting the brownie's melody. The little man was surprised to see his cantrip countered.

"Scaramouche! *Scaramouche!*" shouted Max, striking the pipes from the brownie's hands before pinning him to the leaves with a bare foot.

"What foul magic is that?" said the brownie.

"'Bohemian Rhapsody,'" said Max with a grin as his senses returned. "Beats nine out of ten fairy spells." His smile slipped. "You seem to know a lot about me, brownie, but I know nothing about you. How about you start answering some questions?"

"Or what?" snapped the tiny man, squirming and punching Max's foot ineffectually. He fished a pinecone out of a pouch on his hip and launched it at Max. It struck him hard across the bridge of his nose, making him see stars.

"That was you lobbing cones at me yesterday?" he said.

"And I'd do it again! Maybe rocks, next time!"

Max reached down with his free hand and grabbed the brownie by his animal pelt jacket. He gave him a shake, irritation and anger getting the better of him. This wasn't Max's style, but all of his frustrations were boiling over.

"Where are those campers?" he shouted. "What have you done with them?"

The brownie raised his little hands as if to shield himself from what was to come. Max saw genuine terror in the fellow's eyes, and it sickened him to the pit of his belly. He could feel the blood pumping through his veins, his head thundering. The little man might indeed know where the campers were, but brutalizing him wasn't going to bring Max any answers. He slackened his grip as the brownie began to speak.

"It's not us what's done nothing," he began. "It's . . ."

His words trailed away as he looked up at Max. His confession ceased abruptly, his eyes wide, no longer fixed upon his tormentor. They were looking past the boy, behind him. Max felt a cold chill settling over him as if the sun had been blocked out. He craned his neck and glanced back over his shoulder.

Being a monster hunter had prepared Max Helsing for many things. But nothing had prepared him for the Beast of Bone Creek.

ELEVEN

xxx

BAREFOOT VS. BIGFOOT

Max didn't need the *Monstrosi Bestiarum* to recognize a bigfoot. The monster towered over him and the stricken brownie, blocking out the light with its massive, menacing frame. Its head was hidden in shadow, the sun shining at its back like a halo. Well over eight feet tall, its body was covered in a shaggy coat of dark black fur. It was as broad as a barn door, as Jed was fond of saying, with muscles that rippled and bunched across those mighty hunched shoulders, where the coat was turning gray. Its arms were hung down to its knees, and two enormous shovel-like hands clenched at their ends. Leathery palms flexed as long, thick digits twitched, the clawed tips like bullets of ivory. Slowly, the monster leaned closer, revealing its fierce face to Max as he scrambled back, paddle in one hand, brownie in the other.

The beast's head was perhaps twice the size of a human's,

the skin dark as ebony, its broad slab of a forehead large and cumbersome. There were pronounced ridges across both its brow and cheekbones, while its nose was flattened, splayed as if it had taken a baseball to the face. The eyes were sunken within its head, circular and golden, and when they caught Max looking at them, they fired right back. It was like being stared down by a gorilla: something smart, something close to human, only not. Max saw an intelligence there, way beyond anything he'd ever encountered in the animal kingdom, and beyond much he'd encountered in the monstrous realm as well. The beast snarled, dark lips peeling back to reveal a frightening set of teeth to the boy and the brownie. Jagged incisors and cracked canines grated against one another, as a deep, gut-curdling growl emanated from the creature's chest.

One huge hand went up in the air, curling into a fist. Then it came down like a sledgehammer. Max tumbled back, pulling the brownie with him, and a shower of dirt erupted from the ground as the bigfoot punched the earth. The other arm shot out, grasping for Max's ankle. The boy narrowly avoided it, half running, half scrambling as his bare feet struck the soil. He hit a tree, catching his breath, turning in time to see a row of broad black knuckles flying toward him like a freight train. Max ducked and the fist pummeled the tree. He felt it shudder against his back, splinters of bark showering him and the brownie. He looked up to see the bigfoot almost on top of him, spittle frothing from between those tusklike yellowed teeth. Max dashed behind the tree,

SASQUATCH

AKA: Bigfoot, Urayuli, Swamp Monster

ORIGIN: North America

STRENGTHS: Enormous muscle mass, heightened senses, stealthy stalker.

WEAKNESSES: Fire.

HABITAT: Remote forest, swamp, and mountain.

This hominid is North America's greatest, most infamous cryptid. It seems every state has its own variant, with recorded sightings numerous. Not unlike the yeti of the Himalayas, the Sasquatch is a hulking wild man of the forest, a missing link between ape and man. Interaction with humankind has not gone well. Many are the instances when hunters, farmers, and foresters have died at the hands of this monstrous man of the woods. Debate within our profession rages regarding whether these are acts of violent, bloodthirsty aggression from the Sasquatch, or those of self-defense.

—Erik Van Helsing, November 17th, 1850

PHYSICAL TRAITS

1. _Feet_—The famous feet of the big foot! Not only do these allow the beast to stalk silently, but the toes are also prehensile, allowing the Sasquatch to grip and seize in the same way as a great ape.

2. _Arms_—Disproportionately long, when utilized in a fight these can strike like hammers.

3. _Teeth_—Powerful jaws are the Sasquatch's deadliest weapon, capable of crushing bones and rending flesh.

—Esme Van Helsing, January 18th, 1865

The indigenous monster of the Americas, the Sasquatch is to be rightly feared. This mindless killer cannot be reasoned with, cannot be pacified. Strike first and strike fast, or be another of the bigfoot's victims!

—Algernon Van Helsing, October 18th, 1946

Okay, should I fear them or befriend them??? Getting mixed messages here, folks. They're out there for sure—those sightings can't _ALL_ be a guy in a _MONKEY SUIT_!!!

MAX HELSING— Jan 21st, 2015

out of its reach, the brownie tucked under his arm like a football.

"Let me go!" shouted the little man.

"If I let you loose, you'll just be an appetizer for the bigfoot, before he gets around to me," he said, wrestling with the brownie. "Stop squirming. This is for your own good!"

Max was running again. The woods were dense here, with dark blankets of shadows looming left, right, and center. He was disoriented, but knew he had to keep heading uphill. That would take them away from the campsite and his classmates. Keeping monster and schoolkids apart was in *everybody's* best interest. As cryptids went, this one wasn't happy. Hell, it was furious.

The beast exploded from the foliage to Max's right, running straight at him, knuckled fists tearing up the forest floor. Max lashed out with the paddle in his right hand, catching the creature across the face and redirecting it into a pine. The tree bowed and groaned as the Sasquatch connected with it, sending roosting birds flying from the branches high above. It looked back at Max, amber eyes flashing with malevolence. Max backed away, trying to find a route through the woods that would be impassable for the bigfoot. He swiped the paddle at the beast, holding it at bay while the brownie squirmed in his armpit. Once, twice, three times it struck across the knuckles of the beast as those enormous feet shuffled forward. The creature roared, jaws open wide as it showered Max with stinking drool.

"Let me go!" cried the brownie. "For all of our sakes!"

The monster seized the bright red blade, wrenching it from Max's hand. With a quick snap, the paddle was reduced to kindling and tossed aside. The beast lurched toward the boy, grasping for him. Max dove forward at the same moment, skidding low as he went between the giant's legs. He came out behind it, leaving the bigfoot clutching at thin air as Max leaped up for a branch. The monster turned, in time to receive said branch in its face, prompting a hideous howl. Max didn't wait to see just how mad he'd made the creature. He'd taken three steps when he let out a scream of his own: the brownie's teeth were sinking into his hand.

Max dropped the little man in an instant. He tripped over a hidden root, landing against a toadstool-riddled trunk as the grubby brownie scuttled free. He was gone in a heartbeat, the bracken swishing with his passing. Max looked up at the bigfoot, who was also watching the brownie vanish into the undergrowth. It stood over the fallen teenager, free to smite Max. Instead, the monster stared at the boy, cocked its head, then turned around. Max lay against the tree trunk, panting, pained, and stunned as the bigfoot sloped off into the depths of the forest.

"You could've killed me. But you didn't." Max whispered to himself as the Sasquatch vanished from sight. "You were . . . protecting the brownie?"

Max rose unsteadily to his tattered feet. If the bigfoot was a peaceful beast, looking after its fellow creature of the forest, then what on earth was responsible for the disappearance of the campers? There *had* been a bigfoot print in the dirt, hadn't there? Yet the fur Max had found snagged on the bushes had been russet, not black. Max was certain of only one thing: the bigfoot wasn't the Beast of Bone Creek.

So what was?

TWELVE

xxx

THE MAN WITH THE ANSWERS

Max sat on the stoop of the general store and shook his head. Beyond the shop, every parking space was now occupied, with trucks, SUVs, station wagons, and jeeps. Cheesy stickers adorned bumpers and windshields—choice examples included HUNTERS WILL DO ANYTHING FOR A BUCK and BORN TO HUNT, although the highlight was a baby sign that read LIL HUNTER ON BOARD. Macho men (and in some cases even more macho women) stomped up the steps in their army surplus boots, slapping one another's plaid-shirted backs with blood-thirsty anticipation. One hunter posed before the carved bigfoot, rifle in hand and blowing a kiss, while her husband took a snapshot with his cell phone. Bone Creek was suddenly a lot more crowded than when the school group had first rolled into town, and Max didn't like it one bit.

"I don't mean to whizz in your root beer, Mr. W, but why do we have to stay in that shack? I've seen cleaner slums!"

It was Boyle's voice. The entire group of students had come into town for a little sightseeing, but Boyle had taken it upon himself to badger the principal at the earliest opportunity.

"Kenny," said Whedon through gritted teeth. "We're *all* going to stay at the camp. There'll be no skipping off into town for a fancy place to stay."

"But—"

"And I don't *care* if you have your father's Amex card. We're *all* staying in the bunkhouses. And that's that."

Boyle and his pals turned and stomped off down the street. Max saw Whedon's smile slip into a grimace. He knew Whedon only endured the boy's torment because of the kid's father. Not that Max was about to feel sorry for Whedon anytime soon.

"I got change!" said Syd, punching Max's shoulder as she skipped out of the store.

"Good stuff," said Max, straightening as the two of them descended the stoop, sidestepping more hunters. "This place is a madhouse."

"You're telling me. The only person who seems happy to see them is the storekeeper. They've gone through his shop like a storm of locusts. Fridges have been wiped out, all the food has been bought up, and his ammo was selling like hot cakes."

Max frowned as a family emerged from the store behind them, laden with food and drink as they made their way to a luxury SUV. As the trunk flipped open, Max spied the guns within. He shivered. He may have been a monster hunter, but he wasn't big on hunting. He certainly never went near firearms. Crossbows and slingshots; that was Max Helsing's style. Old-school weaponry, and even then only used against creatures that were a danger to mankind. He watched as Mom, Dad, and the twins fastened themselves in before pulling away from the store.

"There goes the happy hunting family," he said wearily as Syd handed him her change, and the two headed to the end of the sidewalk. "I swear, this has all the makings of a disaster movie. Every man and his dog has turned up ready to go bigfoot hunting. I wouldn't mind, but bigfoot isn't even responsible!"

"I wonder how word got out?" said Syd. "Seems like every big-game enthusiast in North America is arriving in town."

Max pointed across the way toward the police station, where Sergeant Earl was talking to a dapper journalist. The reporter's immaculate black coiffure quivered as he held his recorder to the policeman's drooping mustache.

"The police?" exclaimed Syd.

"Not officially," replied Max. Walt stood behind his uncle, a goofy smile of excitement on his face as another carload of grizzled-looking hunters arrived into town. "The sergeant's nephew reckoned he'd found a bigfoot print near the campsite, but from what I could tell, his uncle was trying to keep a lid on things. Seems Walt isn't singing from the same hymn sheet as Earl."

"Did *you* see the footprint?"

"I told you about my encounter, Syd," Max whispered. "Bigfoot could've ripped my arms out of their sockets and used them as Q-tips but chose not to. He was defending the brownie. No, something else is responsible for the campers going missing. That fur I found was russet, not black. And there were no other tracks that I could see, only hoof marks from deer trails."

Earl shook hands with the reporter and waved good-bye, pushing his nephew back into the station before him like an admonished toddler.

"Well, this is it," said Max, as they arrived at the ancient-looking pay phone on the street corner. It was fixed to the red stone wall of the bank, where bushes had grown around it after years of neglect. Cursing Whedon for having confiscated his cell, Max stared at the machine for a moment. It was a huge slab of ugly metal, covered in bird droppings and cobwebs, with a circular dial and cord handset attached to a pressure plate.

"You used one of these things before?" asked Syd.

"Nope. How hard can it be?"

Max spent the next few minutes losing his change and mind simultaneously, mistakenly pouring Syd's money into the machine at every opportunity. Even the reporter was observing Max's antics, apparently finding the boy's drama more entertaining than interviewing the horde of hunters. Finally resorting to reading the instructions on the machine, Max carefully fed the remaining coins into the slot and made the call. Moments later, Jed answered and Max recounted what had occurred since they'd arrived in Bone Creek.

"I'm gonna have to look into this, Max," said Jed. "Ain't heard much about monstrous activity in the White Mountains. Gimme the night to research things and I'll see what I can turn up."

"Get Wing on it too. He'll find you all the latest rumors and supernatural news from the Weird Web. If there have been any strange sightings in these parts recently, Wing will find them." Max paused for a moment. "This is unusual for New Hampshire, right? Y'know, bigfoot. I'm not taking crazy pills, am I?"

"Sasquatch activity is recorded in most of the United States, although particularly prevalent in some areas more than others. Most infamously you've got the Pacific Northwest, top of the heap being Washington State. Then there's plenty of bigfoot sightings in California, Oregon, even across the country, way down in Florida, where you've got all that swampland. Great place for a cryptid to hide out. But New Hampshire? That's a new one on me."

"This one was no killer, Jed."

"So you say."

"And there's the other stuff," said Max. "The rock drake, the water nymph, the brownie. That's more than just a coincidence, right? Something's going down in Bone Creek; I can feel it."

Jed chuckled down the line. "You sound like me now.

Listen, can you get back to this phone sometime in the morning?"

"I'll try to. Won't be easy. Whedon's got us all on lockdown back at the lodges. He's only brought us to town today for shopping, but it seems like every crazy with a hunting license has descended upon the town since yesterday."

"You be careful. I don't just mean about the monsters, son. It's the people you oughta be worried about, especially those weekend warriors."

"I'm way ahead of you, Jed. We'll be keeping our distance. How's Eightball?"

"He's fine. Pining for you, though. Lots of excess drool and more gas than usual. He's been sleeping on your bed, poor pup."

"Oh, man, you *promised* to keep him out of my room, Jed! It's gonna take ages to get his stink out of my sheets! And the slobber stains too!"

More chuckling from Jed.

Max growled as he caught on to what Jed was finding so funny. "He hasn't been on my bed, has he?"

"Nope."

"You haven't allowed him in my room either."

"Correct."

"You really are a meanspirited old devil, aren't you?"

"Yep."

"Take care, Jed. I'll speak to you tomorrow. Somehow."

Max hung up, stifling a smile. It was good to hear his mentor's voice.

"Couldn't help but hear you talking about the bigfoot there, Sport!"

The speaker was behind Max, making him start with surprise. He and Syd turned to find the reporter stepping out from the bushes beside the pay phone. How long he'd been there, Max couldn't tell, but it was clear he'd been eavesdropping on his conversation.

"Guess you couldn't," said Syd, "what with hiding in the shrubbery there and listening in on a private phone call."

"Hey, hush now, Precious—I was talking to Sport, here."

Max had never seen Syd lost for words, but the reporter had succeeded in achieving that very phenomenon.

"The name's Lyle Cooper. Write for *Grapevine*—you may have heard of us?"

He held a card out to Max, which the boy didn't take. Cooper reached out and popped it into the breast pocket of Max's jacket.

"You're a real piece o' work, you know that?" said Max, batting Cooper away and taking Syd by the arm. He tried to step around the man, but the shiny-haired journo remained in their way, blocking their route. "You gonna step aside? Or do we call the police? 'Journalist Stalker Harassing Minors'—that's going to make a swell story, isn't it?"

"I tell you what *will* make a swell story, Sport," said Cooper, his white teeth shining bright as he pulled a roll of bills out of his jacket pocket. "Whatever you can tell me about the Beast of Bone Creek. Word is you kids are staying in the lodges on the river, real close to where those folks went missing."

Max stared at the roll of bills. There had to be two hundred dollars there, and then some.

"Don't know what you're talking about," he said, following Syd as she barged past the reporter. "We saw nothing."

"Yeah?" said Cooper, pursuing the two as they made their way back down the street in the direction of the school bus. "I heard your little chat on the phone back there. Who were you talking to?"

The man continued to call after them as they hurried back to the bus.

"Better I pay you for that information than find out about it myself. Because I will, Sport. I promise you that. Lyle Cooper always gets his scoop!"

THIRTEEN

xxx

THE BRITISH ARE COMING

"This is too easy," said Boyle. "I want a moving target, a real animal to aim at. Not a butt-ugly fake warthog!"

Max's mind was elsewhere as they made their way along the trail, stopping intermittently to fire arrows at rubber animals that were placed strategically around the forest. This was field archery. Each mannequin bore a multi-colored target, the bright yellow bull's-eye marking the kill shot. There were five kids in their group—Max, Syd, Boyle, Ripley, and Shipley.

"Why have you and I never gone on a date, Perez?"

Max tripped as he walked along, and heard Syd's gasp of horror. Boyle carried on.

"Why do you keep giving me the cold shoulder? I cannot for the life of me see the appeal in hanging around with Helsing."

Max winced as he felt the older boy flick his right ear

from behind. He bit his lip and walked on. He made a point of staying out of the conversation; Syd was more than capable of handling Boyle. Better, if anything. Instead, Max scanned the maze of firs, eyes flitting from one trunk to the next, scouring the dark places between. His sense of unease was constant now.

A distant gunshot echoed through the forest. The sound of birds taking flight followed. It wasn't the first gunfire they'd heard recently.

"Hunters?" said Shipley. "You think they found bigfoot?"

Max hoped to goodness they hadn't found the Sasquatch.

"You're quiet, Helsing," said Boyle. "*Wet* gives? Something *dampened* your spirits? *Water* you thinking?"

His friends laughed in unison, clearly appreciating Boyle's river-related puns. The bully's grating guffaw was like a knife down Max's spine. He yearned to take a swing at him, but Whedon's threat was still ringing in his ears.

"Hey, Helsing." Another shove in his back. "I'm talking to you."

"Leave him alone, Boyle," said Syd, but the bully ignored her, planting a booted foot on Max's rump. He fell forward, sprawling in the bracken.

"You know what makes you and me different, Helsing?"

Max turned back to the bully, his fuse snapped.

"Besides halitosis and chronic body odor?"

Max saw the look of shock on the faces of Boyle's friends, but he also spied Syd's smile. Boyle snarled.

"You'll never have a chance with Perez."

"What are you talking about?" Max's astonishment was shared by Syd.

"You're like a kid brother to her," said Boyle. "You could never bag a date."

Max laughed. *"Bag a date?* She's my friend. Not that you'd know what one looks like, Kenny." Max pointed at Ripley and Shipley. "You've *bought* Tweedledum and Tweedledee here through intimidation. They're lapdogs. Flunkies. And they'd drop you like a hot potato if your dad lost his job tomorrow."

Boyle looked to his friends, but they'd suddenly taken a keen interest in their bootlaces, the undergrowth, the trees. The bully stepped up to Max and smiled.

"Tell you what, Helsing," he said, jabbing Max in the chest with a finger. "Seems we're both bickering over the same thing here."

"We are?"

"Perez," said Boyle with a casual wave of the hand in her direction. "So here's what we do. You and I each take a shot at the next target. Whoever gets nearest the bull's-eye wins Perez."

"Say what?" said Syd, suitably shocked.

"Yeah," said Max. "What she said."

"Whoever wins," said Boyle, "gets the girl. At the very least, I'm expecting a kiss."

"Listen up, Boyle," said Syd, her rage simmering. "I ain't some prize that's on offer. And I sure as hell won't ever be claimed by a creep like you. The only kiss you'll be getting is from my fist, and I don't give a damn who your daddy is."

Max placed a hand on her shoulder and pulled her back.

"Let's do this," whispered Max.

"Are you out of your *mind*?"

"I've never been thinking clearer, actually. Let him think he's gonna win you—"

"MAX!" Syd protested, but he interrupted her tirade.

"Hear me out, Syd. We both know you're not an object to be fought over, but this is a great opportunity to get him off our backs for good. I want to wager something else the other way. I've got a plan, I swear."

"But what if he wins?" she hissed.

"Hey," said Max, sticking two thumbs up and aiming them at his chest. "This is me you're talking to."

Syd shook her head as Max turned back to Boyle.

"We'll take that wager," said Max. "But I don't want to win this maiden's fair hand. She fell for me hard long, long ago."

"Don't push it, numbnuts," growled Syd.

"If I win, you get off my back. Permanently. And I don't mean just me. You quit bullying. Period."

Boyle didn't even hesitate. He spat on his hand and held it out. Max slapped it with his palm, and the deal was done. The two boys took their places, standing side by side. Through the trees, down an incline, and partially obscured by bushes was a life-size rubber dummy of a stag. At the center of its broad chest, Max spied the target, as big as a dinner plate, the bright yellow circle marking the bull's-eye.

Boyle stepped up to the mark, nocking an arrow in his bow. "Pucker up, Perez. This kiss better be good."

Boyle let fly, the missile hurtling through the forest, straight toward the fake deer. The beast juddered as it was struck in the chest. The arrow had found the bull, narrowly missing the red ring that surrounded it.

"Boo-ya!" shouted Boyle, going nose to nose with Max. "Beat that, Helsing!"

Max turned his spit-flecked face away. "Say it, don't spray it, dude."

Boyle was clearly a competent archer. What he didn't know, though, was that this wasn't the first time Max had held a bow. Jed had long ago converted the unremarkable-looking garage at Helsing House into a training arena, with all manner of archaic weapons decorating the interior walls.

Max brought the bow up, arrow set, string drawn taut across his cheek. He allowed himself to breathe once, twice; third time was the charm.

The arrow took flight.

The kids went up on their toes, peering over the bushes and down the incline toward the stag. The second arrow quivered beside the first, a touch farther toward the center of the bull's-eye. That is, dead center. Max turned to a stunned-looking Boyle as Syd high-fived him.

"So, about our deal, Kenny—"

They all heard the unmistakable *twang* of a bow, followed by a resounding *thud* as a third arrow found the target. All heads turned that way, as Max and Boyle both peered through the trees at the peppered stag. The final arrow had also found the bull's-eye, splitting Max's in two, the severed parts curling away like a freshly peeled banana skin.

Booted footsteps sounded in the forest behind them as a towering figure emerged from the shadows. The young man was as big as a brick outhouse and clad in black biker leather, looking every inch the Terminator on steroids. A gigantic longbow was slung over one shoulder, while an enormous ax head poked up from across his back. Syd was already smiling before he spoke.

"Robin Hood." Abel Archer smiled, winking to the girl. "He's got nothing on me."

Some folk rubbed Max the wrong way. Whedon was high on the list. Boyle also had a divine ability to set Max's teeth on edge every time he opened his mouth. But there was one person who made Max prickle with irritation like no other, whenever his lantern-jawed chin loomed into view: Abel Archer.

"Now then, my dear sweet things," said the smooth-voiced Englishman. "Who here has anything useful to tell me regarding the Beast of Bone Creek? There's a shiny dollar in it for you."

Sure enough, a silver dollar appeared between the thumb and forefinger of a black-gloved hand. Archer played it across his fingers. He was only a few years older than Max, but Archer had years of monster hunting under his belt, many of which had been kills. That wasn't Max's way. Where possible, the boy from Gallows Hill tried to relocate and protect many of the monsters he encountered. Archer shared no such interest.

"No takers, chaps?" he said, showing the coin once more to the kids.

Boyle slapped it out of Archer's hand, and only the Brit's lightning-quick reflexes stopped it from flying into the undergrowth.

"Who invited Harry Potter?" said Boyle, sneering at Archer. Boyle was a good six inches shorter than the Brit. Max had seen just how tough Archer was, and knew a freckle-faced grunt from Gallows Hill would provide no contest to the giant should he choose to take him down.

"I seem to have upset you, young fellow," said Archer. "Do accept my sincere apologies if we've got off on the wrong foot. Perhaps it was my crass offer of monetary compensation for any pertinent titbits I could elicit from your traveling companions? Maybe that's what's got your knickers in a twist?"

Boyle didn't answer. He was still trying to process Archer's words and translate them into American English.

"Abel," said Syd with a smile.

"Ms. Perez," said Archer, bowing his head politely. "Radiant as ever."

Max took hold of Archer by one enormous bicep and pulled him away. "Hey, Boyband. Let's you and I have a chat, okay?"

"Adieu, my carrot-headed acquaintance," said Archer,

saluting Boyle casually as Max hauled him back into the undergrowth. "Until we next cross wits!"

"Wow," said Max when the two got a bit of distance from the others. "I never thought I'd see the day where you and I had something in common."

"What's that?" asked Archer, tousling his fashionable mane of hair. "Monster hunting?"

"No. An enemy in Kenny Boyle."

"Yes, he's an odious little weasel, isn't he? How does one tolerate his company?"

"One doesn't," said Max. "Look, what the hell are *you* doing here?"

"Could ask you the same thing," said Archer, leaning against a tree as he took in the scenery. "Last time I saw you I was saving your bum in Gallows Hill. How did you end up here in the wilderness?"

"It's a school trip."

"You came bigfoot hunting on a school trip? That's a bit rich!"

"No!" said an exasperated Max. "That all happened since we got here."

Archer nodded as he peered around the tree, back toward the huddle of teens who were watching the pair suspiciously. Only Syd didn't have a look of concern. Truth be told, she looked rather pleased to see Archer, much to Max's annoyance. He had no reason to be jealous, but somehow the stupid Brit had managed to charm his friend with his stupid hair, stupid good looks, and stupid accent.

"Seems you're a trouble magnet then, Max," he said, plucking a twig from a tree branch.

"Must be, if you're here."

Archer opened his jacket, revealing not only rows of knives and smaller weapons, but also black cord snares and tripwires.

"Sasquatch is quite the draw for any hunter. Especially if monsters are one's specialty."

"So you're here on a trophy hunt?"

Archer leaned forward and put an arm around Max's shoulder. It felt like someone had laid a log across his back.

"I've got a client who alerted me to this sighting."

"The story only broke this morning!"

"I'm nothing if not on the ball," said Archer with a smile. "Got here as quick as my Harley could bring me. There's a whole host of hunters turned up in town."

Max sighed. "I saw them. Weekend warriors, Jed called them."

"The amateurs, sure, but there are some hard-core pros among them too. I've gotta bag this furry fiend before anyone else does. It won't be an easy one."

Max snapped his fingers. "Here's an idea: why don't you *not* hunt it, and if there *is* a Sasquatch in Bone Creek, you can leave it alone?"

Archer's smile slipped. "You seem to be forgetting the first rule of monster hunting, Max. The clue's in the job title: monster *hunting*. These are killers. We kill them before they kill any of us. Like those poor saps who were camping on the riverbank."

"We don't know they're dead yet," Max cut in. "They could be lost anywhere in the White Mountains."

"You know as well as I that those two are dead."

Max was shaking his head, but a grim part of him suspected Archer was right. It was preposterous to believe they'd simply gotten up and gone for a stroll in the middle of the night, leaving everything behind. Bigfoot might not have been the culprit, but something wicked was at play in the woods.

Through the forest, Max could hear the familiar voice of Principal Whedon, squawking angrily and calling for his young charges. He and Archer turned at the sound.

"Who's the little guy with the lip caterpillar?" asked Archer.

"My principal, and if he finds you out here talking to us, he'll lose his tiny mind."

"I've seen better-looking hobgoblins." Archer's smile vanished as he spoke to Max now. "It's not too late for you to jump on board. There's a good bounty on this bigfoot. I'll go seventy-thirty with you; that's a big bag of notes, chap. A damn sight more than whatever that journalist offered you for assistance."

"You saw that?" asked Max, wondering how much of his business over the last day Archer had witnessed.

"Lyle Cooper, reporter for *Grapevine*. Writes a column

called 'The World of Weird.' Raining bullfrogs, UFOs, Elvis sightings—you know the kinda thing."

"He was a real buttmunch."

Archer's great barrel chest rumbled with a belly laugh. "Now *there's* something we agree on. Think about it, Max: you and me, brothers in arms, the bright new future of monster hunting. We'd make one helluva partnership."

"This client of yours. Who is it?"

Archer shrugged. "A sorcerer in Palm Springs. Needs the heart and a few more components for a particular spell. Something to do with summoning a sand demon in the desert. Are you in then or what?"

"I was never *in*, Archer. You and I are chalk and cheese. You seek to kill where I seek to save."

Archer gave Max a look that suggested the younger boy might've grown a second head. "Save them? You're mental. The only good monster's a dead monster."

"There are plenty of monsters out there that mean us no harm. I don't want your blood money."

Archer stretched. "Suit yourself. I'll let you pass on this one, but you do realize at some point in time you're going to come running to me for help. You'd better hope I'm in a benevolent mood when that happens. Rejection can really hurt a man."

More shouting from Whedon, much nearer now, told Max that he needed to be getting back. He turned to go.

"Oh, and just so you know, it's not entirely about the

bloody money," said Archer. "I'm going home with a prize as well."

"Whaddaya mean?" said Max, pausing before returning to face the wrath of Whedon.

"A Sasquatch scalp," said Archer as he was swallowed by the shadows of the forest. "That trophy's all mine."

FOURTEEN

xxx

THE LAST SUPPER

Max's eyes were clenched shut, the noise chilling his bones to the marrow. A chorus of chomping and tearing, rending and ripping, as teeth tore into flesh in an orgy of ravenous destruction. He'd heard those sounds before—in the sickening din of feasting zombies, ravenous werewolves, and vampires lost in a blood-blind feeding frenzy. These were the sounds of nightmares, of terror and torment. They kept the norms awake at night. They came with the territory for Max.

He opened his eyes.

For a mob of hungry kids, the students of Gallows Hill Middle School could make one heck of a racket when eating hot dogs and burgers. Admittedly, it had been a long day, which could transform even the most mild-mannered individual into a bit of a monster. The police investigation at dawn seemed like weeks ago, and the hours since had been action packed. A late meal by the fire was bringing the traumatic day to an end, with students and teachers alike exhausted. Principal Whedon and Mrs. Loomis sat on a log across the fire pit. They made an unlikely pair of bookends, both yawning as the day's rigors caught up with them.

"Slow down," said Max, as Syd inhaled a hot dog the size of a skateboard. When she smiled, her whole face distorted. She looked grotesque, and she knew it. Max chuckled. "I can see what Abel Archer sees in you."

"You fink cho?" replied Syd, her words distorted by her head full of food. "I'm *irridigible*."

"I'm going to assume the word you were trying for was *irresistible*," said Max. "It's hard to argue."

One by one, as the meals were finished, paper plates were tossed into the fire. Whatever preservatives had saturated the burger and dogs ensured each dish went up in unholy green flames. The children cheered, drawn to the blaze like moths. Max clambered over his log and turned his back to the fire, reclining so that he was facing the river. The light of the moon had transformed it into a shimmering field of silver. *Let the others have the flames*, thought Max. *I'll take the cold moon every time.* His reverie was interrupted as Syd flopped down beside him, wiping her greasy face on the sleeve of her hoodie. Stifling a belch, she gave him a dig in the ribs.

"Yep, irresistible," repeated Max.

"What's your problem, grouchy pants? It's Archer, right? You don't like him. What is it? The looks? The accent? Are you seriously peeved he's here?"

"Ha!" said Max, a little too indignantly. "Would you listen to yourself? I couldn't give a flying rat's ass about Boyband. He's a big lunk o' dumb, and furthermore he's bad news."

"You sound like my mom now."

Max wagged a finger. "Then your mom speaks a lot of sense." The two of them laughed. "Nah, Archer's just one more piece of a disturbing jigsaw. Something's going on in these woods. The creatures, the bigfoot, the backpackers—"

"You think they'll find them?"

"Frank and Sissy? I'm hoping so. But the longer this goes on with no sign, the more I'm fearing the worst."

"I'm amazed they haven't told us to pack our bags and head home to Gallows Hill," said Syd.

"Why should they? Two adults have gone missing. As things stand, no crime has been committed."

"Still," said Syd, shivering as she looked up and down the river at the trees along the opposite bank. "These woods. Man, they're creepy."

Max couldn't argue. He stared directly ahead, across the water, to the great swathes of pine trees that loomed over the creek. Like Syd, he could see shadows shifting within the darkness, could hear the strange sounds as the forest came to life. Upstream, twinkling fireflies floated across the water, drifting from one bank to the other.

"I'll keep you safe, Perez," said Boyle, appearing between them from the other side of the log.

"Speaking of creeps," muttered Syd. "Thanks, Boyle, but I'll take my chances."

"Don't tell me Helsing's your knight in shining armor?"

He clipped the back of Max's head, causing him to turn and face the fool.

"What happened to you quitting your bullying, Kenny? I won that contest, or is your memory selective?"

Boyle came right up to Max, putting his forehead onto Max's and pushing hard. His head was solid as a rock. Max grimaced.

"Once the English dude turned up, he voided the bet."

"Lucky you," said Max, jerking his head away from Boyle's, aware that Whedon would be watching them from across the camp.

"Listen," whispered Boyle. "Keep it under your hat, Perez, but I'm heading out to carve me a yeti tonight. I'll bring you back a souvenir."

Max shot Boyle a dark look. "It's a bigfoot, Kenny. Not a yeti."

"Whatever, numbnuts."

Boyle headed back to his friends.

"Maybe we should try to stop him," whispered Syd. "He could do something stupid."

"No chance. That knucklehead's all mouth. He wouldn't dare go into the woods at night. I hope you appreciate all his bravado's for your sake, Syd. It takes a great man to act so persistently dumb."

Max pulled the tuft of russet fur from his pocket. If not bigfoot, then what? He twirled it in his fingers, tugging it taut, the coarse fibers strong as wire. He sniffed it gingerly, the musky scent bestial, acrid. To a norm, it would have prompted a primordial memory, a deep-rooted fear of the dark places, of hellish horrors, of things that go bump in the night. To Max, it reminded him that things were going to get mad, messy, and monstrous—and soon.

LYLE COOPER WATCHED IT ALL FROM HIS HIDING PLACE across the creek from the camp. Stakeouts were arduous affairs at the best of times; spying on a group of schoolkids would be frowned upon by any right-minded civilian, but this was a *big* story. Those kids knew something about what was going on in these woods. Cooper's hunches had never let him down before, and this occasion was no different. Cooper simply had to watch and wait for the kid to lead him to the story.

Cooper checked that the feet of his tripod were stable before looking through the camera lens, focusing in on the boy. He was leaning on a log, girlfriend by his side. That girl had attitude in spades. The two of them were staring directly his way. If he didn't know better, he'd think they could see him. They couldn't, of course. Cooper was well versed in picking the most secluded, secretive places from which to secure his scoops. The local police thought he was staying at Greenwoods' Guesthouse, after leaving him with express instructions to stay away from the forest. Fortunately, those two officers made the Keystone Cops look like Holmes and Watson.

He reached into his rucksack and pulled out his flask of coffee. The lid spun off, and he took a swig. The steaming brew warmed him, perking him up as he readied himself for a long night. His other hand brushed his immaculate coiffure of slick black hair. Ladies loved the hair. Back went the flask as the journalist kept his eyes fixed ahead. The opposite bank had been where all the activity had happened. Just upstream was the spot where the two from Minnesota had been camped. Many of the hunters had already set off higher into the mountains, seeking out the deepest, wildest parts of the forest, but that gut feeling told Cooper they were on the wrong trail. The beast would return to the site of its first attack; he was sure of it. And when it did—*FLASH*—the photo would be his.

Cooper had spent a career being mocked by so-called "serious" journalists. They took great delight in belittling his stories, especially those that featured in *Grapevine*. Cooper was no fool. Most of those stories were indeed hokum—sensationalist nonsense that was just there to shift numbers. It might have been made-up gossip, but some was his best work. "I Married a Martian" was still the most read article on the *Grapevine* website, and had secured him guest appearances on a number of late-night cable talk shows. Those TV spots in turn helped to promote his book, *The World of Weird*. Of course, if this story broke—the first pictures of undisputed proof of the existence of bigfoot—his career would go stratospheric. Interstellar. Hell, maybe even Lyle Cooper could marry a Martian!

The snapping of twigs behind caused him to sit up straight on his folding stool. That annoying raccoon was back, on the scavenge. There was a still-warm tuna melt in Cooper's rucksack, destined for his belly: he'd be damned if he was going to lose it to some jumped-up giant squirrel. He reached slowly down and picked up a branch from the forest floor. It felt heavy, good in his hands. It would feel even better when he'd whacked that raccoon with it.

"You picked the wrong guy to pinch a panini from, varmint," whispered Cooper, turning to strike the animal.

There was no raccoon behind him.

What starlight found its way through the trees was suddenly blotted out, as a great shambling shape lurched out of the darkness. The beast's body was coated with a wiry, rust-colored hair that bristled across its leathery flesh. As broad as an ox and with an enormous barrel chest, it towered perhaps eight feet tall, dwarfing the seated reporter as he craned his neck to look up. This was not what Cooper expected. The beast's hand shot forward, seizing him around the throat. Then the journalist felt himself being lifted into the air.

Cooper kicked the stool away, legs jerking frantically as he danced to the hangman's jig. He looked into the monster's face, expecting to find no intelligence there, only the mindless indifference of nature. Instead, the gaze that held his was cruel and cunning, the beast's yellow eyes widening and then narrowing as it measured up its victim. The reporter felt the monster's clawed fingertips digging into his neck, squeezing his windpipe.

Cooper brought his right hand back before lashing out with his makeshift club, aiming for the brute's grotesque face. The beast's other hand came up, seizing the heavy branch and tearing it from Cooper's grasp. The man watched as, seemingly in slow motion, the creature raised the branch high above that terrible, monstrous head. It came down with lightning, sickening speed.

The first strike split Cooper's temple, flattening that glorious, pampered coiffure. The next strike broke his skull. He was dead by the time the third strike descended.

FIFTEEN

xxx

HEAD COUNT

"I want all of you to get your stuff together!" shouted Principal Whedon, his voice making the walls of the boys' lodge tremble. "Now!" he added.

Yesterday had been crazy, but the bedlam Max awoke to this morning was something else. He looked across to JB, who was already sitting up in his bunk, blinking as he retrieved his glasses from beneath his pillow. Max jumped out of bed and scurried into the corridor, where he found a frantic-looking Whedon standing by the lodge door, peering outside.

"What's going on, sir?" asked Max, trying to shape his mop of brown hair into something that resembled order.

"Trouble, Helsing," said Whedon, without looking back. "The very worst kind you can imagine."

Max trotted over, bare feet slapping the boards as he peered around the principal and peeked outdoors. He saw

Sergeant Earl stride past the porch, heading around the bunkhouse. He caught the sound of radio interference as men and women spoke into walkie-talkies. Whedon suddenly did a double take when he realized Max was almost perched on his shoulder.

"Are you deaf, Helsing?" he squawked, mustache bristling like a wire brush. "I said get packed. Right now. We're leaving."

"But what's happened, sir?"

Whedon's face was ruddy and blotchy, eyes twitching, his voice a whisper. "There has been . . . a murder."

"Who's been murdered?" Max gasped.

"Can't say. Don't know the details. It's across the river there, on the other bank."

Bizarrely, at least for Max, this was the first time he'd ever enjoyed a conversation with Whedon where he hadn't been trying to bite the boy's head off. In the rear of the bunkhouse, Max could hear the other kids all rising, getting their gear packed, and bickering with one another. Only he had bothered to come and ask questions.

"So we pack our bags, sir. Then what?"

"Mrs. Loomis and I have been asked to ensure we're out of here pronto. Mr. Gideon has arranged for us to move to a guesthouse in Bone Creek. I strongly suspect I'll be driving you all straight home, though. I think we've had enough excitement for one week."

More of the boys were emerging from their rooms now to hear what had transpired. As they came forward, Max stepped back, slipping through the mob and returning to his room. JB cut a bedraggled figure in his pajamas, shoving his belongings into his backpack, as Max passed by and raised a finger to his lips. JB looked confused as Max took hold of the sash window and raised it quietly. Then he was craning his head to peek outside.

Sergeant Earl stood a short distance away, patting Walt's back as his nephew emptied his stomach's contents onto the grass.

"Let it out, son," he said, within earshot of Max. "Ain't nothing to be ashamed of."

Beyond them, fifty feet away on the opposite side of the creek, a team of deputies worked, stringing up yellow crime scene tape along the bank. Even from this distance, Max could see the trunk of one fir tree was painted red with blood.

"Just ain't natural, Uncle Earl." Walt wheezed. "Only a couple of body parts left behind. The rest of him gone." He clicked his fingers. "Just like that. Seems whatever killed him dragged him into the water to cover its tracks. That's one wicked beast we're looking at that's done this. Newspaper man comes to our town, seeking out a story, and this happens to him!"

"He was a gossip columnist. For *Grapevine*," said Earl. "Bigfoot must have drawn him here. Him and all the hunters. We've got you to thank for that, Walt. Hope you're happy now."

"Sorry, Uncle."

Earl checked his watch. "We got a busy day. Frogmen will be here within the hour. Sheriff's department says the FBI has already been in touch. Coming in by chopper. This place is gonna look like the set of a Die Hard movie by the time we're done."

"Well." Walt sighed. "It's no longer a missing person investigation. Somebody's been killed, by an animal. Or . . ."

Earl looked his nephew up and down. "Or what, Walt? The Beast of Bone Creek?"

Walt took off his hat and wiped his brow, the heat and stress of the morning clearly getting to him.

"They found prints, Uncle Earl."

"Bigfoot prints?"

Walt nodded. Earl sucked his teeth. Max closed the bunkroom window.

"Hey, JB," said Max, reaching up to Whedon's bunk. "Keep an eye out for me." He grabbed the principal's backpack and hauled it down. Dropping it onto the floorboards, he loosened the drawstring and dove in.

"What on earth are you doing?" whispered the bespectacled boy.

"Cover for me," said Max. "I'm begging you, buddy."

The smaller kid stood at the door, fidgeting nervously, as Max rummaged through Whedon's belongings.

"That's stealing," hissed JB.

"Can't be stealing if I'm taking back what's mine," said Max. "Bingo!"

Out came his cell phone. He punched a button to turn it

on, before throwing it onto his pillow while it came to life. He tugged on his ratty jeans, slipped into his Chucks without untying them. Torn limb from limb? Bigfoot prints found as well? Sasquatches were fiercely territorial, like many alpha predators. Had they somehow encroached upon a bigfoot's turf? But he'd *met* that bigfoot. It had been defensive, not aggressive, protecting the brownie.

The phone was ready for use. Max snatched it up and hit redial. In the other room, he could hear Whedon doing a head count, calling out all the boys' names.

"Helsing?"

"Here, sir!" shouted Max to Whedon, before creeping into the corner of his room, out of the line of sight of the door. Jed answered. Jed *always* answered.

"Jed."

"Max, thank goodness it's you," said his guardian. "The White Mountains, or more specifically Bone Creek: you're not going to believe this, son—"

"Reckon I am," replied Max as Whedon continued to shout names. "You've got to get up here. Things just got real."

"Well?" shouted Whedon, louder now. "Has anyone seen him?"

"Wait a minute, Jed," said Max, holding the phone to his chest so he could better hear the principal in the common room.

"One of you must have seen him," Whedon said, the pitch of his voice rising with panic. "Anybody?"

Max heard frantic footsteps now as Whedon kicked

open every door of the lodge, checking every room. The last room he entered was the one he shared with Max and JB. The small boy stumbled aside as the principal came in like a whirling dervish. Max hid the phone behind his back.

"What is it, sir?"

"I can't find him," said Whedon, eyes twitching.

"Who?"

"Boyle," he said, his face now draining of color. "I can't find Kenny Boyle."

IT WAS THE DRIPPING SOUND THAT SLOWLY ROUSED Kenny Boyle to consciousness, a steady, staccato *drip drip drip* that echoed inside his head. One eye opened, lazy and heavy, the lashes held together by something sticky. His vision was blurred and out of focus, the surroundings dark, dank, and murky. His mouth tasted salty, metallic, from the tip of his tongue to the depths of his throat. A foul stench clogged his nostrils, reminding him of Seamus, the family's Irish wolfhound back home in Gallows Hill. Whenever he came in from a walk in the rain, he'd stink the whole house up, his steaming, damp coat carrying the reek of whatever he'd rolled in. This was that odor, only worse.

Kenny tried to lift his head off the floor, but it felt heavy and cumbersome, as if twice its usual size. His other eye slowly peeled open, yet still his vision remained clouded, distorted. He clenched his eyes shut, casting his mind back to the events that had brought him here. His recollections were disjointed. He'd been boasting at supper, trying to show Perez how tough he was. What had he promised her again?

His eyes were open again, his vision clearing gradually, but the gloom remained. Slowly, the chamber he was in began to shimmer into focus. The ground and walls were rough and misshapen, with puddles gathered here and there that reflected a light source from around a corner. Was that daylight? Was this a cave? Either his eyesight was shot or the illumination was faint. Kenny prayed it was the latter, but the skull-thumping headache he was suffering suggested a concussion.

He'd promised Perez he was going to catch the bigfoot, hadn't he? Better than that, carve one up. It was partly for the benefit of embarrassing Max Helsing; that jerk really grated Kenny's gears. Kenny found him arrogant, cocky, a know-it-all. He always had that smug grin on his face, the one that said *I know something you don't*. One of these days he was going to knock him out. Then everyone would see how clever Helsing was.

Claiming he was off to hunt a bigfoot was one thing; acting on it was another. After waiting until Whedon's snoring in the bunkhouse had reached peak drone, he'd climbed out of bed, fully dressed. With his friends covering for him, he'd jumped out of the window. Ripley and Shipley had wished him good luck, but he'd had no intention of going on some monster hunt. Instead, he'd crept off into the bushes on the camp's edge, settling down with a chocolate bar to kill a half hour. The plan had been bulletproof: return at the appropriate time, breathless, filthy, and with his hair full of twigs. In his pocket he had a ragged bit of fur he'd stripped from some roadkill earlier. That would've been enough to convince the other kids—and most important Perez—he'd encountered, fought, and evaded a bigfoot. He would be a legend.

Kenny struggled once more to rise, levering himself off the ground with his forearm. With his elbow locked, he took a deep breath, squinting as he searched the shadows. He felt like he'd been flattened by a truck, which had proceeded to reverse back over him again. He caught something suddenly in the corner of his eye: a glint, something shining, only for the briefest moment. Kenny moved his head, trying to focus on what he'd seen. There it was: a golden glimmer on the ground, an arm's length away from him. He reached forward and clenched the tiny metal object as he dragged it back toward him.

Kenny could feel the cold metal within and the chain outside, trailing against his knuckles. He opened his hand slowly. It was a golden crucifix, fixed to a dainty, fragile necklace. Kenny recognized it. He'd seen it before, very recently. He tried to think back, but it hurt so much, the pain in his head intensifying. And why was his face so wet?

Lifting his free hand tentatively, he ran it across his brow and temple. It came away sticky. Even in the darkness, he could see the unmistakable sheen of blood on his fingertips. It was in his hair, across the bridge of his nose, and in his eyes. Clumsily shuffling into a seated position, he shoved the necklace into his pocket. Where *was* it from? His brain at last shuddered into gear, and the memory of last night's horror returned with a bang.

They were freeze-frames of his encounter in the forest. The sound first of all, a deep grunting snort that had caused him to look up. The giant shadow, a monstrous silhouette in the woods. The shaggy fur, the enormous frame. The eyes blazing a sickly yellow. The teeth bared. The teeth gnashing. The teeth opening as the beast lunged for him.

Kenny tried to stand, frail as newborn deer, his head woozy as he staggered to one side. He hit the wall with a thud, trembling fingers clutching the rough rock as he fought to remain upright. Every time he blinked, he saw those eyes, burning in the darkness, gold on black. A noise ahead suddenly, toward the light. Kenny's head came up, his blurred and bloody vision struggling to make out what was happening. A heavy snort, followed by a shadow growing upon the wall. It shifted as the ponderous footsteps approached, footsteps that confirmed he was facing a fiend from his worst nightmares.

Kenny stumbled back, away from the dim light, into the recesses of the rocky chamber. The panic that he'd felt last night was back, multiplied tenfold, as he fumbled in the darkness. His hands searched the walls, looking for a way out.

The creature was close now, stepping nearer on those dread feet, its yellow eyes burning with wicked glee. The crucifix! Kenny remembered now. It belonged to the woman, with the guy, the ones who were camping. The ones who had gone missing. What had become of them? What would become of Kenny? He sobbed for his mother. He wailed for his father. But nobody came. There was no rescue for the boy from Gallows Hill. Only the darkness, and the horror, and the Beast of Bone Creek.

SIXTEEN

xxx

VACATION VACATED

The White Mountains had rarely looked prettier. Clear blue skies bloomed bright and brilliant, while the treetops shimmered with the passing wind. The snowcapped summit of Mount Washington loomed large, big brother to its smaller but still mighty neighbors. Below the peaks, rivers rushed and brooks babbled, few as picturesque as the crystal clear rapids of Bone Creek.

But this idyllic scene was now blighted. Police officers took photos, sheriff deputies gathered evidence, and scuba divers searched the waters as the creek wound its way through the mountains down toward the Saco River. And a party of schoolchildren from Massachusetts made its way up a stepped woodland path, laden with luggage and heavy hearts.

"Get your gear up there as quick as you can," said Principal

Whedon at the base of the slope, ushering the children on their way. "I want your bags back in the bus *tout de suite!*"

All the while his eyes darted back to the camp and across the water to the hubbub of activity on the opposite bank.

"Mr. Whedon," said Sergeant Earl, sidling up to the teacher. "Walt will guide you back into town. He'll make sure your party gets settled in at Greenwoods' Guesthouse. I would, of course, ask that you remain there. Once I'm wrapped up down here, I'm gonna need to interview you. You know as well as I do that the business with Mr. Cooper happened across the river from where you were staying, but don't you worry: we're not looking at any of your party as suspects."

His smile was meant to be reassuring, making his droopy mustache flicker, but Whedon didn't react. Earl continued.

"I doubt there's much you'll be able to tell me—it's clear you've all had an awful shock—but these are just formalities. I don't want to cause your students any further distress. Once we're done with the questions, you can be on your way, back to Boston."

Whedon smiled nervously and mopped his brow. "Thank you, officer. We'll, er . . . we'll be waiting for you there."

From the middle of the procession of kids, Max caught the conversation. As the police sergeant made his way back to his staff on the jetty, Max couldn't resist having a quiet word with Whedon.

"Hey, sir. I was wondering: have you actually *told* the police that Boyle is missing? It's just that, well, it doesn't look that way to me."

When Whedon turned to Max, his ashen face was slack with worry. He grabbed Max, jerking him away from the other kids and pulling him close.

"He's not *missing*, Helsing."

"Sir," said Max warily, his voice low. "Boyle *is* missing."

The principal shook his head, sweat beading on his brow. "Boyle said he was heading to town to get a room in a hotel. We all heard him. I just need to get over there and knock on a few doors. He'll turn up in no time."

Whedon was unraveling before Max's eyes. The bluster and arrogance that made him the King of Gallows Hill Middle School were evaporating. He should have been informing the police and calling Boyle's father. Thinking the boy would be holed up in a hotel was just clutching at straws, wasn't it? He couldn't *really* believe what he was saying, could he?

"He'll turn up in town," whispered the principal. "Just you wait and see, Helsing; he'll turn up."

Max had a sickening feeling that whatever the journalist Cooper had fallen foul of, it was the reason Boyle had vanished too.

"Um, listen, sir," said Max, hitching his thumb back at the lodge. "I think I might have left something in the bunkhouse. Can I just dash back and get it?"

Whedon wasn't listening, his mind elsewhere as he continued to wave the other students up the log steps while watching the cops go about their business. Max backed up, bumping into JB coming the other way.

"Dude," said Max, patting the smaller boy's arm. "Can you tell Syd that something's popped up?"

"Popped up?"

"Yeah. A work thing. She'll know what that means."

"*I* know what you mean," said the shy bespectacled kid. Max arched an eyebrow. "What? You think everyone who lives in Gallows Hill has their heads up their butts? Weird stuff goes down. All the time. And you're usually involved. I'll let Syd know she shouldn't worry, and you'll catch up with her later."

"Wow," said Max, more than a little stunned that JB was savvy on the supernatural, even if only in a small way. He bumped fists with the kid and walked slowly until he was out of sight of Whedon, then dashed back to the lodge. He went in through the rear window again—Earl was at the front of the building, in conversation with a man from the state police. Hauling his backpack in after him, he opened it up. Loaded as it was, it would just slow him down, and there was only one thing he needed from it. He tipped the bag out onto the bed. Spare clothes, matchbox, comics, and souvenirs showered down. A squeaky toy for Eightball, a snow globe for Wing, beef jerky for Jed, a half-eaten bag of gummy worms—the bed was littered. Last of all came what he was seeking: his messenger bag. It went with him everywhere, on every job. Throwing it over his shoulder, he paused before grabbing the candy and shoving it into the bag. Always be prepared. He dashed through into the common room, mindful of the rotten, creaky floorboard, and quickly rooted through the kitchen area. Then he was back through the bedroom and clambering out the window.

"Who've we got here?"

The voice made Max start as he landed on the ground. He turned, surprised to find their tour guide standing there, hands on hips, looking stern.

"Mr. Gideon!"

"Just Gideon, Max. What on earth are you up to, young man? Don't you know you need to catch up with your classmates? They're all heading back to town."

"I, um . . . forgot my bag," he said sheepishly, before patting his satchel. "Silly me."

"Indeed, young man. Silly you." His smile was weary, as if the weight of the world were upon his shoulders. "You know, Max, I truly am sorry about all of this. Still, at least you're all safe and sound, eh?"

Safe and sound? So Whedon hadn't told Gideon about Boyle's disappearance yet, clearly hoping he could resolve the matter himself.

"This really wasn't what I had planned for you and your friends, you know?" said the tour guide.

Max shrugged. "I didn't remember seeing animal attacks, death, and disappearances in the brochure. Don't sweat it, dude. This isn't on you."

"No," said Gideon, looking over his shoulder at the forest that bordered the adventure camp. "This is Bone Creek itself. I should've believed the gossip."

"The gossip?"

"The Beast of Bone Creek. I never believed in bigfoot. Never believed such a monster could be roaming these beautiful mountains." His face drained of color. "Doing such terrible things."

"Hey, it may just be a bear or a wolf, Gideon. Don't leap to conclusions."

Gideon's usually cheery demeanor had slipped, replaced by one of grave concern. "I've lived here long enough to hear every tale. And I've chatted with Ike Barnum enough to know there must be some truth in them too."

Max had heard that name before. "The hermit, right?"

"Indeed. Nobody knows Bone Creek like Old Ike. He's the best tracker there is around these parts."

"Why haven't the cops brought him in to help them with the search, then?"

Gideon whispered. "They reckon he's touched in the head. Not all there. I've heard Sergeant Earl say he's a liability."

"Do you think he's crazy?"

"Well, he does have an overfondness for pickles and chewing tobacco, and he doesn't much like strangers, but that hardly makes him crazy. Eccentric would be a kinder description. They should've enlisted his help from the beginning, once that poor couple vanished."

An idea blossomed in Max's mind.

"Where does Barnum live again? You did mention it, last time we chatted."

"Did I? He's way up beyond High Crag, where we rappelled the other day."

"Oh yeah, that's right." Max snapped his fingers as if he were trying to recall the conversation that had never taken place. "It's easy to find because of the . . ."

He left it hanging.

"Oh, his cabin is up past the waterfall, maybe half a mile, on the patch of woodland where the twin streams meet. Easy to miss, just as Barnum likes it." Gideon suddenly looked hard at Max. He stroked his goatee and eyed him suspiciously. "A lot of questions here about my old pal the hermit. You weren't thinking of paying him a visit, were you?"

Max kept his best poker face. "Criminy, no. I've had enough of Bone Creek. I just wanna get home now."

"Good kid," said Gideon. "Leave the manhunt to the professionals."

"Take care, G," said Max, shaking the man's hand.

"You too, Max Helsing. Now get a wiggle on, before they leave without you!"

Max nodded and set off toward the tree line and the path that led up to the parking lot where the school bus was waiting. He looked back just once. The diminutive tour guide was standing at attention, performing an immaculate scout's salute. Then Max was gone, up the log steps. Once out of Gideon's sight, he hopped off the staircase, vanishing into the cool, dark shadows of the pine forest.

SEVENTEEN

xxx

THE HUNT

Max knew he was being stalked.

The last of the Van Helsings shared the same keen senses as his forefathers, picking up on things that others might have missed. A terrified scream in a chorus of cheers. A smell, sweeter than flowers, that promised rot and ruin. A pair of eyes, watching in the darkness. A branch snapping in the woods. Whoever, or whatever, was following him, it was doing so from a distance, but drawing ever nearer. He'd felt its presence for a good hour. The brownie? Perhaps. The Sasquatch? He hoped not. The true Beast of Bone Creek? Max's pulse quickened. He ducked behind a big pine, flattening himself against the trunk as he waited for what might come. He lifted the flap of his messenger bag, hand slipping in to close around the polished wooden length of his lucky stake. Out came Splinter, his family heirloom, the weapon's shining silver tip ready to dish out some damage.

A distant gunshot sounded, causing Max to flinch. He hated firearms, and he'd heard plenty in the White Mountains this day already. Max's breathing was shallow, allowing him to better listen to his approaching foe. The footsteps were steadily getting louder, twigs breaking under their weight. Could it be the Beast? Would it dare attack in broad daylight?

As his pursuer rounded the tree, Max leaped out, stake descending. He changed the angle of its scything action at the last moment, narrowly avoiding a shocked Syd as Splinter's silver tip connected with the trunk above her head.

"Whoa, Mr. Stabby!" she cried out, arms whirling as she stumbled back and threatened to land in a nearby nest of brambles. Max reached out with his free hand, catching her.

"What the heck are you doing, following me like that, Syd? You could get yourself hurt. Or worse! Why didn't you call out or something?"

"Call? Sure, that's what we need to be doing, Max." She tugged herself free from him, bristling with annoyance. "You do realize the woods back there are swarming with cops, and the woods up here are full of hunters."

"If you shouted you were coming, that would've stopped the hunters from mistaking you for a wild animal. Creeping around in the forest is one surefire way of getting buckshot in your butt!"

"It's also a surefire way of alerting the police that we're snooping around up here."

Max stashed his stake back inside his messenger bag. "I gave JB explicit instructions—"

"Stop right there," she said, punching his shoulder. "You don't *get* to give me instructions. Especially through poor JB. News flash, Helsing: I'm not your sidekick. I do what I want, remember?"

"Remembered." Max rubbed his arm. "I can't believe you've been following me through the woods for an hour. I thought I'd covered my tracks."

"Through the woods for an hour? I took the creek path. I only picked up your trail ten minutes ago, and that's because of the noise you make. I swear, a deaf, blind tortoise could follow you with ease."

Max looked back into the emerald wilderness. His skin prickled, that feeling of unease remaining. The two of them set off, a pair of grumpy companions.

To their left, the river rushed by, the water providing a musical melody as they hiked in silence. It was Max who eventually spoke.

"How did you give Whedon the slip?"

"It wasn't difficult. JB helped. You know, I think he might be a bit more aware of the weird shenanigans that go on than you might think. You have to watch the quiet ones, I guess. Whedon's super worried about Boyle. I guess we all are."

Max grunted. "Whedon's lost it, big time. He hadn't even told Gideon that Boyle had gone missing! He seriously thinks Kenny's going to turn up safe and sound." Max shook his head. "I can't stand the guy, Syd, but if he's out there, I'll find him. And you'll help me."

"Damn right," she said.

"Y'know," said Max, pulling out his cell and holding it up before him. "I've just realized, Jed's on his way up here. I should call and tell him what we're doing." He rolled his eyes. "No signal. I'll try again later."

"Hush!" she hissed, grabbing his shoulder and hauling him low into the bracken. She pointed through the lush undergrowth, toward the river. There, standing in the shallows, was a handsome young buck. Max let out a quiet whistle.

"Have you ever seen anything so beautiful?" asked Syd, her smile lighting up her face. It was rare for Max to be lost for words, but all he could do was watch the buck as it drank from the river.

"It's a whitetail," whispered Syd. "See where he's growing his antlers, on the crown of his skull? They shed their antlers each year."

"Since when are you the expert on all things deer, city girl?"

"Since I read the pamphlet about the White Mountains. You know, the one they gave us before we came? Jeez, Helsing. Do you ever read anything?"

"Spell books, the *Monstrosi Bestiarum*, pizza delivery menus—just the important stuff."

"He's lucky it's not hunting season," said Syd, as the

buck suddenly threw its head back and shook his sable coat. "Come September, he'll want to—"

The crack of gunfire nearby made the pair of them jump, then duck down.

"Are you okay?" asked Max. She nodded as they both raised their heads.

The buck was staggering through the shallows, that big proud chest now stained crimson. It let out a pained bellow, snorting as it tried to keep its footing. A second gunshot sounded, and the deer went down with a splash, back legs kicking as it struggled with its dying breaths. Syd made to rush over to the animal, but Max held her back. From the tree line on the opposite side of the river, three figures emerged, rifles in hand.

One guy wore full camo gear from head to foot, even his hat sporting a wide variety of twigs and leaves. The man who followed him had made less effort, his white Green Day T-shirt hardly hunting attire. The last of the trio wore a red plaid shirt with matching hat, the white fur–lined earflaps sticking out at right angles from his head.

"Did you get him?" asked Green Day.

"Hell, yeah," said Camo, his rifle still aimed at the dying deer.

"It's still alive, dude," said Lumberjack, leveling his own gun at the buck in the water. Max and Syd looked away as the firearm dealt the killing blow.

"Three shots," whispered Max. "That poor creature. One should have done the trick."

"It's not even hunting season," Syd said tearfully as she watched the three men celebrate their kill.

"What do we do with it now?" asked Green Day.

"Haul it outta the water and leave it on the bank," replied Lumberjack. "We can pick it up later."

"But something might get to it," said Green Day. "Y'know. Wolves, bears . . . bigfoot. That's what we're out here lookin' for, ain't it?"

"Hell, yeah," said Camo.

"I say we drag it to camp," said Green Day.

"Come on, that'll take all day," whined Lumberjack. "If something else comes along and eats it, so what? Like you say, it's bigfoot we're here for, right?"

"Hell, yeah," from Camo.

"Seems like a waste," said Green Day.

Camo shrugged and turned around, making his way back to the forest. Lumberjack and Green Day grabbed the butchered buck by its hooves and dragged it across the rocks, through the water, toward the bank. Syd fought back her anger as they unceremoniously dumped it on the grass. The hunters shared a quick high five before the other two followed Camo back into the woods.

Max placed a hand gently onto Syd's shoulder. "We need to move, while daylight's still on our side."

Syd sniffed again, nodded, and followed her friend, looking back just once at the slain whitetail on the shore.

EIGHTEEN

xxx

ONE-MAN CAVALRY

Jed stood on the porch of the Greenwoods' Guesthouse and checked his phone. He had a signal, but it was awful faint, and there sure as heck weren't any messages from Max showing up on it. He pocketed it and looked down the street. It was a pleasant evening in early spring, and the sleepy town of Bone Creek was resting easy. He could hear kids playing in a garden that neighbored the guesthouse. He could smell barbecue across the street. The sound of an old Louis Prima hit drifted out of an open window nearby, the regular clipped sound telling him it was an old vinyl recording. Jed's favorite. It was a tranquil, mellow world, far removed from the hustle and bustle of Gallows Hill. But it was perplexing that folks were so relaxed, considering the horrors that had so recently played out not five miles away.

Jed looked back down the porch to where Principal

Whedon sat in a wicker chair, rocking back and forth, leafing through the local phone book. Mrs. Loomis, the school nurse, was in the building, keeping the students and young teachers as calm as she could, all things considered. Many of them, understandably, just wanted to go home now, but they had to stay put for the foreseeable. Since arriving in Bone Creek and getting directed to the school group's accommodation, Jed had quickly grilled the principal for what he knew. That hadn't taken long.

"Boyle went out in the night and didn't return. And Max and Perez disappeared today. That's all you know, Irwin?"

The principal didn't look up from his phone book. "Boyle has come *here*, Mr. Coolidge, to Bone Creek. He quite clearly stated that he was seeking out alternate accommodation, as the bunkhouses weren't to his liking."

"You *really* believe Boyle's soaking in a bubble bath and deciding what to watch on pay-per-view at this moment?"

"That's what he said he was going to do." His fingers were frantic as he flicked through the pages, writing down guesthouse and hotel addresses. "I simply need to pay each of them a visit and find our wayward teen."

"There are *three* children missing, Irwin. Boyle, Max, and Syd. Three. Not just the chief of police's brat. What are you doing about finding the other two?"

"The tour guide, Mr. Gideon, is searching the woods for them now. They'll turn up," he muttered.

Jed crouched, hiding the discomfort he felt in his stiff bad leg, his face up close to Whedon's.

"Why so fixated on the Boyle kid? Scared of what his father will do when he finds out the golden child is missing?"

"He must be in a bed-and-break—"

Jed's hand smacked down onto the phone book, stopping the principal's search with a loud clap.

"And if he doesn't turn up in town? What then? Have you informed Boyle Senior of what's happened? Have you called Mrs. Perez? Do *any* of the parents know what's going on here?"

Whedon's wild-eyed sweaty face told Jed all he needed to know. Max's guardian narrowed his eyes.

"What's Chief Boyle got on you, Irwin? I get that he's a powerful man, but there's something more, isn't there? Did he do you a favor, Irwin? Is that it? What did he make go away? What will he do when he discovers you've lost his only son?"

A tear broke from Whedon's eye, racing down his cheek and disappearing into that bristly mustache. He opened his mouth, then snapped it shut. Jed growled. That was all he was getting from the principal on this occasion, but there was clearly a lot more to the story. When he got home, he'd start digging.

Jed rose tall, his back creaking as he straightened it.

"Looks like it's up to me to haul your sorry ass out of the mire. I'm going to bring these children back—all three of them. You can thank me later."

"If Chief Boyle finds out about this—"

"He *won't*, Irwin. But I need you to understand that not

only has Max stuck his neck out for this kid, but he's stuck his neck out for *you*, too. When all this is over, and your little world returns to its hunky-dory state of play, I hope you can think about cutting Max a break."

Whedon nodded, but Jed was already walking away from the principal. From his vantage on the other end of the porch, he saw a jeep pull up outside the guesthouse. A short middle-aged white guy in a khaki shirt and shorts jumped out and tried to grab four huge tubs of fried chicken out of the backseat. Jed made his way down the steps to lend a hand.

"Bless you, kind sir," said the flustered man as Jed caught a bucket about to topple.

"No problem. I'd hate for you to lose your dinner . . . or part of it."

"Oh, they're not for me," said the man. "I can't get away with this kinda food."

To Jed's eyes, he looked like Curly from the Three Stooges. As they walked toward the inn, Jed shivered.

"Bit chilly, are you?" the man asked.

"Not used to this chill evening air."

"Yes, the temperature really drops at nighttime," said the man. "You feel it up in the woods for sure."

The man led Jed back toward the Greenwoods' Guesthouse. "These Southern fried offerings are for the school group that's staying here."

"You mean the kids from Gallows Hill? I'm one of the parents. Jed Coolidge." Jed extended a hand, which the little fellow managed to shake while still balancing three buckets of wings and drumsticks.

"I'm Gideon! I was their activity coordinator until this morning. Awful business." He sighed, shaking his head.

"Of course, you're the tour guide. Whedon mentioned you to me."

Gideon glowered in the direction of the principal, who was sitting at the far end of the porch.

"Do you know he didn't tell me right away that the children were missing? I've been rushing around all day, trying to track them down in the woods. I'm only here now to drop off some food for the other kids, and then I'm heading back out there. So long as these students are missing on my watch, I'll do all I can to find them."

He was silent for a moment as he continued to glare at Whedon. "He's a character."

"That's one word for him," said Jed with a growl. "You can't *imagine* how much it pains me to say this, but he's not a bad guy. He's just spineless."

"Which of the little angels is yours?"

"I'm Max Helsing's guardian."

"Oh, I'm so sorry. I wish I'd seen what he was up to sooner."

"Up to?"

"Indeed," Gideon whispered, his little goatee beard bristling as he chewed his lip with embarrassment. "Young Max was picking my brains about Bone Creek. I'm sorry, I didn't realize he was interrogating me about where to search for his friend!"

Jed's grin was humorless. "Yeah, he's a cunning little swine, isn't he?"

"Your words," said Gideon, "not mine. But what a pleasant young man. I hope to goodness he and Syd find young Kenny. I can't bear to think of what might befall the three of them."

Jed handed the fourth bucket of chicken back to the man, balancing it on top of the other three and obscuring Gideon's face from view. As the adventure camp coordinator took the first tentative step up to the guesthouse porch, Jed remembered he was missing one crucial bit of information. He snapped his fingers, which in itself almost caused the man in khaki to drop a hundred pieces of chicken all over the steps.

"Sorry, Mr. Gideon."

"Just Gideon," said the curly-haired man, hovering on the steps.

"Yeah, I meant to ask: how far did you get with your search?"

"You're not thinking of going out there, are you?" Gideon said, catching the brief glance Jed gave Whedon.

"I'm not the kind of guy who can sit back and do nothing."

"I tried to warn Max: the woods are an awful dangerous place, especially after what's gone on. I know the forests and hills of Bone Creek, as do the police who are out there. With all due respect, it's no place for an amateur. You really are best leaving the manhunt to the professionals, Mr. Coolidge."

Jed tried not to react. There was nobody better equipped than he to find the kids. Gideon, the police, the sheriff deputies, the park rangers . . . they didn't know *what* they were dealing with.

"Where d'you think he went?" Jed asked once again.

"Higher into the mountains. There's a hermit who lives up there; maybe he's gone to pick his brains. I'm sorry I'm so vague; you must think I'm a real ninny!"

"Don't worry—you've been a great help already."

Jed turned to leave. Gideon's voice stopped him.

"I'll be informing the police about the missing students, Mr. Coolidge. The principal may be a good man, but I can't stand by and let these children remain in peril."

"Gimme until the morning, Gideon. Max and Syd are mighty resourceful. You never know; they may actually find Boyle. If they're not back by sunrise, go ahead and call in the SWAT team."

Gideon wasn't smiling. "I'm making no promises."

"Hope the kids enjoy their chicken," Jed said, before turning and setting off down the sidewalk toward his station wagon. It was rocking as he approached. In the passenger seat he could see an excited Eightball hopping around, slobbering all over the upholstery and licking at the windshield. He was going to need wipers on the inside of the car at this rate. And air fresheners. Lots of air fresheners.

He passed by the excited pup toward the back of the vehicle. There was a real nip in the air, and Jed had been in such a hurry, he wasn't even sure he'd packed a jacket. He flipped the trunk and looked inside at the clutter of gear, everything a self-respecting monster hunter might need. Pickax, short sword, crucifix, crossbow, holy water, smoke bombs, silver darts—it was all there, and more. And there was his old duster, the trench coat that had been with him on more horror-hunting escapades than Max had enjoyed hot dinners. He grabbed it, yanking it out of the trunk with a snap.

"You've got to be kidding me," said Jed as he saw what lay beneath.

"Surprise!" said Wing Liu, waving from his hiding place.

NINETEEN

xxx

UNEXPECTED ANSWERS

The hike to High Crag felt more arduous than it had when they'd first arrived in Bone Creek. Knowing there was a monster loose in the forest with a taste for human blood had a way of sapping one's energy. Combine that with two days of pretty much solid stress, and Max felt like he needed a vacation after this vacation was over. The ascent up the cliff path, with the sun beating down from above, was a killer. Thankfully, the spray from the waterfall helped cool them while they climbed. More than once he found himself looking back, down the steep rocky path. Try as he might, Max couldn't shake the feeling he was being watched.

They paused for a drink once they'd reached the summit of High Crag, filling their water bottles from the creek before it tumbled over the cliff top. In the distance, below, red and blue lights flashed in the heart of the woods, no doubt at the camp parking area. A little beyond that, they could see the rooftops of Bone Creek town. Whedon and the kids must be there by now. Jed, too, hopefully. Max checked his phone for a signal once more; no luck. Screwing the lids tight on their water bottles, the two monster hunters set off once more, following the creek. They were glad to get a bit of shelter from the sun as they dipped into the tree line for shade.

"There's something in the air," Max said abruptly.

"Pollen?" Syd quipped.

Max looked at the backs of his arms, where his hairs stood on end. "I felt like this when I went rappelling with Gideon and Boyle. On top of the cliffs, it's like there's an intensity. It's hard to explain."

"You get an A for effort," she replied, keeping her eyes peeled as they walked side by side. "So the hermit lives up here? Somewhere near the stream?"

"Where it forks," muttered Max distractedly, glancing back the way they'd come.

Ahead, there was the sound of a whipcrack, followed by a whooping shriek. The two halted instantly, looking to each other with alarm, as a string of colorful obscenities echoed through the trees. Max recognized the voice and smiled at Syd.

"There's someone I want you to meet."

He took her by the arm and pushed on, parting the bushes ahead. The brownie was suspended five feet off the ground, a black cord tight about his ankle, the other end wrapped around a branch overhead. He twirled and cursed, struggling in vain to get free of the trap. The ears of his rabbit-skin hat hung limp in the most forlorn fashion. Max stifled a laugh.

"Release me, Van Helsing!" shouted the brownie, struggling to rise and reach the snare about his ankle. His panpipes lay on the earth beneath him, out of his reach.

"What's that? I think there's a magic word missing. . . ."

"*Please* release me," hissed the forest fairy, his filthy cheeks growing redder with each passing second.

Max tapped his chin with his forefinger, contemplating the request. "You were dead set that I wanted to kill you last time we met. You even bit my damn hand! Monster killer, you called me. Why was that? Tell me and I'll set you free."

"Set me free, *then* I'll tell you."

"With all due respect," said Syd, walking around the suspended imp and inspecting the rope, "you're in no position to haggle, little dude."

Max grinned, glad to have Syd by his side. She gave the black cord a twang, causing the brownie to judder.

"Don't know what this is made from, but it's strong as steel!"

Max recognized the material. He'd seen it recently, tucked inside the jacket of England's greatest teen monster hunter and the planet's biggest dork.

"Abel Archer," said Max. "The snare is his handiwork." He looked around the clearing and then back to the brownie. "No sign of your bigfoot pal though. So we're going to let you down. And I can only hope you'll reciprocate this act of kindness. Okay?"

The little man nodded enthusiastically. Syd was already shinnying up the tree trunk, making her way to the branch that supported the offending rope. Whipping a penknife out of her belt, she set to work on the bindings.

"Sheesh, what is this stuff made from? I can't even cut it with my knife."

"Knowing Archer, it must be some kind of state-of-the art black-ops gear that his lordship's invested in. Maybe a blend of Kevlar and frost giant butt whiskers."

"I can't cut it. Trying to pick the knot loose now," she called down.

"No rush," he replied, patting the brownie's upturned head and giving him a gentle push. The man of the forest spun slowly, irritation writ upon his dirty face. "You don't mind hanging around, do you?"

Max picked the panpipes off the ground and brought them to his lips.

"I wouldn't, if I were you," said the little man. "In the hands of the untrained, those pipes can be dangerous."

"I played a mean recorder in elementary school," said Max.

"Did your recorder induce a brain hemorrhage when you hit the wrong note?" Max stopped instantly, as the brownie grinned. "No, didn't think so."

The little man's smug look vanished in a flash as the rope came loose overhead and he fell toward the ground. Max snatched him out of the air, cradling him like a newborn.

"It's a bouncing baby brownie!" exclaimed Max in his best new-father voice.

"Gerroff," grunted the little man, jumping out of Max's arms and landing with a thump in the soil. He reached up to grab for the pipes, but Max held them high.

"We made a deal, remember? We've already cut you down."

"You get your pipes back when you answer some questions," said Syd, swinging upside down from the tree bough above like a true acrobat. She landed deftly beside Max. "You can start by telling us your name."

The brownie huffed for a moment before gathering what few shreds of dignity he had left.

"My name is Kimble. And please be careful. Those panpipes are the key to all my good work."

"I've been hearing these in the forest since I got here, haven't I?" said Max.

Kimble took a sarcastic, over-the-top bow. "Yours truly. That's me trying to keep the harmony in the forest. Not easy, all things presently considered, I can tell you. Without these pipes, I'm just a grubby wee fellow who wanders the forest. With them, I can cast spells, glamour people, perform all kinds of brownie magic upon them. I'd have done so to you if you hadn't called upon your own dark magic to counter my spell."

"'Bohemian Rhapsody,'" said Max proudly to Syd, who rolled her eyes with a sigh.

Kimble continued, growing more animated. "I can embolden the most frightened spirit, and calm the wildest beast. I can make a heart feel love, a soul feel hope, a mind forget. They're as important to me as your *Monstrosi Bestiarum*, Maxwell. Without them, my magic won't work."

"Whoa," said Max, grabbing Kimble by his rabbit-eared hat and pulling him forward. "You seem to know an awful lot about me, yet I know diddly-squat about you."

"You're not the first Van Helsing to come to Bone Creek, Maxwell. One of your great-great-great-whatevers came hunting this way in the late 1800s."

"Hunting bigfoot?"

"Who's telling this story?" Kimble glowered at Max. "Bernhard Van Helsing—what a twisted soul he was. He turned up in the White Mountains, tracking an ursanthrope."

"An ursa-what?" asked Syd.

"Werebear, for want of a better word," explained Max. Kimble nodded.

"Indeed, a shape-shifter who could turn into a bear. Originally a Scot, he went by the name MacMillan—he was a gambler, a huckster, a confidence trickster, plying his trade right across the Wild West. That is, until he killed a Pinkerton agent and was chased back East, back to where he had family, here in this valley. He wasn't alone when he returned, though. MacMillan brought trouble to the White Mountains in the shape of a Van Helsing."

Kimble plucked a juicy millipede off a fern. He proffered

it to Syd and Max, both of whom recoiled. With a shrug, he popped it into his mouth and slurped it down.

"Mmm, tickly. Anyway, Bernhard Van Helsing cut a bloody path through Bone Creek. Here was a fellow who killed for pleasure, and he wasn't fussy about what he put to the sword. Black bears and bugbears, wolves and will-o'-the-wisps, foxes and fey folk. You know, there was a clan of dryads who once protected this forest?"

"Tree nymphs," said Max, nodding. "I already met the water nymph in the river."

"One of many, Maxwell, but their tree-bound cousins called the woods their home for many centuries. Shy, peace-ful beings that tended the trees throughout Bone Creek. That is, until Bernhard turned up. Slew the lot of them as he sought out the werebear, for no reason other than sickly, cruel pleasure."

"I'm sorry," said Max, feeling the overwhelming guilt of his forefather's wicked deeds.

"Old Bernhard slaughtered all manner of creature, both fairy and natural, as he tried to find MacMillan. Did he find him?"

"I'm guessing no?" said Syd.

"Precisely," said Kimble. "Bernhard came across a human settlement up here on a tributary of the Saco River, known to be MacMillan's family home. The mad monster hunter butchered innocent men, women, and children before MacMillan finally arrived, enraged and trans-formed. Van Helsing and the werebear died that day,

atop the falls that were named after their titanic strug-
gle, locked in mortal combat, while the river ran red with
blood. This region never got its name because of the white
zinc in the mountains, no matter what anyone tells you. It
and the falls were named after what happened that dread
day. Battle Falls, Bone Creek: we have a Van Helsing to
thank for that."

"I've never heard that story before," whispered Max
quietly. "Never heard of Bernhard, either."

Could one of his ancestors have really committed such
atrocities? This Bernhard sounded worse than any monster
he'd ever encountered. The brownie reached forward and
patted the boy's knee.

"It's not all bad, Maxwell. There was another in your
family, a kinder soul, who paid Bone Creek a visit. Esme,
her name was."

Max's ears pricked up. "I know of Esme. She's one of the
main contributors to the *Monstrosi Bestiarum*."

"Well, she wanted to put right the wrongs of Bernhard.
Even went so far as bringing other waifs and strays from
the fairy world here and helping them relocate when their
homes became too crowded with dangerous humans."

Max's heart soared to hear this.

"She'd turn up on occasion, bringing another fey
stranger into the fold. Then she stopped coming. We figured
she'd died. But by then, we were a community. Looked after
ourselves. There hasn't been another Van Helsing here in
well over a hundred of your human years. Not until now."

"How do you know so much about *me* then?"

"You Van Helsings give off a vibe," said Kimble. "I'm guardian to this woodland and all that lives within it, so it's my job to monitor what goes on here, who's coming in and out and suchlike. I figured trouble wouldn't be far behind you, and I was right."

"Wait a minute," said Max. "What's happened in Bone Creek this week—I had nothing to do with it!"

"Maybe you didn't cause it on purpose. But look at the facts: you turn up and bad stuff happens. Does that happen to you a lot?"

Max didn't answer. Trouble found him, without a doubt. Kimble continued.

"Something profoundly wicked is at work in these woods. Fairies, nymphs, and all manner of harmless monster have been getting killed, snuffed out by who knows what. The Sasquatch, a powerful but peaceful creature, is getting framed. The young male you met yesterday has vanished, fled the forest as far as I can tell. Any sane fellow, human or fairy, should be hightailing out of here."

"I'm going nowhere, not until I find Boyle."

"The missing boy?"

"He's out here somewhere and he needs our help."

"If you were right-minded, you would run."

Max knelt down beside Kimble, his knee cushioned by the mossy ground. He looked hard at the brownie, who gave him the same stare back.

"I'm a monster hunter, Kimble. I can't run away from a

fight. There's something bigger and badder than a bigfoot out there, and it means to harm humans, fey folk, and cryptids alike. I'm going nowhere until I stop it. I'm making a vow to you, Kimble: I'll protect your people in this forest, just as Esme did before me."

The brownie reached out and placed a tiny hand over Max's, giving it a squeeze.

"You're all right, Maxwell. For a Van Helsing."

Max handed the brownie his pipes back and then stood.

"We're off to speak with Barnum the hermit. In the meantime, move everyone deeper into the woods. Head to where no man has gone before, to where no man can *reach*, and wait there until the storm has passed."

"I'll tell them to hide, but there's no guarantee they'll listen to me," said Kimble. "The fey folk of Bone Creek are a willful bunch. If you feel eyes upon you in the darkness, remember there's a chance it could be a friend."

"I'll keep that in mind when we're running and screaming." Max turned to Syd. "You ready?"

"Sun's going down," she said as she prepared to follow Max. "This is going to be a *long* night, isn't it?"

"Be lucky, Maxwell," said Kimble as the teenagers set off into the woods. "Be safe."

TWENTY

xxx

TRACKING 101

"Jed! Jed! Are we there yet?"

Jed Coolidge slowly exhaled and turned. His flashlight dazzled Wing Liu, who was scrambling up the woodland path behind Jed with all the grace and coordination of a true city dweller. The boy was panting, knees and elbows coated in dirt, the sleeve of his jacket shredded after an altercation with a bush. His glasses were speckled with sweat and mud, and his big eyes blinked as he looked pitifully at his companion.

"You have to be kidding me, Wing. You can't be tired already!"

Eightball had been leading the way since they'd parked up on the side of the road, not far from the camp parking lot. A single patrol car had been stationed there for the night in case there were any developments. Eightball had led Jed and Wing into the forest, sniffing as he searched for Max's scent. Now the pup was walking behind Wing, urging him on with nudges from his nose. Wing wiped a grubby hand across his brow, leaving a filthy smear.

"I'm just not used to this." The ten-year-old wheezed, leaning hard on Jed's arm as he gathered his breath.

"The great outdoors?"

"Exercise."

Jed grunted. "You're a fraction of my age, I'm carrying all the gear, *and* I have a bum leg."

"I'm strong in a different way," said the boy as his breathing slowly returned to normal.

"A completely useless way?"

"Far from it. My parents have spent hours, and many dollars, strengthening my *brain*. I have mental aptitude, an inquiring mind, and super smarts."

"Perhaps you should trade some of those super smarts for some old-fashioned common sense."

"How come?"

"Because you're standing in a pile of dung, kid."

Jed tried not to laugh as Wing pulled his sneaker out of the fecal surprise and proceeded to do the dance of the dog droppings. He wiped, dragged, and even kicked out from the knee, sending poop flicking with resounding splats into the surrounding bracken.

Eightball growled as Wing stopped hopping, the devil dog's eyes flashing bright and white.

"What's got his hackles up?" asked Wing.

Jed crouched, his left leg remaining locked at the knee.

The old wound always returned to haunt him. He'd been on the receiving end of a charge from a minotaur many years ago, when the beast's mighty horn had gored a hole clean through his leg, curtailing his career in the field.

"Easy, boy," said Jed, putting his flashlight on the forest floor and patting the rolls of fat on Eightball's neck. They felt hard, like coiled rope.

The hellhound dipped his head, snarling at something unseen in the darkness.

"Maybe he can smell bigfoot," whispered Wing.

The boy picked the flashlight up off the ground. It was slender, a foot-long cylinder of dull black metal, but rather than having the cold feel of steel, it had the texture of polished wood. Instead of an On/Off switch on the barrel, there were a series of strange symbols.

"Hey, are these runes? What kind of cockamamie camping store did you get this from?"

Jed looked up from Eightball and snatched the flashlight from the boy's hand.

"Gimme that back!"

"Keep your hair on, Jed," grumbled the kid.

Jed sighed. "Wing Liu, stowing away in the trunk of my car was the single dumbest thing you've ever done. For all that intelligence, you really have zero wisdom."

"I left a note for Mom."

"I know you did, and I've spoken to her. I told her that we're staying at a guesthouse while we get Max, so I can bring you home to her tomorrow. Trust me, Wing: lying to your parents does *not* make me happy. Now I'm stuck with you by my side as I try to find Max, Syd, and the Boyle boy, in dangerous terrain where no doubt a supernatural horror is at work. You read those old reports, Wing; Bone Creek has history."

After he'd received the call from Max, Jed had gone into research mode. With Wing's help, he'd discovered that there had been sightings of bigfoot reported in the New Hampshire press, but no evidence had ever been captured. The ever-resourceful Wing had uncovered an old scroll signed by one of Max's ancestors, Esme Van Helsing: an agreement between herself and the fairy folk of Bone Creek that she would ensure their protection against humankind. The message had clearly never made it to the other Van Helsings.

Eightball was still snuffling around, and his nose led him to the offending sole Wing was now scraping with a stick. The hellhound's eyes flashed white, and his chest hummed as if he might belch fire at any moment.

"Jed!" exclaimed Wing. "Can you shine your fancy flashlight this way? I want to take a closer look at this dooky."

Jed grabbed the boy's ankle firmly, holding him steady as he focused the beam from his flashlight onto the stinking shoe. Eightball got in closer, his growl steady as an idle chainsaw. The hellhound's eyes glowed white-hot as he took another tentative sniff at the sneaker. Jed could now see tiny bone fragments in the foul sludge, crushed and splintered by powerful teeth.

"I think it's monster mash," said Wing.

"You could be right. You think so too, huh, Eightball? Good dog." Jed patted the pup as he straightened, his back creaking. "This is a predator that's done this, and judging by the size of the deposit, it's a big one."

"So it could be bigfoot?" asked Wing. His voice carried that unusual cadence that was somewhere between excitement and total pant-soiling fear. Jed never tired of hearing it from norms.

"Could be." He patted the boy's shoulder reassuringly. "Good find, Wing."

The old man opened his leather haversack and reached inside, pulling out a glass bottle that was corked and sealed with wax.

"What's that?" asked Wing as Jed picked the seal away and bit the cork. It came away with a *pop*!

"Wood musk. I bought it from Odious Crumb a few years back, when I was heading into the wilds on some monstrous goose chase. It's a fairy concoction, used to mask their scent from predators. We have to douse ourselves with it to kill our scent. Only one drawback." He shook the bottle. "It smells absolutely foul."

He tipped a hearty glug of it over the boy's head, which made him splutter and retch. Eightball got a shower too; the stinking potion hissed as it hit his boiling skin. Lastly, Jed poured it over his own head.

"Smells bad, don't it?"

"And stings the eyes," added Wing. "Burns the flesh, too. Any other side effects?"

"Give it a moment," said Jed. "How's that?"

"It doesn't sting anymore. And the smell's vanished!" said Wing with surprise.

"You're effectively scent-free now. The only way you'll leave an odor is if you make one."

The three of them walked on, Eightball leading the way, nose to the ground. "So we're following whatever beast dropped its breakfast back there?"

"I figure, chances are Max and Syd could already be on its scent and have successfully tracked it. That's the best-case scenario."

"What's the worst?" asked Wing.

"The beast is already tracking them. And it's still hungry."

TWENTY-ONE

xxx

THE DEAD HOUSE

If Max and Syd hadn't known about the hermit's shack, they would have walked straight past it. Hidden away on a promontory of land where two mountain streams converged, it was surrounded by scrub, obscured from sight. Pushing their way through the tangle of undergrowth, the two kids found themselves standing before the solitary building dwarfed by the forest and mountains. It was a single-story structure, its timber walls warped and weather-worn, covered in veils of moss and cobwebs that fluttered in the cool night breeze. The window frames were broken, the shattered glass reflecting the moonlight. The shingle roof looked like it might fall in at any moment, while a crooked stone chimney rose like a stubby gray finger. If the horror movie industry had a location guide magazine, Max and Syd were surely looking at the cover photo for the latest edition.

"There's no way this place is lived-in," said Syd, breath steaming before her face.

"Gideon said Barnum lived up here. We've come this far."

"Max, do you not . . . feel it?"

He knew exactly what Syd was talking about, for he felt it often. He and fear were old acquaintances, and he knew exactly how to deal with that old devil: face it head on. He squeezed his friend's forearm and gave her a warm smile.

"Syd, if you want to hang back, that's cool. I've done this kind of thing before. It's perfectly normal to be scared."

"Would you listen to yourself?" she said. "I'm not some damsel in distress, Helsing. How many times have I saved your butt?"

"Who's counting?"

"I'll stay out here on watch. If Barnum shows up, I'll holler. Likewise, if you get into any trouble, shout and I'll come running."

"You sure?"

She shrugged. "Someone has to haul your ass out of the fire. It's usually me."

Max nodded and set off across the bleached grass toward the ramshackle building. As he approached, he allowed his own light beam to pass across the shack. It looked abandoned, a ruin from a bygone age. Nobody could live here. Then his flashlight picked out the big jar of pickles beyond a broken window, glowing like unearthly green eggs in a specimen jar.

"Mr. Barnum?" he called, suddenly remembering it was

probably best to announce one's arrival when trespassing on the land of a crazy old mountain man. "It's Max Helsing. We met in Bone Creek the other day, at the general store. I know it's late, but I was hoping I could ask you a few questions?"

He kept walking, stepping up to the door.

"Mr. Barnum?"

He knocked on the rotten timber, and the door creaked open. Max looked back at Syd, who stood thirty feet away in the moonlight. She ushered him onward, nodding enthusiastically. Max smiled and turned back to the shack, his smile instantly slipping.

"Nope," he whispered. "As vibes go, this isn't a good one."

He stepped over the threshold, swinging the flashlight in broad sweeping arcs so they took in as much of the room as possible. A rusty tin basin sat on a table by the window, a stack of pots towering within it, housing a mob of fat flies. A rustic rocking chair was positioned in front of a stone fireplace that was covered in thick layers of black soot. Beside the chair was a chest doubling as a table, a tumbler and an empty bottle on its lid. The decor was decidedly grim, with a macabre collection of animal skulls adorning every bit of wall space. A big bear skull took pride of place above the hearth, while the majority of bleached, bony heads had belonged to stags. Antlers twisted and fought with one another, cluttering the timber panels. The chill reminded Max of a morgue.

"Mr. Barnum?" said Max hopefully. He stepped through

the room, stumbling over detritus. Empty tins of chewing tobacco, glass bottles, and tin plates littered a stained circular rug. There was a smell, all too familiar to Max. In his thirteen years he'd seen a fair few dead bodies—some of them even walked and talked. Unless he was very much mistaken, he was catching that distinct whiff in the air right now. He tried to find the source of it, but the stench was fighting with many others that occupied the shack.

At the back of the hut, a bed occupied the corner of the room. The wall above the bed had yellowed scraps of parchment and notes pinned to it. Max edged nearer, letting his flashlight run up and down it. There was a shape beneath the stained gray sheet, distinct and lumpy. Max gulped as he walked closer, gripping his flashlight in his right hand while drying the palm of his left on the leg of his jeans. He held the light like a club, ready to strike should anything happen. *Should anything happen?* Max shook his head. Something *always* happened. He was Max Helsing, for goodness sake.

He grabbed the sheet and whipped it back. There was no body. Clothes littered the mattress, jumbled together, stinking and soiled.

"They don't need washing," said Max. "They need incinerating."

His flashlight drifted over the notes. They were ramblings, scrawled in the most illegible hand. One appeared to be a map scribbled onto an aged scroll with curling edges, held in place by a single rusty tack. Max leaned close, inspecting it. Without a doubt, this was the surrounding countryside, with the hermit's shack, Battle Falls, Bone Creek, and the camp all marked out. What made the hairs tingle on the back of his arms were the red circles. The river below the falls was marked; could that have been the water nymphs? The cliffs had a mark too, where he'd encountered the rock drake. So what was the additional red circle, with a cross scratched through it, not far from the hermit's shack? It appeared to be farther upstream, toward one of the mountain's rockier regions. And what did the cross mean? Max grabbed the scroll, the tack pinging off, and stuffed it into his pocket.

He wandered back to the center of the shack, collapsing into the rocker. He let it tip back, creaking on its runners, and considered the situation. Barnum had been Max's best hope of finding Boyle. If it weren't for the giant pickle jar by the sink window, Max would've been convinced the old hermit no longer lived here.

His eyes passed over the chest beside the chair, and the tumbler and bottle. He picked up the bottle and placed it on the floor. Taking the grubby tumbler in his hand, he shone his flashlight on the drinking vessel. It was empty, but whatever the last contents had been had left a dark residue in the bottom of the glass. Max sniffed it, dabbed it with a fingertip. It came away sticky, red. Blood? He placed the tumbler on the floor and lifted the lid of the chest.

There was poor old Barnum. The hermit's corpse was folded up inside the heavy valise. He had been drained of blood, his parchment-thin skin clinging to his bones, lips peeled back in a terrified death mask. Max was rising, up out of the chair, suddenly springing to life, but he wasn't alone.

A cloud of black soot exploded from the chimney as a scrawny shape crawled out of the stone chute, landing on the ground beside Max. Between him and the door, the floor suddenly erupted, the circular rug taking off into the air, sending the rubbish that had littered it flying. A trapdoor had crashed open in the floor, allowing the second hidden vampire to pick its moment to reveal itself.

"Oh boy!" shouted Max, trying to maneuver himself into a better position between the two monsters who circled him, keen to keep him between them. "I do love a surprise party!"

The first vampire was clearly an adolescent, the flaps of skin connecting its arms to its torso still only wafer-thin. Dead black eyes, like those of a shark, fixed on Max as the creature dipped its pale white head up and down, gauging its enemy. It hung back, awaiting the command of its master.

Max kept the big one in his sight line. It was probably the maker of the adolescent. While the smaller creature was skin and bone, the mature one was solid, its broad chest revealing the unmistakable pronounced rib cage of an adult. The wings were more substantial too, powerful enough to grant it flight, not that there was room in Barnum's shack. Its flesh had a pale blue hue that seemed to glow in the flashlight's beam. It hissed, showing Max those

VAMPIRE, MATURE

AKA: lamia, vampir, vampyras, wampir

ORIGIN: Transylvania, Europe

STRENGTHS: Great speed, high intelligence, immunity to many conventional weapons, telepathy, regeneration.

WEAKNESSES: Daylight, Holy Water (blessed), and items of faith. Fear of the Christian <u>crucifix</u>. Aversion to garlic and silver. <u>Wooden stake</u> to heart is ideal method of dispatch.

HABITAT: Anywhere dark and removed from daylight: tombs, crypts, caves, disused buildings, and tunnels.

The Mature vampire (also referred to as a "Stage III") is infinitely more dangerous than its Adolescent counterpart. Shedding the more human features of a Stage II, the Mature enjoys the added power of telepathy. This mind control allows the fiend to beguile and command the feebleminded.

—Erik Van Helsing, January 13th, 1853

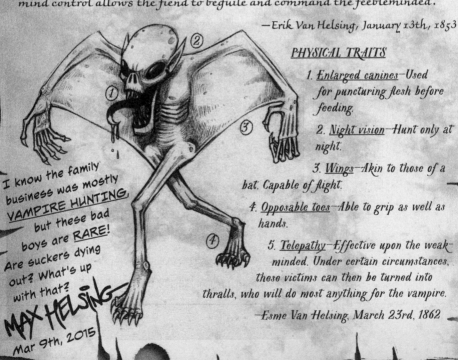

PHYSICAL TRAITS

1. <u>Enlarged canines</u>—Used for puncturing flesh before feeding.

2. <u>Night vision</u>—Hunt only at night.

3. <u>Wings</u>—Akin to those of a bat. Capable of flight.

4. <u>Opposable toes</u>—Able to grip as well as hands.

5. <u>Telepathy</u>—Effective upon the weak-minded. Under certain circumstances, these victims can then be turned into thralls, who will do most anything for the vampire.

—Esme Van Helsing, March 23rd, 1862

I know the family business was mostly <u>VAMPIRE HUNTING</u>, but these bad boys are RARE! Are suckers dying out? What's up with that?

MAX HELSING

Mar 9th, 2015

trademark canines, its jaw yawning open to reveal more rows of smaller razor-sharp teeth lining its throat. A sinuous black tongue snaked out of its throat, undulating and glistening as it ran across those terrible fangs.

"Have to say, this was the last thing I was expecting tonight. You guys are too kind. . . . Did you bake a cake?"

Max stepped around the rocker. "Are we going to play games?" He grabbed the arm of the chair. "What are we drinking?"

"You, Van Helsing!"

The words sounded in Max's head, the psychic attack almost stunning him, as the pair of vampires surged forward.

Max's first volley was at the adult sucker, the flashlight flying from his hand and striking it square in the face. He heard the glass lens crack along with the vampire's nose as the creature crashed wide of him in a screeching, half-blind fury. The adolescent was leaping, though. And Max was falling, deliberately. He dragged the rocking chair with him as the fledgling vampire landed in its spokes. Max twisted and turned, keeping its mouth from his face. Its hands and forearms reached through the bars in the back of the rocker, long taloned fingers clawing at Max's chest. The boy from Gallows Hill twisted the chair around counterclockwise, and the vampire's arms were both trapped between the struts of timber. Max roared as he forced it around, the monster screaming. Another yell from Max as he forced it home. *Snap!* One vampire arm went like a stalk of celery; then the other followed it. Max pushed the chair and wailing monster aside.

He didn't have time to catch his breath. He rolled forward, and not a moment too soon, as the adult vampire's clawed toes struck the floorboards where his head had been a heartbeat before. Max could see its face was torn, the blue skin running dark with black blood where the flashlight had struck it dead center.

"Yikes," said Max. "Looks like I've ruined your good looks."

"The King in Yellow comes for you, Van Helsing."

Max was running for the door, hurdling the maimed adolescent on the floor. He stamped on the chair as he passed over it, crushing its frame and sending daggers of wood into the young sucker's flesh. The adult was faster though, diving across the room like a bolt of pale blue lightning and blocking his path. Max leaped clear of it as it lashed out with one of those long disjointed legs again, narrowly missing him with its clawed toes. He ended up in the kitchen, the adult close behind. Max jumped onto the wobbling table, reaching for the windowsill and knocking over the tin washtub, which landed with a clang. He grabbed at the window frame, trying to force it open, but it was hopeless. Instead, Max caught the palm of his left hand on the broken glass. It came away bloody. The sucker made a gurgling sound of anticipation, its mouth stretching as the black tongue pulsed and quivered with excitement.

"A drink!"

"Bottoms up," called Max, tossing the jar of pickles at the monster. The glass shattered as it struck its head, shards peppering the blue flesh, vinegar dousing it, surging down its throat and across its torn, bloody skin. The vampire screeched and staggered as Max leaped off the wobbling kitchen table and hit it like a linebacker, or the best impression of one he could muster. Boy and vampire raced across the room, the sucker temporarily blinded. Max drove it into the wall across the shack, skewering the fiend on a multitude of antlers. The fight slowly drained from the vampire, along with rivulets of foul black blood, as Max wheeled away from the twitching terror. He took a breath and turned around.

The adolescent was there, towering over him, throwing its broken arms around the boy's shoulders to overlap in a lover's embrace and pulling him close. Max felt it draw him in, heard the splintered bones protruding from those fractured limbs grating together against his back. He tried to knee it in the groin, or what groin the monster had, but its clawed toes dug into Max's Chuck Taylors. The jaws snapped, the hideous tongue licking Max's cheek as it closed in.

The creature stopped suddenly, the dead shark eyes swelling as if they might pop. Max looked down and spied a crooked spindle from the rocking chair protruding from the adolescent's chest. The broken limbs went loose as the monster toppled lifelessly to one side. Syd stood in its place, her hands trembling, coated in its black blood.

"Holy smoke, Max!" she said, clearly shaken. "Are you okay? It looks like a bomb went off in here."

"Trust me," whispered Max, hugging his friend. "It was like this when I got here."

TWENTY-TWO

×××

A FOREST PAINTED RED

The game had changed and the chatter had ceased. Eightball was hunkered down, his tiny legs carrying his spherical body over roots and rocks. His head remained dipped, nostrils flaring as he stuck to the scent of their quarry. Wing followed the hellhound, remaining exactly where Jed could see him. He'd told the kid he had to keep him safe from harm, and that meant keeping him close at all times. They traveled in darkness now, their passage dependent on the moon and starlight that found its way through the tall pines.

They'd been tracking the beast for almost an hour now, the trail leading them west, ever higher. Jed had buttoned Wing's jacket up and lent him his flat cap; the old man could feel the cold in his bones, so chances were that the boy was suffering too, though he wasn't complaining now. Wing had proven himself invaluable in recent months, helping Jed to catalog Helsing House's tumbledown library. He often came to help when his homework—of which there was a great deal—was done, and nothing ever seemed too much trouble for him. If ever a monster hunter was destined to remain a base controller and not a field agent, Wing was that monster hunter.

As they walked, Jed lifted up his flashlight and gave it a quick inspection. It was older than him. A lot older. To the uninitiated, and at a glance, it probably did look like a regular flashlight. Jed kept his arthritic hand tightly clasped around it.

Soon their walk became a scramble, as the path became more rugged. They were traversing an incline of near forty-five degrees, Jed and Wing pushing and pulling each other uphill. Now it was Jed's turn to make too much noise, cursing as his bad leg slowed his progress. And it was Wing's turn to be there for him, helping him climb. Eightball would stop on occasion, waiting for the humans to catch up before continuing on his way.

Their route slowly leveled out. As the dog trotted along the forest floor, Wing and Jed pushed through the bushes.

"I could actually get used to this," said Wing. "Maybe I should ask my mom and dad if they'll let me—"

Jed's hand was suddenly on Wing's shoulder, gripping him hard enough to silence him. The boy's eyes went wide as he looked at his companion, but Jed's gaze was fixed upon the bushes. He grabbed a handful of branches, pulling their emerald leaves closer and into the starlight. They shone, spattered with speckles of blood. Wing went pale.

Hush. Jed mouthed the word, and Wing read it loud and clear.

Jed reached down slowly, his hand settling on Eightball. The dog didn't make a sound. His flesh, normally so loose and wobbly, was suddenly hard and hot as sheet metal, fresh from the furnace. A paw print lay in the packed earth before Eightball, larger than Jed's hand. Some kind of bear, perhaps? Jed's eyesight wasn't what it had been, especially in the half-light. He ran his fingertips over the imprint, felt them dip into its hollow. It was big and heavy, for sure. He rose back to his full height.

Jed advanced, slipping between the branches as the hellhound stalked forward slowly. Wing was now behind, his feet going where Jed's went. Ahead, in the woods, they could see the flickering light of a fire, sending shadows dancing through the gloom. They could also hear a growling sound, the snapping of jaws, and the rending of flesh.

With luck, they might surprise the beast, catching it unawares as it feasted. It had been too long since Jed had been on the hunt. His battling days had begun on the streets of New York City. Brawling had led to boxing, the boy from Brooklyn making a name for himself as Killer Coolidge. His success had brought him to the attention of Algernon Helsing, and the rest was history. It was coming back to him, the old thrill of the approaching fight, the chance to go toe-to-toe with a worthy opponent. Humans provided a certain challenge, but nothing came close to a battle with a monster.

Right in Jed's path, snared on a low-hanging branch, was a red plaid hunting hat. It hung limp, one of its fluffy white earflaps soaked with blood. Jed maneuvered around it, finding a huge pine to duck behind. He pulled Wing close, placing the boy's back so that it was against the rough, rippled bark.

"You stay here," Jed muttered, and Wing nodded. With a big hand firmly set against Wing's chest, Jed chanced a peek around the tree trunk.

A neglected fire popped and crackled in the center of a small clearing, its flames dying as it slowly burned out. Empty beer cans littered the ground. Three men lay sprawled around the fire, still in their shredded sleeping bags. Their gear was strewn around them, their rifles leaning against a nearby tree.

One hunter wore a flannel shirt that matched the hat Jed had found flung in the bushes. His chest had been ripped open, and steam still rose from the exposed inner workings of his torso. Beside him, a second hunter's carefully chosen camouflage outfit had clearly not saved his skin; he lay facedown, covered in the fluffy white filler from his sleeping bag, the wool sticking to his blood as if he'd been tarred and feathered. The final hunter's Green Day T-shirt had been torn in two and painted red, as had the man himself.

The hunters weren't alone, either.

Jed counted four of the most enormous wolves he'd ever seen, their monstrous heads buried in the slaughtered hunters as they worried organs and hunks of flesh loose from the still-warm corpses. While one pawed at the camouflaged body, two of them fought over the remains of the T-shirt's owner. The biggest of the bunch, its fur black and oily, had the flannel shirt all to itself. It threw its head back, gorging on a rack of ribs like a glutton. Mighty jaws cracked as it ground the bones to crunchy pulp, swallowing the lot in one gulp. The wolf was easily the size of a grizzly, its fur flecked with blood and chunks of meat.

"Eat your fill, boys," said the monster, its voice booming from its vast, shaggy chest. "It's been too long since we enjoyed the taste of man."

The other wolves didn't answer, still lost in the feeding frenzy. Jed had never encountered any beast such as these before. Big wolves, yes, but none with the power of speech. The alpha smacked its lips, a pink tongue slurping gore off its huge, knifelike teeth as it returned its head to its dinner. Then it stopped. The black wolf lifted its head. Jed heard it growl. He could feel himself shrinking back, making himself smaller, his only thought to keep Wing safe. Even Eightball backed away now, his tiny paws silent as he took a tentative step into the shadows. One of these terrors, Jed might have been able to face, and eventually kill. But four of them? He was hopelessly outgunned.

"What's the matter, Grimgrin?" said another wolf, lifting its head from its meal as it noticed its brother's agitation.

"We're not alone, Fellfang," replied the black-furred pack leader. "I smell humans in the air once more."

Jed clasped his hand over Wing's face, clamping the

boy's nose and mouth closed. He raised his forearm to his mouth, trying to blanket his own breath.

Fellfang sidled up to Grimgrin, his head low and subservient. Grimgrin snarled, snapping at him, but Fellfang held his ground.

"Where does this scent come from, brother?"

Grimgrin sniffed at the air again. "North of here, not far at all."

"Eat, brother," said the smaller wolf. "One meal at a time. We finish here, then we follow your scent. And we find the next human. And we feast once more. The night is young."

The wolves returned their attention to their meals, hurrying down the remains of the dead hunters. Jed stared at Wing, then gestured that they were leaving. The two backed up, Eightball alongside them, all three grateful beyond words that they were covered in wood musk.

"Are we heading out of here?" whispered Wing when they were out of earshot.

"Not yet," said Jed, skirting the bloody campsite as they headed north. "We need to find the poor sap who's nearby. I don't think he realizes he's on the dessert menu."

TWENTY-THREE

xxx

X MARKS THE SPOT

Max held the scroll in both hands, checking he had indeed found the right place. Syd peered over his shoulder at the map, then looked ahead. Partially obscured by scrawny trees and threadbare bushes, the fissure in the rock seemed unremarkable. A stream trickled out from within, joining up with a faster-flowing body of water at their backs, which would eventually reach the waterfall that tumbled to Bone Creek below. The crack in the mountain was perhaps twenty feet high at its tallest point, widening to a gap of six feet at its base.

"So come on, dude. What does the X stand for?"

"We're about to find out," said Max, stepping forward across the babbling stream bed, flashlight in one hand, stake in the other.

"You sure you're gonna need that?" asked Syd, following

him and gesturing to the ancient silver-tipped wooden spike.

"After what happened to poor Barnum? Heck, yeah. And besides, Splinter goes everywhere with me, Syd. He's stuck by me through some pretty rough times."

"You do realize that you've not only named your stick, but you're also projecting feelings onto it?"

"It's a monster-hunter thing, Perez," said Max, stepping through the rocky arch. "You wouldn't understand."

"I worry about you sometimes," she muttered as she went in after him, glancing back as they were swallowed by the mountain.

The twin beams of light cut through the darkness, illuminating a twisting avenue in the rock, the walls leaning in on either side. It felt to Max that two mountains had met, crashing together and leaving the narrowest gap between them. Their feet splashed in the stream bed that passed for a path, the sound echoing deep into the tunnel as they continued forward. Gradually, the space began to open up, the ceiling growing taller until they found themselves in a vast, vaulted cavern. Stalactites and stalagmites threatened to meet one another, glistening with mineral deposits. His flashlight picked up other colors sparkling in the walls of the huge cave, hinting at gems and precious metals aplenty. Max had joked about the existence of quicksilver ore in the mountains, but now it wouldn't surprise him one bit to find a clan of gnomes in this secluded, secretive corner of the White Mountains.

"This place is beautiful," whispered Syd, smitten by the surroundings.

"Yeah, caves always tend to start out that way, before the hordes of goblins show up looking to tear our faces off."

"Could it just be a regular cave?"

"Why would Barnum have not only marked it on his map like other paranormal hot spots, but also put a dirty red cross on it?"

Max threw the light straight up into the ceiling of the cavern, and regretted it instantly. The dark rock suddenly came to life as thousands of winged creatures disengaged from the roof. They swept down, a squealing storm of wings and fur. Syd screeched, and Max joined her, as the colony of bats rushed around their heads, mobbing and dive-bombing them as they made for the exit en masse. In the commotion, Max's flashlight fell to the ground with a clatter, the light instantly extinguished. When the last of the bats had vanished, he reached down, searching for it. Syd threw her own beam across the floor to help. His heart sank as he saw the smashed bulb within the already broken glass.

"Crapsacks," he grumbled, standing again.

"So," said Syd, managing a faint smile. "Max Helsing is scared of bats?"

"You screamed too!"

"Yeah, but I don't profess to being a monster hunter."

"Hey, I've faced some pretty heinous beasts in my time!"

Syd smirked. "Don't worry, Max. It's perfectly normal to be scared."

The two laughed as their heart rate returned to something approaching normal. As they quieted, they returned their attention to the cavern. Pools of water had gathered here and there, their depth immeasurable, and Max had no intention of investigating further.

"Shine your light back over there," said Max, as Syd's beam caught something pale lying on the dark ground: a bar or stick of something, white against the absolute blackness. The two stepped carefully over, walking around the puddles and pools and rock formations. They rounded a huge stalagmite in the recesses of the cave and found the white stick.

"Wouldn't you just know it?" said Syd, as the flashlight picked out the stripped bone on the ground. Gradually, she began to find others, strewn about, piled in heaps, broken and gnawed on by whatever called the cavern its home. Max crouched and picked one up. It could have been a human femur, but could've equally been the leg bone from a large deer. Teeth marks ran up and down its length—extra large, naturally. Max stood still, listening, while Syd swirled the flashlight around her.

"Nobody's home," she said.

"Correction," whispered Max, grabbing her flashlight and turning it off. "Nobody *was* home."

He led her to the stalagmite, colliding blindly with the twisted tower of petrified minerals. Syd flinched when Max's lips brushed her ear, his voice a warm whisper.

"Listen."

They both heard it now: a shuffling, splashing sound, as feet hit water, coming through the passage they'd entered by. Max and Syd remained still as statues, hugging the gray pillar, unable to see a thing. The footsteps drew closer, heavy and slapping against the cave floor. Grunting, burbling, hacking, and coughing. It was almost on top of them.

Max leaped out and flicked on the flashlight.

His aim wasn't great. The beam hit the creature somewhere around its chest, illuminating the dead black bear it was carrying. The bear's neck was broken, lolling over a huge gray arm as if the animal were a slumbering infant. Max let the light shoot up the enormous body, the monster already recoiling. The beam finally reached the creature's head, around fifteen feet off the ground. Max saw the monster's eyes go wide with horror, as its irises retracted with the speed of a camera shutter. It was too late for the cave dweller, though. The flashlight had done its work.

"Troll!" shouted Max, as much to himself as to Syd, as the giant dropped the dead bear and crashed toward him.

Max dove one way, Syd the other, as the troll bounced off the stalagmite, cracking its shin. It staggered back, striking its head on a low-hanging stalactite and collapsing to the ground with an earthshaking crash. It lay there, wheezing for a moment, before its fingers scrabbled around and into one of the pools. It wailed, tossing the stagnant water into its blinded eyes, trying to restore its stolen sight.

"What's you done to Murdo's eyes?" shouted the troll. "You's blinded 'em, is what you's done!"

MOUNTAIN TROLL

ORIGIN:
Norway

STRENGTHS: Great strength. Immune to many physical attacks. Regenerates.

WEAKNESSES: Low intelligence. Slow. Calcification in sunlight. Avoid melee confrontations and rely upon ranged weapons.

HABITAT: Mountains, caves, gulches, subterranean environments.

Although originating in Scandinavia, trolls have done a tremendous job of traveling to most corners of the globe. The mountain troll can be found in the high places of the world, most comfortable in near-arctic conditions. While they're known to prey upon humans, their favorite foods are cattle and sheep. They come out only at night, as sunlight can turn them to stone. Likewise, they have a severe aversion to any bright light.

—Erik Van Helsing, October 13th, 1848

PHYSICAL TRAITS

1. _Armor_—Should you foolishly find yourself in a fight with a mountain troll, know this: their flesh is as tough as the rocks they're supposedly born from.

2. _Limbs_—Arms and legs are truly brutal weapons. Steer clear at all costs!

3. _Regeneration_—Not only is the mountain troll impervious to most weapons, it also enjoys the luxury of rapid recovery. Wounds heal over, sword slashes seal shut. Take nothing for granted. Removing the head is the only way to be certain they're slain!

—Esme Van Helsing, August 1st, 1870

With the help of a local guide, I found a nest of these foul fiends, high upon the north slope of Mount McKinley: a mother, a father, and three infants. Esme's advice was sage— removal of their heads was the only way to be sure. Those five stone skulls may be mistaken by hikers for boulders. Only I shall ever know the truth.

—Algernon Van Helsing, February 12th, 1943

Wow, GRANDPA!! Five of them. <u>DEAD</u>. Even the kids . . . #SPEECHLESS

MAX HELSING
Sep 19th, 2015

Syd was already pulling at Max's arm, trying to encourage him to leave, but Max held fast.

"No, Syd," he said as the troll gnashed his teeth and balled his fists in anger. "Boyle could be here, somewhere in this cave." Max kicked some of the bones aside. "If he hasn't already been eaten."

The troll turned his head toward the bones that Max had kicked, his attention fixed upon the two kids.

"Who's you to be 'ere in Murdo's 'ome?"

"I'll take this," Max whispered to Syd, warily stepping forward to the blind monster. "The name's Max Helsing. And you'd be Murdo, right?"

The troll growled, turning his head one way and then the other as Max let the light wander over his grotesque frame. This was a mountain troll. His gray flesh was the color of the rocks around them, and where one might have expected to find hair—he was, after all, naked—great clumps of moss and lichen grew, peppered here and there with a variety of odd-shaped fungi. His feet were broad and flat, as were his hands, while his large knobby head was covered in growths, as if he had gone through some strange process of rapid calcification. He reminded Max of the earth elemental he'd encountered in the Undercity, only minus a great many of its better features, not least charm and personal hygiene. The canines of the troll's jaw jutted up like a pair of hippo tusks, almost touching the bags of dark flesh that gathered beneath his eyes. The eyes were pale, like saucers of milk, the irises at their centers flickering like moths around a flame at night. The tiny dots were lost, looking anywhere but at Max and Syd.

"What's you wanting in Murdo's cave, Maxelsing?"

"We came here looking for answers," said Max, trying to deepen his voice and sound authoritative. After all, the troll didn't know he was speaking to a scrawny human kid, did he? "The deaths, down in Bone Creek; your doing, right, Murdo?"

"Why would Murdo go killing down there? Murdo's got all 'e needs up 'ere on the plateau. Murdo's 'appy 'ere."

"Don't lie, troll. You're the one who killed those people—admit it. Tell us what you've done with our friend!"

The troll scratched his throat, slate fingernails scraping like chalk on a board. "Murdo eats animals, Maxelsing. Not 'umans." He chuckled and smacked his lips. "Not anymore, anyways."

"So you're reformed, then? You're not partial to the odd manburger?"

"Murdo 'as to live near the 'ermit. 'Ermit would kill Murdo if 'e knew Murdo were eating 'umans."

Syd tugged Max's sleeve. "So Barnum and the troll knew all about each other? Maybe the map was just marking up this lair for Barnum's peace of mind then? A reminder to steer clear?"

Max nodded and turned back to the troll. "If you *haven't* been killing folk and kidnapping them, then who has? What do you know, Murdo? Tell us and we'll leave you in peace."

"Leave Murdo in peace?" The troll laughed, his bellowing

chortle loosening stones from the ceiling that showered down around the cavern. "You's gone and blinded poor Murdo! 'Ow's that leaving in peace?"

"Ah, quit whining," said Max. "It'll be temporary. You'll have your eyesight back in no time."

"Will he?" whispered Syd.

"Haven't a clue, but we'll be long gone by then." Then he was back to the troll. "Go on. Tell me what you know about the one that's responsible for the attacks."

The troll pulled himself upright, taking hold of the tall stalagmite for support and straightening before the pair. Syd gulped as the gray giant cleared his throat.

"Murdo may be big, but Murdo also be slow. 'E don't think too 'ard about stuff. 'E keeps 'imself to 'imself. The Sasquatches . . . they're the bosses of Bone Creek. This was their land before any of the rest of us came 'ere. They welcomed us. Let us live 'ere. Keep out of sight of 'umans and be at peace."

This all fit with what Max had heard about Esme Van Helsing's work, just as Kimble had recounted.

"Others always come to Bone Creek. Fairy folk and monsterkind alike. Looking for new beginnings. Trying to get along. Then something new came and changed everything. There's always something new. . . ."

"What *new* thing came knocking, Murdo? What came to make a home in Bone Creek?"

The troll ran a hand along his rib cage, where Max could see a long white scar, recently healed over. "The stranger came knocking. It fought Murdo. Told Murdo to stay in 'is cave. Bone Creek belonged to the stranger now." The troll scratched the wound, the great jagged line about a foot in length. "But Murdo's gotta eat. So Murdo leaves the cave at night. But Murdo always looking out for the stranger. Murdo scared of stranger."

"Aw," said Syd, tilting her head.

"Really?" whispered Max, rolling his eyes. "Murdo, the stranger: was he a Sasquatch?"

The troll shook his head. "Not Sasquatch."

"Can you describe him?"

"Murdo can describe 'im. But after Murdo's eaten."

Max nodded. "Fair enough, if you must, but be quick. Our friend's life depends on us finding this fiend, and when we do, things will be better for *everyone* in Bone Creek, Murdo. You, the Sasquatches, every monster that lives in these mountains. You won't live in fear anymore."

The troll wasn't listening. He was scratching his stomach, which rumbled like a volcano about to erupt. He snapped the centuries-old stalagmite from the ground with an effortless *crack*, and in one fluid motion swung it at the kids. Max and Syd both dived, landing awkwardly as the giant stone club whooshed over their heads. The troll sniffed at the air once more.

"Stay still, little 'umans."

"But I can help you!" shouted Max as Syd pulled him away, flashlight arcing wild in the darkness as she searched for the tunnel out of there. "It doesn't have to be like this!"

"Troll's gotta eat!" bellowed the monster, lurching after the pair on his great, flapping feet, his belly growling like a caged beast.

"What do we do?" screamed Syd as the two stumbled toward the exit.

"You're already doing it!" yelled Max. "Run! I'm right behind you!"

TWENTY-FOUR

xxx

THE DYRE DUEL

Jed was running, and it wasn't pretty. That bum leg of his was managing to snag itself on every passing root, rock, and rut in his path. More than once he hit the ground, Wing quick to help him to his feet. Eightball whimpered. Hellhound he may have been, but he was just a puppy in the shadow of those giant wolves. All the while they glanced back into the night, searching the swathes of darkness between the trees. Time was against them.

"Do you even know where we're running?" asked Wing. "This looks a lot like blind panic."

"North," said Jed.

"And you know which way north is?" No reply told Wing all he needed to know. He whipped out his cell, hit a few buttons, and within seconds he had a GPS compass on the screen. Then they were moving again, bearing north at last. "What kind of beasts were those back there?"

Jed shrugged, his heart crashing like waves against the cliffs of his ribs.

"Why don't you check *your* phone, Jed?"

Jed pulled his phone out and looked at it, utterly confused. "What good will that do?"

Wing's exasperated sigh reminded Jed of a disgruntled schoolteacher when dealing with a dunce. "I've spent the last three months scanning and uploading as many pages as possible from the *Monstrosi Bestiarum* onto our encrypted database. Your phone, the computer at Helsing House—they're all now linked up and accessible via the Cloud."

"What cloud?" asked Jed, looking up, utterly bemused.

Wing snatched the old man's phone and gave Jed his own, the compass still lit up. "Why do I bother?" muttered the boy as his fingers danced across the touchscreen. "There!" he said in a matter of seconds, showing Jed the screen. "Just what I thought!"

Jed snatched the cell back. The phone showed him all he needed, a digitized page straight out of the Van Helsing monster manual: *Dyre Wolf.*

"I was sure I'd seen a rumor somewhere online of dyre wolves in New Hampshire," said Wing. "Looks like I was right after all. Wing shoots! Wing scores!"

Jed squinted at the beast's description in the half-light. It made for grisly reading. If there were a crueler sentient pack animal out there, Jed had yet to encounter it. The dyre wolves were a throwback to a time when monsters and animals shared the earth. The arrival of man had pushed

DYRE WOLF

AKA: "Canis lucifus," devil wolf

ORIGIN: North America, Northern Europe, Russia

STRENGTHS: Thick pelts, huge paws, fierce jaws, high intelligence. Hunt in packs. A true alpha predator.

WEAKNESSES: Very few physical frailties. Like werewolves, they have a weakness to silver.

Bloodlust might be exploited, as they lose all reason.

HABITAT: The veiled lands between worlds, where monsterkind and mankind meet.

Not to be confused with the prehistoric dire wolf (<u>Canis dirus</u>), the dyre wolf is a highly intelligent pack hunter that possesses the power of speech. One and a half times the size of a gray wolf, dyre wolves have been ridden on occasion by goblins in battle. While some are trained as guard dogs for demonic forces and powerful magicians, others remain wild, hunting in packs. Voracious carnivores, their favorite prey are humanoids of any kind (man, elf, dwarf, gnome, etc.). —Erik Van Helsing, May 8th, 1850

FIELD ACCOUNT–THE WOLF OF WILLOW COUNTY

The brutal death of a shepherd boy brought me to this curious case, with a witness describing the killer as a monstrous wolf that could speak. My instinct told me lycanthrope—the attack occurring the night before a full moon was a big clue! I set up a trap during daylight, lying in wait for the returning fiend, only to encounter three great, grisly wolves that afternoon. While I was unable to dispatch all three of them, a silver saber to the heart of their pack leader was enough to break the spirits of his brothers, who fled.
                              —Esme Van Helsing, April 17th, 1868

Very Important Health Tip: NEVER leave home without <u>SILVER</u>!

MAX HELSING

Jun 12th, 2015

the dyre wolves back, virtually wiping them out. They had since lived far away from humankind, preying exclusively upon other magical beasts. Max's great-grandfather had been the last Van Helsing to face one down, a lone male that had crawled out of the Undercity to hunt the homeless of Gallows Hill. How on earth would Jed fare against four of them, with only a ten-year-old bookworm for backup?

"We've been heading north for a while and haven't seen anyone," said Wing, staring at his compass as Jed urged the breathless boy on his way. "Maybe the dyre wolves were mistaken?"

"Don't reckon," grunted Jed, shoving his own cell back into his pocket. "The pack leader, the one they called Grimgrin, got the scent on the wind from up here."

The image of the monstrous wolves devouring those men in greedy gulps was seared onto Jed's mind's eye. Jed doubted there was anything left of those hunters now. He expected the wolves were already on their way.

Eightball whimpered a few feet in front of him as they crashed through the forest, but it was too late. The hellhound flew up into the air, a loop of black cord tight about his belly. His rolls of fat bulged around the noose, which looked like it had nearly cut him in two. As for Jed, a different trap awaited him, as that accursed leg triggered a trip wire. He was able to shove Wing aside just in time as a weighted net fell from the boughs of the tree overhead, catching him as sure as a fly in a web.

The "spider" lay nearby, sleeping on his bedroll beside

a woodland pond. He looked up, yawned, and smacked his lips.

"Well, bless my socks," said Abel Archer. "If it isn't the oldest monster hunter in town! Talk about a rude awakening."

"Zip it, boy, and get me out of this damned net!"

"Now, now, Mr. Coolidge," said Archer, stretching where he lay as Wing dashed over to Jed to try to wrestle him out of his bonds. "You come crashing in here, making a hell of a racket, no doubt waking half the forest, and you expect me to just jump to it like some peasant? What an astonishing lack of manners."

The next words out of Jed's mouth were even more color-ful. The young Brit glanced at Wing.

"Such language! And in front of a minor, too."

Wing gave the muscled teen a boot in the shoulder.

Archer chuckled. "You get the first one for free." When Wing attempted a second kick, Archer deftly swept the boy's legs out from under him and he landed unceremoniously in the pond.

"You really are the *rudest* people." Archer sighed. "Now, I know why Max is in Bone Creek. And I know why *I* am in Bone Creek. But tell me, Mr. Coolidge—and I'll release you and your funny little dog if you behave—what are *you* doing in Bone Creek?"

"Right now," snapped Jed, "I'm trying to save your sorry ass, but I'm having second thoughts."

Archer laughed as Wing dragged himself out of the

pond. "I can assure you, Mr. Coolidge, my arse is anything but apologetic, and—"

Even with the net draped over him, Jed was able to make a clumsy leap across the clearing. He landed in the dirt beside Archer, making the brash youth jump.

"Quit the flowery talk, you dunderhead, and get me out of here. There's a ravenous pack of dyre wolves on its way, and it's *your* scent they've taken a shine to."

Jed and Archer eyeballed each other for a split second. Then Archer whipped his bowie knife from his belt, catching the net and sawing through it, right up the middle. He was only halfway through the job when the undergrowth burst apart, and four enormous wolves pounced.

Archer was a blur of sudden, violent movement. The nearest and biggest, a black-furred monster, caught an army boot to its jaw, sending it skidding away. The next lunged in, openmouthed, only for Archer's bowie knife to tear a strip off its tongue. It yelped as the hulking young hunter followed with a punch on the nose. That was enough to make the other two hang back as Archer seized hold of a damp Wing and tossed him up into the tree bough overhead. Wing moved quickly, scrambling along the branch until he could haul Eightball up to safety.

"The black one's the leader." Jed gasped as he tore the cut net in two and rose. "Called Grimgrin."

"Cool name," said Archer, nodding approvingly.

"Grimgrin!" shouted Jed. "A challenge for you. Your champion versus ours. You win, we're in your bellies before sunup. We win, you're out of here, never to return. Winner takes all."

"Takes . . . all?" growled the big black wolf. "What's to stop us from taking all anyway?"

"Don't mistake us for those chumps you just filled your face with." Jed puffed his chest out. "You're not facing one, but *two* of humankind's greatest monster hunters, Jed 'Killer' Coolidge and Abel Archer."

Archer gave Jed a thumbs-up and wink for the name check, which the old man promptly ignored.

"So whaddaya say? Who wants to fight me?"

Archer leaned across to Jed. "I thought you were talking about *me* as the champion, Grandpa."

"I'll fight you," said Grimgrin, taking the bait.

Jed lifted his black flashlight and ran his fingers along its length. A light appeared on its end.

"That's your plan?" said Archer in disbelief. "You're going to clobber it with a flashlight?"

"I'll fight you, Jed Coolidge," said Grimgrin, "and I'll crush your bones and suck the marrow dry. I'll—"

Jed was leaping, flashlight in hand. As he brought it around, it extended a further three feet in length, transforming into an elegant staff in an instant. The telescopic weapon struck Grimgrin across the snout, a flash of light exploding where it connected with the wolf's muzzle.

"Some folk really love the sound of their own voice," grumbled Jed, swinging it back the other way. It glanced across Grimgrin's brow, leaving bright sparks with its passing.

"Elf magic?" roared the dyre wolf, as his brothers howled in horror. They snarled and snapped at Archer, who promptly reached for his ax.

"You recognize the magic of the Undercity?" said Jed, driving the black beast back. "You should have stayed there, Grimgrin."

Jed jabbed the wolf in the chest. The nightwand had been a gift from an elf sorceress, way back in Jed's youth, in return for a noble deed. More than that, it was a lover's gift from a life that might have been. The telescopic staff was just one of its many uses, while the illumination tended to exhaust its energy. Its charge was limited, and already almost spent. Jed just had to keep Grimgrin moving a bit longer.

The nightwand came around again, but the black wolf was faster. Grimgrin's jaws snapped around the staff's middle, the light blooming at its end as the monster's eyes narrowed. The dyre wolf's laugh was a demonic gurgle as he ignored the ball of magical light. Jed booted Grimgrin in the head, causing the wolf to dislodge his jaws from the nightwand as he staggered back, hindquarters slipping into the pond with a splash.

One of the other wolves jumped forward, its jaws clapping together inches away from Jed and causing the old man to stumble. Archer's ax swept about, cutting a scarlet gash along the smaller wolf's flank.

"Back, Fellfang." Grimgrin laughed, shaking his soaking coat like a dog that had been in the sea. "We had a deal with

these men. We shall stand by it. Then we shall eat our fill."
Grimgrin's cackle was joined by that of his brothers. "Is that
all you've got, Jed Coolidge? A trinket from the Undercity?
An elfin plaything? It isn't even a proper weapon!"

"Isn't it?" said Jed, diving forward and plunging the
nightwand's end into the pool. He shouted out the ancient
words of magic, taught to him by the sorceress who had
lived a dozen mortal lifetimes. The magical staff unloaded
everything into the pond, discharging all its stored lightning in one bright and blinding flash. Grimgrin thrashed in
the churning water, the elf magic coursing through the huge
dyre wolf. His limbs locked, his muscles contorted, and his
organs ruptured one after another. The other wolves looked
away as Grimgrin, their alpha, their leader, enjoyed a grisly,
glorious death. When his smoking corpse splashed down
into the pond, blood streaming from every orifice, Jed knew
the job was done.

He turned wearily toward the other three wolves, who
had begun a chorus of growls.

"We had a deal, Fellfang."

The beta wolf's snarl was cut short when Abel Archer's
ax smashed into the ground, a mere whisker away from
his face.

"That could have been your skull, wolf," said the
Englishman. "Now scurry on home with your tail between
your legs—there's a good boy."

Fellfang turned and ran, his brothers fleeing with him.
Jed collapsed and dropped the wand, which reverted back

to normal size, as Wing and Eightball climbed down out of the tree. Archer picked up the black tube of dull metal, his eyes wide with wonder as he tried to read the runes.

"I wouldn't try to decipher it if you're a novice with magic," said Jed. "Last person who did got his face scorched off."

"You have to tell me who your outfitter is, Mr. Coolidge," said Archer, giving the cylinder a swish through the air as Wing and Eightball rushed to Jed's side. "I simply must pick up one of those."

"It's one of a kind," replied Jed, as he received a hug from a boy and a lick from a dog. He winked at Archer. "Like me."

TWENTY-FIVE

xxx

BATTLE FALLS

The flight from the cave hadn't gone quite according to plan. Running hell for leather through the cavern, Max and Syd had gotten separated when the teenage monster hunter charged headlong into a handily situated stalagmite. The girl had run on, Max yelling to her to head down the cliffs.

When Max finally emerged from the cave, Murdo the troll was right behind, squeezing out of the fissure in a (very) blind fury. If the monster's sight had been fully functioning, Max's number would've been up. As it was, the troll was dependent upon his other senses. His ears and nose kept him on Max's heels, as the boy bounded, splished, and splashed his way toward the head of the waterfall.

If the moon and stars hadn't been out that night, there was a fine chance Max Helsing's monster-hunting career—and more important, his life—would have ground to a halt atop those cliffs in the White Mountains. The glow of the heavens guided him down the stream and all the way to Battle Falls. Without the stars' guiding light, he might have run straight off the crags.

Max collapsed onto a boulder beside the top of the waterfall. The water looked like polished glass here, the moon's reflection rippling on its surface as it raced away off the plateau. Max looked about, panting for breath, trying to work out exactly where the path down was located.

"Okay, Max," he said to himself, as behind, in the darkness, he heard the troll drawing nearer, throat gurgling and belly growling as he came. "The exit should be . . ."

He looked one way and then the other, but it was hopeless. He was completely turned around. He pulled Barnum's map out of his pocket.

The ink markings ran in rivers of their own from the sheet. Max's numerous falls and flounders in the stream had ensured the scroll was as soaked as his undies. He tossed it to the wind, which carried it off the cliffs and down to the forest below.

"Maxelsing!"

He turned, sick to the pit of his belly, as the mountain troll splashed closer, swinging his stalagmite club and striking the riverbed. Water and pebbles erupted, showering the boy and sending him staggering closer to the cliff's edge. There was nowhere left to hide. Max looked at Splinter in his hand. He shrugged; it was hardly the ideal weapon to have on hand in a scrap with a troll, especially one wielding a giant stone club, but it was better than nothing. If only he'd packed a bazooka for the camping trip.

"Hey, Murdo!" shouted Max. "What say you and I have a little chat, eh? See if we can't hammer out an understanding, an agreement of some kind, where we both get what we want? Mano a mano. Guy to guy. Whaddaya say?"

"Mmm," said the troll. "But Murdo wants to eat Maxelsing."

"Yeah, Max Helsing isn't keen on that. I was thinking more we could hook you up with a lady troll. That's what your cave really needs—a woman's touch. Believe me, back home in Gallows Hill, the contacts I have in the Undercity? I guarantee I can bag you an interested party. We can really sell this: fresh air, great views, eligible . . . umm . . . bachelor?"

"Murdo not interested in lady trolls," said the stony-skinned fiend, shaking his enormous head, blind eyes still staring into space.

"Ah, how rude of me to assume. Perhaps a nice fellow, then?"

The troll stomped his foot. "Murdo just wants to eat Maxelsing!"

Max sighed. "Are you *sure* I can't persuade you that there's more to life than eating me?"

The troll chuckled, saliva drooling from his tusklike teeth. Even though the monster wanted to eat him, Max didn't look on the troll as a bad guy. Trolls ate people, on every continent. That's what made them trolls. At least this one had been reformed for some time.

Max suddenly made to run along the plateau, away from the waterfall and the troll. The stalagmite descended, smashing the crag and crumbling the cliff edge in front of and around Max. He leaped back, splashing into the river and instantly feeling the fast-flowing water pull at his ankles. He waded the other way, keeping a healthy distance from the waterfall's overhang. Again, the club came down, the river exploding as if a depth charge had gone off. Max stood there as the water came back down, soaking him from head to foot.

The troll's hand shot forward, frighteningly fast, making a clumsy grab for Max. Murdo succeeded in knocking him over, the current seizing Max and pulling him toward the falls on his belly. Before he could disappear over the edge, Max felt the troll's hand grasp him by his messenger bag and drag him back, out of the river and into the air. Max twisted and turned, caught up in the satchel strap like a rabbit in a snare. He got a great view of that big ugly face as Murdo brought him closer, the monster's belly now snarling with wild anticipation below.

The troll stopped suddenly, his blind eyes shifting left and right, as his nostrils flared and his ears twitched.

Max covered his face as something flitted past, missing him by inches. When it hovered a short way from his face, Max saw it was a will-o'-the-wisp, a fairy of the forest. Of course, this wasn't a breathtakingly beautiful sprite like the kind Peter Pan kept in his pocket. Although its top half was roughly humanoid, its lower portion was that of a swollen bug, bloated abdomen glowing like a floating Chinese lantern. It hovered before the helpless boy for a moment, before zigzagging through the air toward the troll's face, buzzing the monster. Max couldn't help but feel touched by the fairy's brave, and admittedly impossible, intervention. What could one tiny will-o'-the-wisp do to save him?

The sightless troll batted it away, once, twice, the fairy coming back for more each time, slowing the fiend and buying Max precious time. It flew around the monster's giant head, a belligerent gnat in the face of a lion. Then the troll snorted, sending the tiny being spinning into the darkness. Murdo grinned before returning to the squirming, dangling boy in his grasp.

Murdo's mouth opened wide, a stinking, saliva-coated tunnel, as he prepared to toss his supper down his gullet. Before the troll could bite down, though, he felt a stabbing pain in his clenched fist as the creature known as Maxelsing struck back. Up went Splinter, again and again, peppering the mighty hand and those filthy fingers. Murdo cried out, releasing the messenger bag instantly as boy and satchel crashed down into the water.

Max didn't wait around. Repositioning his bag, he splashed away along the shallow river, trying to get to safety. He felt, rather than heard, the troll's next furious attack, as the wind whooshed around him. Max flopped forward with a splash as the stone club swept past and over him. If it had connected, the entire forest below the cliffs would've been speckled with bits of Max. He rolled over as the troll roared,

WILL-O'-THE-WISP

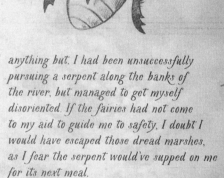

AKA: *ignis fatuus, hinkypunk, friar's lantern, ghost lights*

ORIGIN: *Europe*

STRENGTHS: *Bioluminescent—a "living light," extremely mobile and agile.*

WEAKNESSES: *Fragile.*

HABITAT: *Countryside, wilderness, areas of magical focus.*

The will-o'-the-wisp has a colorful past, with reports of them ranging from the helpful through mischievous to malignant. Tiny fairies, no larger than a thimble, they appear as glowing balls of light when in flight at night. Upon closer inspection, they have a roughly humanoid torso and head, while the abdomen resembles that of an insect. It is this lower portion that provides the bioluminescent light source. They are utterly harmless physically, although some have been responsible for leading travelers into treacherous and deadly areas such as swamps and quicksand. If in doubt, avoid interaction.

—Erik Van Helsing, October 13th, 1852

FIELD ACCOUNT–THE HUDSON RIVER

While not doubting that some will-o'-the-wisps are belligerent beings, the ones I encountered upon the shores of the Hudson in upstate New York were anything but. I had been unsuccessfully pursuing a serpent along the banks of the river, but managed to get myself disoriented. If the fairies had not come to my aid to guide me to safety, I doubt I would have escaped those dread marshes, as I fear the serpent would've supped on me for its next meal.

—Esme Van Helsing, March 5th, 1871

The will-o'-the-wisp is a conniving, cunning fairy, capable of fooling the finest of minds. Do not dither should you encounter one, trying to decide whether it is wholesome or harmless—smite it, as you would a wasp or a no-see-um. Take no chances, regardless of what my predecessors suggest.

—Algernon Van Helsing, November 22nd, 1940

You're all heart, Grandpa! Is there anything you actually LIKE???

Apr 17th, 2015

aware of exactly where he was, spittle splattering the boy and the river.

A bird suddenly flew by, narrowly missing Max before smacking the monster's face. Then another, swooping by the other way and raking a broad, bulbous cheek. A third was followed by a fourth. The troll cried out, and Max smiled.

The rock drakes mobbed the troll, fluttering and flapping around his face and neck, striking and stabbing with tooth and talon. They spat acid at the monster, and it hissed and sizzled as it struck Murdo's flesh. The monster screamed, lashing out blindly, club swinging, fat fingers snatching at and missing the flying lizards. He wailed as he tried to reach his exhausted meal. Max continued to retreat, wading back, away from the melee and closer toward the relative safety of the waterfall's overhang.

The troll raised his powerful arms, mighty hands balled into fists. He was about to strike Max when a series of shrill, sharp notes caused him to falter. His expression changed from fury to fear, as the tune became a jaunty jig. The tiny figure of Kimble appeared among the reeds on the river- bank, mouth moving across the panpipes as he wove his musical magic. Murdo retreated in a blind panic, swing- ing his club as if it might physically keep the tune at bay. The troll crashed into a tree that promptly snapped in two and noisily toppled into the river. He let loose a terrible cry that made Max's blood run cold. Murdo cowered as the drakes continued to mob him, driving him back upstream, back toward his cave. The brownie remained on the bank, playing his pipes, guarding the beaten boy in the river. He turned slowly and looked at Max, who managed a smile and a wink. Kimble did the same, and Max's spirits lifted.

They dropped seconds later when the felled tree collided with him, pushing him toward the top of Battle Falls. He tried to hurdle it, but only landed on the trunk as it went over the edge. Max ran up its length as it tipped, trying to get back to the cliff top, but it was hopeless. He was going down, and the tree was coming with him. Max brought his feet up and kicked away from the tumbling tree, changing his angle of trajectory so that his plummet carried him away from the pine. He only prayed it didn't carry him away from the churning water below.

As the top branches of the tree struck the Dead Pool, Max landed with a *splash* a short distance away, caught up in the torrent of water. He went deep, drawn into the frigid plunge pool's maelstrom like a doll in a washing machine. Almost deafened by the noise of the rushing water, he still managed to catch the sound of the tree smashing into the water above him. He tried to swim clear, kicking frantically, but he was beaten down by the mighty trunk, forced toward the depths of the icy pool. The cold was overwhelming, paralyzing each limb. Bubbles streamed from his mouth and nose as a branch speared him in the guts, threatening to puncture his flesh. A torn belly was the least of his worries as his precious breath escaped.

Max saw lights flashing before his eyes, white against the dark, turbulent water. This was it, his brain starved of oxygen, the end approaching. Before he could be dashed against the boulders that littered the riverbed, he felt hands seize hold of him by the armpits. He felt legs kicking beside him, fighting the current as he was carried to the surface. Exploding from the water, he snatched a lungful of air, spluttering as half the river seemed to find its way in as well. He floundered, sinking once more as his rescuer took hold again.

"Stop struggling, Helsing, or you'll drown both of us!" shouted Syd over the roar of the waterfall.

Max was a competent swimmer, but not great like Syd. He wasn't used to swimming fully clothed, certainly not in freezing, turbulent waters such as the Dead Pool. His numb hands clawed at her shoulders as he disappeared beneath the foaming water and took Syd down with him. She kicked hard, yanking him roughly, trying to get distance away from the strongest currents at the river's heart.

Suddenly, shimmering shapes sidled up alongside them, brushing against their heavy limbs. Max felt bizarrely buoyant as a host of silver-skinned water nymphs carried them through the waves toward the shore. There were dozens of the aquatic fairies, working as one, leaving the fierce current behind as they helped Syd haul Max to safety.

As they neared the shallows of the gorge, Syd's feet found the pebbled riverbed and she was able to scramble toward the rocky bank. The fairies splashed clear like a shoal of startled fish, their scales shining brilliant in the starlight. Syd snatched Max by the collar of his bomber jacket and dragged him the remaining distance to the rocks. Throwing him onto his side, she pulled him by his belt, forcing him to spew water across the stony beach. Max coughed and hacked, rolling onto his knees as he retched up the last remnants of the Dead Pool.

He looked at Syd, who sat panting for breath beside him, her eyes fixed on the water and the departing nymphs, the river rippling as they sped away.

"Is this where you attempt mouth-to-mouth?" Max asked, teeth chattering as he tipped water out of his messenger bag. Syd looked up as a tiny light drifted down from above, like a feather in the wind. The will-o'-the-wisp came to a fluttering halt, inches away from her face, awaiting their next move.

"In your dreams, Helsing," she whispered, shivering as the misshapen fairy bug danced before her eyes. "In your dreams."

TWENTY-SIX

xxx

GRATEFUL FOR GIDEON

By the time Max and Syd limped into Bone Creek Camp, the will-o'-the-wisp lighting and leading the way, the two teens had reached a joint conclusion: they needed help. This was too big a task for the pair to handle alone. Max, of course, felt like he could face down any monster (although a double-shot espresso right now would've done wonders for his energy), but the sheer vastness of the wilderness was crippling their search for Boyle. He could have been anywhere out there, and without the help of someone they could trust, time was running out.

"I'm not sure we should tell him," said Syd as they passed the boathouse on their way into camp. The fairy flitted ahead of them, waiting for them to catch up, like an obedient puppy that was off the leash. A thin veil of mist was settling over the creek, rising off the river and rolling through the woods. "He could freak out."

"Gideon? I don't see how we've got any choice," said Max. "He's a good guy, and we're lucky he's here. What we have to tell him might be alarming, but we're between a rock and a hard place and someone's dropped a boulder on us. Until we hook up with Jed, it's just you and me, and that scenario leaves Boyle with slim to no chance of surviving."

"Have you tried calling Jed?"

"Do I look stupid?" said Max, before sheepishly shoving a hand into the pocket of his still damp jeans. "Don't answer that," he added as he fished out his phone. He turned it on. The screen glowed, then went off, then came back on again. Then was off once more.

"Probably not the best idea to take it swimming with you," muttered Syd.

"You don't say?" Max sighed as they walked past the bunkhouses, the mist partially obscuring them in the darkness.

Max trudged along, scuffing the grass with the toes of his Chucks. He looked up as they approached the third lodge, situated a little deeper into the forest that neighbored the creek.

"Thanks, Syd. Y'know, for back there. Fishing me out and saving my bacon."

She punched his arm. "You'd have done the same for me. Besides, it was your fairy fan club who stopped you from drowning. I just got you on dry land."

"That was pretty amazing," said Max with a sigh. "They all helped me—brownie, rock drake, water nymph, will-o'-the-wisp. I don't think I can rely on the help from a mountain troll anytime soon though."

Syd's chuckle was weak, her thoughts lingering on their hopeless predicament.

"We'll find Boyle, Syd," said Max, although the words rang hollow.

"Maybe Gideon has a landline we can use," said Syd, as they marched up the steps to his lodge. It was bigger than the one the kids had stayed in, and resembled a home more than a bunkhouse.

"One can only hope," replied Max as he rapped on the door. "Gideon? Wake up, Mr. G! We need your help."

They waited for a moment, hoping that a light might come on and a nightgown-sporting tour guide would appear at the door. There was no light, and there was no sign of Gideon, either.

"Perhaps he's a deep sleeper?" said Syd, cupping her hands around her face as she peeked through a window pane into a darkened room.

"You wanna come up here?" asked Max, turning to the will-o'-the-wisp that hovered a short distance away from the house. "Maybe throw us a little light?" The ugly fairy remained where it was, close to the surrounding trees. Max shrugged and turned back to the house.

He knocked again. Still no answer. He felt a sinking feeling come over him.

"Or maybe he's in trouble," said Max, trying the door handle. It was locked.

"Back up, monsterboy," said Syd, pushing Max aside as she pulled her key ring from her pocket and a crooked pin from her mop of dark hair. Nestled between the keys to her bike lock and to her mom's front door was the pick she was after. She slotted it into the mechanism, adding the hairpin alongside it. As the girl jiggled the lock and the key ring jangled, Max took a look in another window. It was pitch-dark within.

"Gideon!" he shouted a final time, but no reply came.

"Open sesame," said Syd. The door creaked open, she pocketed her keys, and the pin went back into her curly mane.

"Where would I be without you?" Max grinned.

"Lost, I'd imagine," said Syd, stepping aside to allow her friend through the door first.

Max fumbled along the wall, searching for a light switch. He flicked the button, and low-energy bulbs began to dimly glow along the timber walls. The floorboards were polished to a rich hue, while the room was handsomely furnished, a big leather Chesterfield sofa facing an old television set in the corner. A bowl of fresh fruit sat on the coffee table in front of the sofa, a couple of magazines neatly beside it. Two well-stocked bookcases flanked a big stone fireplace, a polished slab of slate running along the floor in front of it. Pretty rows of pinecones and candles decorated the hearth, placed in a precise fashion. A large painting of a woodland scene graced the chimney, while the flowers in the vase on the dining table were a lovely touch. Max couldn't help but smile wryly. The eccentric Gideon had class, and a style all his own.

"Gideon?" he called, as Syd stepped into the lodge behind him. "We need your help. Are you there?"

"This place is like the inside of a chocolate box," said Syd.

Max was looking for the telephone but having no luck. He passed the TV and paused.

"I wonder if the Beast of Bone Creek has made the national news?" he muttered, pausing to turn it on.

"We're not here to watch TV," said Syd, leaning across the table to take a hearty sniff of the flowers.

"That's good," replied Max, "because this set's broken." He flicked the switch up and down, but the screen remained black.

"That's disappointing," said Syd.

"You wanted to watch TV too?"

"No, numbnuts; the flowers. They're not real, they're plastic."

Max walked to the coffee table and picked up a shiny red apple from the bowl. He took a bite.

"Max!"

He spat it out.

"Wax," he said, wiping his tongue on the sleeve of his filthy bomber jacket as he dropped the phony fruit upon the polished wooden floor. He reached down. "And these magazines are two decades old, Syd."

Max straightened, looking around the room once

more with fresh eyes. He headed straight to the bookcases to browse the shelves. Max could spot a rare tome a mile away, and these bookcases had plenty of collector's items. While none of them at a glance sent alarm bells ringing, they were predominantly about nature, specifically that of North America, and a few on Europe. Many of the books were written in foreign tongues—Max had to guess they were German, judging by the proliferation of umlauts in the texts.

"The cupboards are bare, Max," said Syd, working her way through the pristine kitchen. "Even the fridge!" she said, slamming the door shut.

Max was still examining the bookcases. *The Huntsman's Heart, Cryptids of the Northern Wilds, The Ballad of the Big Bad Wolf, The Green Man Cometh*. Names like those got Max's Helsey sense all a-tingle. There were classics here too, woodland tales of Greek and Roman myths alike.

Syd reappeared in the room after checking the bedroom at the back of the lodge. "He's not here." She rejoined Max by the fireplace as he peered at the books. "This is weird, right?"

"Just a little. He hasn't even got *The Half-Blood Prince*."

The punch to the arm was well deserved on this occasion. Max glanced down and gave it a rub. That was when he noticed that the floorboards, polished immaculately elsewhere around the lodge, were scuffed in front of the bookcase.

"Freaky painting," said Syd, cocking her head as she took

it in. Max pulled back from the bookcase and joined her. The forest scene was debauched. Festivities and feasting were fully under way, where nude women danced with fauns and other horned men, wrapped in one another's arms while they cavorted and capered. The humans fed their companions grapes, held goblets to their lips, their throats running red, while the creatures of the forest watched in wonder. A man sat upon a throne of antlers at the painting's center, a slaughtered deer laid out before him. Max recognized the figures from Jed's tutoring on deities from every mythology around the world, even those that had died out.

"Is that red wine those guys are drinking?" asked Syd.

"You'd hope so, but somehow I doubt it."

"There's something inscribed along the frame. Do you see that?"

"Well spotted, Nancy Drew," said Max, stepping closer to read it. "Looks like a verse from a poem:

For Dionysus, the Father, Lord, and God of all the Wild

We offer thee the Husband, and the Wife, and Virgin Child

We offer the Song, the Feast, the Wine by endless flood

An offering so bountiful of Flesh and Bone and Blood."

They were silent for a moment, before turning slowly to each other. Syd tapped the painting with a fingertip.

"Okay, this doesn't sound good. The husband and wife?"

"Could be the campers," said Max, his hand flitting along the bookcase now, going from one shelf to another as he searched for something. "And I think we know who the virgin child could be."

"Boyle?" said Syd. "What are you looking for?"

"This," said Max, jabbing his forefinger upon the spine of a leather-bound book.

"*The Children of Dionysus*?" said Syd. "Who are they?"

Max pointed at the painting. "Them. Just step back a touch, Syd," he said, shooing her away from the bookcase before continuing to explain. "Dionysus was the Greek god of harvest, fertility, and wine. Oh, and ritual madness. They say his parties were the *bomb*."

Max seized the book's spine and pulled. There was a groaning, grinding noise as gears lurched into life, a ratchet cranking as the bookcase swung out toward where the pair were standing. Max reached across and gently pushed Syd's slack jaw back into place, closing her mouth. The bookcase ceased moving with a clang, revealing a staircase carved into the rock that led down into darkness. He looked at Syd, who shook her head.

"No way, dude. This is your gig. You go first."

"At least gimme the flashlight, then," he said snatching it from her as he pulled Splinter out of his jacket pocket.

As Max descended the stairs, a smell from below rolled up toward him, a heady combo of blood, rot, and efflu-ence. Syd gagged as she followed him down. Max let the flashlight's beam strafe the passage, strange marks at head height on either side of the tunnel catching his attention. It looked like something had scraped the rock, cutting furrows into the walls.

"Is this a natural cave, or man-made?" whispered Syd, still gagging.

"Geology was never my strongest subject, but I bet it's natural, though it's had some work done."

The passage curved around, opening out into a longer chamber. The walls were rough and untouched on one side of the room, water trickling from the rock, no doubt originating from the nearby creek. The opposite wall had been reinforced, crude brickwork and timber beams supporting the ceiling. A filthy, stained sheet had been pinned to the top of the wall, where it met the ceiling. Max spied the edge of a wooden frame poking out from behind the blanket, indicating some kind of window that let natural light into the room. Not that *that* had happened in a long, long time. Crates and metal shelving lined this wall, loaded with the usual paraphernalia one would expect to find in a secret, sinister, stinking cellar: specimen bottles, axes, hammers, bones, and bundles of herbs and twigs. Taking pride of place on the shelving were two oversized plaster of Paris feet, their soles covered in dried earth.

"Looks like we found our killer bigfoot," whispered Max.

Then there was the workbench. The heavy table was hacked and chopped all over, as if a butcher had been at work. Beside the table, on the floor, stood a white plastic barrel that bore a hazardous material symbol. Max took a closer look. Unless he was mistaken, the drum contained a lye-based acid, the kind used to dissolve pretty much anything, including body parts. He straightened and shuddered. A collection of cleavers and bone saws were suspended from a beam above it. Max let his flashlight run along its length. There was more besides butcher's tools hanging from the beam.

"Helll . . . sssinnnnng . . ."

The faint voice came from the rear of the chamber, a muffled, weary croak. Max brought the flashlight back around, shining it deeper into the subterranean recesses. There, at the back of the room, a trio of shapes hung by bound hands from hooks in the ceiling. Max recognized the nearest instantly.

"Kenny!" said Max, rushing toward his suspended classmate. A rope was tied around his mouth, the boy's face bruised, his matted hair bloodied. Max placed his stake and flashlight onto the floor and grabbed Boyle by his thighs, hoisting him up. Boyle's bound hands fell forward, coming loose from the butcher's hook, as he flopped across Max's shoulder. Max lowered the bully gently onto the damp floor. His fingers fumbled with the rope and unhitched the knot. Boyle gasped for breath, one eye closed shut, the other wide with fright.

"Max," said Syd excitedly from a short distance away. She stood beside two more suspended, wriggling victims. "It's Sissy and Frank! They're here too!"

"Helsing," Boyle whispered. "It's . . . it's a monster . . ."

"I know, Kenny," said Max, glancing up at Syd, who was already lifting Sissy off her hook.

A door slammed in the lodge above.

"Honeys, I'm home!" a familiar voice called. "I see you've invited some friends over to play."

Booted footsteps crossed the floorboards quickly. Then they were on the stone staircase, heading down into the cellar. Max helped Syd lift Frank from his hook. Then Max was moving, dashing to the workbench.

His blood ran cold. The footsteps had changed. The sound of shoe on stone was suddenly replaced by something sharp and clipped, striking the steps like a chisel against marble. Like a hammer against bone. Like a hoof against rock.

TWENTY-SEVEN

xxx

THE DEVIL WALKED IN

"What a night it's been, Max Helsing," said Gideon.

The flashlight remained abandoned on the floor, its beam reflecting off a puddle and sending rippling light bouncing off the wall. All the children and campers could see of the little man was his flickering shadow advancing through the corridor as he descended the stairs, backlit by the lamps in the lodge. His footsteps echoed sharply as they struck each rough step.

"Yep, it's been a wild one, hasn't it?" said Max, leaving the bench and his companions to approach the short tunnel that led into the room. "I don't know about you, but I'm tuckered out and ready for bed."

"Don't worry, Max," said Gideon. "You'll have plenty of time to sleep soon enough."

"Aw, Gideon, that just sounded plain sinister, dude. Why'd you have to do that?"

As Max reached the tunnel, Gideon arrived at the base of the staircase, not ten feet away from the boy. Max glanced back to his friends, checking they were okay, before snapping his head back around to the camp coordinator.

Although he was just a silhouette, lit from above, Max could see that Gideon had ditched his boots. The man's feet had transformed into a pair of shiny black hooves.

The Beast of Bone Creek wasn't a bigfoot. The killer was a satyr, and he'd been hiding in plain sight, right under their noses all along. This satyr wasn't the happy little faun one might find in a children's book. This monster was the stuff of nightmares.

"You don't mind if I get out of these, do you?" said Gideon, beginning to unbutton his khaki shirt.

"If it's all the same, I'd rather you didn't."

"You must know your Greek myths and legends, Max, following the rhyming verse and finding my little playroom. I hope you liked my painting, too?"

"I'm more of a Dr. Seuss man. That painting was a little grim for my tastes."

"Heavens, no! What could be more joyous than a series of unspoiled offerings to Dionysus?"

"You mean sacrifices?"

"Sacrifice . . . offering . . . po-*tay*-to, po-*tah*-to. The whole blood ritual *is* indulgent, I'll admit. But once I bagged those two lovebirds, well, it was all too good to resist! Your pal Boyle was the missing ingredient for the festivities." He clapped his hands. "We're all set now. You're cleverer than

you look. I clearly underestimated you. Bravo, Max. Bravo."
He shook the shirt off and tossed it aside.

"So the painting and the poem are what? The recipe for something sinister and sordid?"

"Sinister? Sordid? Step away from those combustible human emotions for a moment, Max. This is my moment, where I transcend."

"Transcend into what, exactly?"

"A greater being, a vessel for Dionysus on Earth. Immortality, divine wisdom, untold knowledge. It will all be mine, and more."

"And killing three innocents will make that happen?"

"The man, the wife, and the virgin child? That union epitomizes birth, beauty, and becoming. Goodness, it's no coincidence that trio feature in religious iconography throughout your world. Could my Lord be any happier with such an offering? The death of those three would be the greatest sacrifice mankind can give."

"Give?" said Max. "There's nothing willful about this. It'd be murder. They wouldn't be giving. You'd be taking."

Gideon shrugged. "And we're back to potatoes."

"Gideon, no offense, but . . . I've been on better vacations. Scratch that—I've been to better funerals."

Gideon's laugh was a shrill giggle as he turned his neck from left to right in quick, sudden motions. Max heard vertebrae pop and bones crack.

"Oh, Max, you and I have gotten along, haven't we? The whole schoolkid-and-mentor thing, where you got to pick my brain and share your troubles, was real sweet. In another time, another forest, we could've been firm friends."

"There's still time for that."

The shadowy figure shook his head, curled tufts of hair bouncing around his ears. Ears that looked a touch longer, more pointed now. "Sadly, there isn't. The end comes to all men and beasts, and your end is upon us."

There was a tearing sound, Gideon's khaki shorts ripping as his thighs began to thicken. Max could hear his breathing growing more labored.

"Can you just tell me one thing?" said Max.

"Ask away, young man," said Gideon, the satyr's voice deeper now.

"What drove you to frame poor bigfoot for a string of hideous crimes? Why can't you share Bone Creek?"

Gideon's laugh was a rasping rattle, his chest broadening as he took another clopping step toward Max down the short stretch of corridor. "Oh, bless you, Max; it's true what they say about you, isn't it? You're the soft Van Helsing. The one who thinks peace is the answer to everything. The one who doesn't have the stomach for the job."

"You seem to think you know a lot about me, Gideon."

The man, or what had been a man, shrugged. Another step closer. "You're a Van Helsing. Your forefathers are the bogeymen to my kind. The monsters whose names we whisper to our children. And you? Well, you're just the Easter Bunny, aren't you? Cute as a button. So young. So . . . tender."

Max stood his ground, holding firm. He couldn't allow Gideon to enter the room. *Keep him talking, Max*, he told himself. *Let him chatter.*

"Tender? I've been called worse."

"I heard tell of a valley hidden away in the White Mountains that was a haven for the paranormal and supernatural. Your ancestor founded this place, did she not? What better place to claim as my own? I've wandered this wretched continent for over a hundred years, seeking a forest I can call my own, a wilderness to rival the Black Forest of my homeland in Germany, and could I find one?"

"Could you?"

"Of course not! Too many damn monsters, and they were always bigger than me. So I came here. I made Bone Creek my home. I picked my moment. And then I set the wheels in motion. I alerted humanity to the presence of our large-footed neighbors."

"You've invited every fool with a gun into these hills," said Max. "Bone Creek is crawling with people intent on finding a monster. Aren't you afraid they'll find you?"

"If they find me, it'll be jovial, cheery Gideon, Mr. Funtime himself. They won't get—" he cast a long-fingered hand over his shifting, twisting torso—"this."

Russet hair caught the lamplight from upstairs. Hair just like Max had found in the bushes at the scene of Frank and Sissy's abduction.

"So you get others to do your dirty work for you?"

"Hard as it may be for you to believe, Max Helsing, I'm

a lover, not a fighter. My kind are not known for violence, although we'll turn our hands if forced."

"And you've been forced to do this?" exclaimed Max angrily. "Innocent people have died, Gideon—"

"And more to come tonight," growled the monster, taller now as he advanced. "In a turf war, Max Helsing, there are always casualties. Let the humans find and kill that wretched twig-muncher. Bone Creek isn't big enough for *two* apex predators. There's only room for one sheriff in this piece of paradise."

Gideon shook his head, the curling tufts growing longer now, joining up with the hair on his chest, his shoulders, the fur that sprouted all over his body. By the half-light Max watched as black nails tore from his slender fingertips. Another step, heavier than before, and now on mighty, muscled haunches. The satyr's thighs were huge, the fur darkest here as it ran down to a pair of disjointed ankles, finally stopping at those big, black hooves. It all became so clear now to Max; the hoofprints he'd seen repeatedly around Bone Creek. He'd dismissed them as deer tracks; how wrong he had been.

"You hurt me and my friends, and others will come. You won't get away with it," said Max. "Jed's already here."

"Jed Coolidge is as good as dead. I sent him searching for you in the forest. I think it's called a wild-goose chase. The last I heard he was heading blindly toward a pack of dyre wolves. They're probably finishing him off as we speak."

It was Max's turn to snarl now. The monster laughed.

"You thought he was going to be the knight in shining armor for you? You've been played, Max Helsing, every step of the way. Did you not wonder why you encountered vampires in Ike Barnum's shack?"

Max hadn't given it too much thought, but it had been quite the surprise.

"I sent them, child! The minute I knew of your intentions, I got in touch with our local undead friends and let them know you were heading there. They were to be your welcoming committee."

Max managed his best cocky grin. "How'd that work out for you, Gideon?"

The monster sighed as he took a final step toward Max, causing the boy to stagger back into the chamber. "Never send a vampire to do a satyr's job."

With that, Gideon arched his back, embracing the final, most painful stage of his transformation. While his body continued to shift, becoming more bestial and savage-looking, the greatest change was to his head. Max heard a violent cracking as Gideon's skull changed shape, teeth tearing from gums, mandibles elongating, jaw jutting. His rosy pink skin shimmered, turning ruddy and then a fiery red. Misshapen yellow eyes rolled wildly in their sockets as he let loose a gurgling wail. Another awful splintering sound from within that monstrous head, and two horns burst from the satyr's temple on either side. They came out bloody, curling in on themselves, twisting and turning as they corkscrewed into the air.

SATYR

AKA: *faun (Roman)*

ORIGIN: Greece

STRENGTHS: Fierce intelligence and charming wit conceals a fearless nature and brutal instincts. Horns are the principal weapon, although many may wield man-made weapons such as staves or sickles. Some magical ability, including ability to shape-shift and fit into human society.

WEAKNESSES: Wine, dance, song.   HABITAT: Wilderness.

The classical vision of the satyr, much like his Roman cousin, the faun, is one of a fun-loving, nature-worshipping, playful soul. In truth, the satyr is more complex. A devout worshipper of the god Dionysus, he has learned to adapt and survive in human society, even assuming the form of man as he seeks out his indulgent and often unpalatable excesses. Truly wild spirits, satyrs can veer with abandon from deeds of kindness to those of abject cruelty. Easily led by passion and the desire to make mischief, they are volatile and mercurial. One would be unwise to make an enemy of a satyr.

—Erik Van Helsing, August 3rd, 1849

PHYSICAL TRAITS

1. <u>Horns</u>—Come in all shapes and sizes. Used for goring the enemy.

2. <u>Hooves</u>—The powerful legs of the satyr ensure that when their cloven feet strike a foe, skin splits and bones break.

3. <u>Mind</u>—Arguably, this is the satyr's greatest weapon. The selfish, playful, and vengeful spirit ensures this creature is utterly unpredictable. Almost like some humans I've met!

—Esme Van Helsing, January 11th, 1869

If it looks like a DEVIL, and walks like a DEVIL, chances are it IS a DEVIL.

—Algernon Van Helsing, October 2nd, 1944

I got one for you, Grandpa: <u>NEVER</u> judge a <u>BOOK</u> by its <u>COVER</u>!!

MAX HELSING
Dec 16th, 2014

Max took a step aside, moving behind the large white barrel he'd positioned in place, and gave it a heavy kick. The plastic shuddered as it toppled over, the lid rattling clear as gallons of acidic slurry splashed across the floor, showering the hooves, legs, and torso of the transforming satyr. As the monster's wails became high-pitched screams of agony, Max leaped for the metal shelves, clambering up their height toward the open window above. Syd, Boyle, and the backpackers were there, already outside, waiting for him, grabbing him by the arms as they hauled him to safety.

Safety was, of course, a fleeting thing. The chase had just begun.

TWENTY-EIGHT

xxx

FOREST OF FEAR

The mist was thicker now, a swirling soup that blanketed Bone Creek. It was thin and wispy on high, drifting around the pine tree branches. Closer to the ground, it became a fog, obscuring root, rock, and river from view. On any other night, it might have appeared pretty, but tonight it provided an additional obstacle to the five humans as they staggered into the forest, the tiny will-o'-the-wisp lighting their way.

"Is he following?" asked Boyle, pushed on by fear and the furious roar at their back.

"Hard to tell," said Max, the other boy's arm slung across his shoulder as he supported him through their escape. "We can wait and see if he follows, if you like?"

"Keep going!" cried a terrified Sissy.

Max looked at Syd on Boyle's other side, helping him along as they put distance between themselves and the lodge. Judging by the grave look of concern on her face, she shared the same worries as Max. They might have saved Boyle and the two Minnesotans physically—for now, at least—but what kind of long-term damage had been done to their minds?

"Maybe you stopped him?" hissed Syd as they scrambled up the incline in the direction of the road.

There was a sharp splintering sound from behind them as a door flew off its hinges.

"It's a nice thought," said Max. He unhitched himself from the bully and let him collapse into Syd's arms. "Listen, you need to get these three up to the parking lot, away from here. The will-o'-the-wisp can lead you there, I reckon." Right on cue, the insectlike fairy shone with a brilliant bright light, as if in agreement. "There's a police car up there, I think. They should be able to keep you safe."

"We're not leaving you," said Frank.

"Frank's right," said Syd, helping a shivering Boyle straighten. "You're coming with us. We'll get up there quicker if we all work together."

"Better I keep Gideon occupied down here. Draw him into the woods. Distract him and buy you guys time."

"That's suicide!"

Max looked mortified. "I hope it isn't!" He gave her a shove on her way. "Now get going, doofus, before it's too late."

Reluctantly, Syd headed toward the road, Boyle, Frank, and Sissy in tow, fairy above her head, looking back at Max all the while as he peeled away in another direction. He dashed through the trees, yelping, whooping, and hollering.

He looked back down the hill, toward the creek, the lodge, and the bunkhouses. The route he was taking ran parallel with the creek, his path bringing him back past Gideon's cabin. Lights shone from the lodge's windows, the warm glow spilling out of the broken front door and illuminating the soupy mist.

"Yo, Mr. G!" Max shouted as he dashed on through the woods. "Do you have a feedback form we can fill out? I found elements of this vacation unsatisfactory!"

An approaching growl in the mist got him thinking faster. Gideon had taken the bait.

"Firstly," called Max, as his slipped and skidded over pinecones, finding his way back down toward the river as it headed downstream. "Hot water was a bit of an issue in the morning shower. Secondly, the blankets in the bunkhouse were a little scratchy. And thirdly, the tour guide was a psychotic, murderous goatboy with terrible fashion sense!"

The ground leveled out suddenly, as Max felt spongy grass underfoot, as opposed to earth, twigs, and cones. He slowed, panting, and turned around. Not so far away, he could see the dim lights from Gideon's cabin, faint through the misty night, but beyond that, nothing. The babbling river had never sounded louder. Max kept his eyes fixed back the way he'd come.

"Come on out, Gideon," he called, steeling himself in preparation for the arrival of the satyr. He clutched his silver-tipped stake in his right hand, raised high, ready to strike out. Max's eyes scoured the mist, now up to his waist, keeping everything obscured beneath. There was no sign of the monster. Had his plan failed? Had the satyr gone after the others? Max was cursing himself for being a fool when a low chuckle sounded in the darkness.

"I see what you've done, boy," said Gideon. "Very clever, getting your friends to scurry off to safety, offering yourself up as bait in return. Clever, but ultimately stupid. You're just delaying their demise. You'll die and then they'll die, and I promise, yours will be a slow and lingering death."

Max concentrated, turned his head, trying to pick out where the satyr was in the darkness. The noisy water muffled the beast's voice and movements, while Gideon's words echoed around the forest in every direction.

"You should have stayed with your friends, Max," he said. "Safety in numbers. Instead, you've left yourself alone. Exposed. At my mercy."

Max turned quickly, trying to gauge where his enemy was hidden, but it was hopeless. He could've been behind any tree, any boulder, even creeping up for a rear attack.

"How about you show yourself, Gideon? Make this a fair fight. Shouldn't be hard, right? I'm just a snotty thirteen-year-old kid, and you're . . . a tubby middle-aged loner with a receding hairline, horns, and hooves."

The satyr's laugh rumbled loud, over the noise of the river.

"Why would I reveal myself to you? I'm not looking for a fair fight here. You're a monster hunter. You may be the last of them—and a poor excuse for a Van Helsing—but I know what you're all about. You're in *my* world now, Max."

The teenager from Gallows Hill realized with horror that he'd played right into Gideon's clawed hands. Max had imagined he'd be able to use his quick-thinking and street-fighting smarts on the satyr, once he'd drawn the fiend away from his friends. He hadn't taken into account that these weren't his streets.

Max edged forward, just a step, thinking about making a run for the tour guide's home. There were bound to be weapons he could improvise with, he'd have a bit of light on his side, and the monster would have nowhere to hide. At the very least Max could pelt the satyr with fake fruit and books.

"Ah, ah!" came Gideon's voice, extremely close by. "Where do you think you're going, Max? We've only just begun to play!"

The monster sounded so very near, Max could hear his skin still sizzling where the acid bath had struck, the stench of burned hair and flesh pungent in the chill air. Then why couldn't he see the beast? Max suddenly realized the problem: the mist. Gideon was hiding *beneath the mist*!

Max was about to reply when he felt something rush past him under cover of the fog. He doubled over as Gideon passed, lashing out with Splinter, but the stake caught only thin air. Then Gideon came back the other way, racing behind Max, claws raking the small of his back. He felt the cuts open up instantly, cold and stinging as he cried out.

"You know, Max," said the beast as he circled. "What you did to me in my cellar was terribly poor form. I do worry for our friendship. . . ."

Max was running full tilt, straight for the trees, away from the river. He'd never been a fan of gloating victory speeches. The mist exploded beside him as the horned horror pounced, landing where Max had been standing a heartbeat earlier. Max could hear the satyr giving chase, his hooves kicking up the earth as he charged Max down. The frantic boy launched himself back into the woods, weaving between trees and trying to shake the satyr off his tail. It was hopeless. The monster knew the forest better than any man. Max's mind was racing. He needed to even the playing field, and that left only one option.

"Come here, Helsing!" cackled Gideon, lurching around a tree toward the boy, his devilish head lit up with murderous glee.

Max let go of the branch he'd seized, allowing it to spring back at the fiend's head. Gideon caught a face full of pinecones, screeching with annoyance. Max ran like hell through the woods, past Gideon's lodge, headed toward the only terrain that felt remotely like his.

Max ran back to the bunkhouse.

TWENTY-NINE

xxx

TURNING THE TABLES

Max sprinted, back through the maze of trees and waist-high mist, toward the boys' lodge. He bounced up the bunkhouse steps and arrived on the porch. He gritted his teeth as he felt his shirt clinging to the flesh of his bloody back. Max straightened, determined not to show the satyr that he was weakened. He clapped his hands and waved at the mist.

"Yo, Mr. G!" he yelled. "I think we've got a leaky faucet, and we're all out of toilet paper!"

He didn't have to wait long. Black horns appeared through the mist, like a smoking devil at the gates of Hell. Gideon strode purposefully through the fog, snarling, eyes glowing like fiery infernos within that demonic red face.

Max spun around and dashed into the bunkhouse, hearing the satyr's hoofed feet stamping up the steps behind him. The beast dipped his head as he navigated the doorway, turning to allow his horns through the opening. The moment he was in, Max launched the oil lamp that had hung from the ceiling. It exploded over Gideon's head, leaving his hideous face soaked in choking paraffin oil. Max retreated toward the middle of the room, relieved to have got a good solid hit in. The satyr charged, head down like an enraged bull. Max stamped a foot, hard. The faulty floorboard shot up, rotten end aimed squarely at the beast's huge chest. The length of timber became a spear, set in the ground to meet the onrushing enemy. It splintered as the satyr struck it, but not before great shards of wood punctured Gideon's crimson flesh, tearing open skin and muscle as he smashed it aside. The monster looked down in disbelief at the daggers of wood that were protruding from his torso. When he looked back up, the next wave of the assault came at him.

Max was in the kitchen, cutlery drawer emptied on the counter, his hands a blur as he threw whatever he found at Gideon. The satyr advanced unsteadily, arms shielding his oil-blinded face, his chest bleeding, as knife, fork, spoon, and rolling pin showered down upon him, followed quickly by the drawer itself. With the utensils expended, Gideon lowered his muscular arms, which were studded with forks, potato peelers, and can openers, only for the huge chili pan to strike him sweetly across the jaw.

"Match point!" shouted Max as the satyr staggered back, a cracked hoof sinking into the fresh gap in the floorboard.

Gideon twisted, trying to pull it free, only for Max to swing back the other way, catching the fiend with a backhand.

"Helsing hits it straight down the line with a winner!" he yelled.

A clawed hand shot out, snatching the frying pan from Max's grasp and turning it on him. He danced back, landing with a thump as the satyr buried the pan into the floorboards as if it were an ax. Max was scrambling back now as Gideon pulled himself free. The boy was up on his feet, dashing for his bedroom at the end of the corridor, opening doors as he went and slowing the monster down. He heard the doors slamming back on their hinges as the enraged satyr followed. Gideon crashed into the bunkroom, seeking the boy from Gallows Hill.

The bunkbed tipped forward, crashing down onto the stumbling satyr and trapping him in the doorway. Max dove forward from behind the toppled bed frame, striking the beast over the head with the tin pee bucket. It clanged hard, crumpling against the shiny black horns. Max snatched up the matchbox from his emptied rucksack, fingers grasping a clutch of them and striking them on the abrasive strip. They burst into life and Max flicked them at the satyr. They showered down over Gideon's oil-soaked face. There was a *woof* as his head and shoulders went up in flames. Then Max sprang back, skidding toward the window as the screaming monster broke the bunk apart. Up went the window, squealing on its runners, as Max threw a leg out.

Gideon dove forward, face on fire, landing on his belly and driving those shards of wood deeper into his chest. He roared, snatching Max's other foot by the ankle, dragging him back into the room. Max tumbled, landing in the debris from the tipped bed, the satyr raising a clawed hand up, ready to rip the boy open. Max's grabbed a mattress and threw it up before him. The black taloned fingers tore through the material, sending springs and filling flying about the room. The satyr pulled it apart, that grotesque, smoking goat head shooting forward, yellow eyes narrowed, sharp teeth set in a vengeful grin.

The snow globe shattered as it came down into the monster's smoldering face. Liquid and white flakes sprayed everywhere as the glass punctured cheek and eye. Max drove it home with an angry cry, twisting the snow globe's base into the satyr's face as the beast bleated in a blind panic and drew back. Hooves came up kicking and thrashing as Gideon tried to pluck slivers of glass from his eye in vain, black blood streaming from the socket.

Max was up, jumping through the window, but the satyr followed, even with only one good eye. Max swung himself out, clinging to the frame as Gideon thrust his bloodied and burn-blistered head through the gap. A horn gored Max's stomach, tearing a bloody gash across his belly, but he clung on. Once both horns were through, and ready to strike the boy again, Max grabbed the base of the raised window and jumped. The paneled sash came down like a guillotine. Wood and glass shattered, ripping into the back of the monster's neck as Max was swallowed by the mist and landed on the wet grass. He rose unsteadily, woozy, just as Gideon began tearing about the broken window frame. He was trapped for now, but the more he struggled, the bigger the hole in the wall became. Big enough, eventually, for him to follow the teenage monster hunter.

Without waiting for the satyr to escape, Max was running again, slower this time, as he sought a place to hide. Syd and the injured trio should have found the cop by now. Help would be on its way, in one way or another. He was exhausted and battered, and the coldness was spreading across his belly. He pulled his bomber aside, saw the red patch on his white tee spreading. As with the wound on his back, he had no idea how deep it was, but he was losing blood. He bounced off the girls' bunkhouse wall, tripping and almost going over. Landing on a knee, he struggled to his feet once more and stumbled on. Behind him, in the darkness, the Beast of Bone Creek worked himself free from his timber trap.

Max was at the boathouse, grabbing the door in a bloody hand. It was chained shut. Cursing, he picked up a rock and pulled out Splinter, placing the stake's silver head over the lock. He struck it once, twice, and on the third attempt the lock broke free. The chain links rattled and the door was open. Max slipped inside, pulling it closed behind him. Then he backed up slowly, careful not to disturb the walls of stacked kayaks and rowboats around him. *This should do the trick*, he reckoned, keeping a hand over the wound in his stomach.

"Come on, Jed," he whispered, praying his mentor might come to the rescue. "Whenever you're ready, old man. Whenever you're ready."

THIRTY

The yo-yo went up. The yo-yo went down. Max sat in the antique Native American kayak at the back of the old boat-house, spinning his old toy, hiding in the shadows. The building was on the water's edge, a launch at its heart where kayaks could be lowered directly into the river. He was waiting for someone, anyone, to kick the door in and save the day. The yo-yo was a means to focus his attention, to keep him awake. He was damp, dog-tired, and had a cut in the guts that hurt like hell.

"You should see the other guy," he whispered to himself.

Max cataloged the injuries he'd dished out to Gideon, or whatever it was he'd become. A satyr, supposedly the guard-ian of the forest, but this one clearly never got the rule book. Acid burns to the legs, lantern to the face, slashed torso from a floorboard, fork wounds to the forearms, concus-sion from a frying pan, bucket to the brain, head set on fire, snow globe to the eye socket, and a wood-and-glass guillotine crashing down upon his neck. If Max thought he'd had it bad, that put things into perspective.

Max had been under no illusions; there were drawbacks to every job, and his unusual line of work was always going to have its downsides. Lousy hours, unexpected skirmishes with all manner of flesh-hungry fiends, curses that kick into gear on one's thirteenth birthday—these all came with the territory. A shortened life expectancy was pretty high on that list of negatives, of course. He'd been aware of the perils since he'd been in diapers. His father had drilled that into him, as had Jed after Dad's untimely death. It was a dirty job, but someone—a Van Helsing—had to do it.

Everyone had their time to go, and Max's was most likely going to be at the hands of the monster. He'd always imagined it was going to be a vampire that finally got him. Let's face it—there was history there. He'd never expected a satyr might be the beast that did the deed. Just showed how wrong a kid could be.

Crack.

A twig snapped outside the boathouse. Max let the yo-yo zip back up to his palm. He held his breath. Footsteps, in the damp grass, heavy ones, were approaching the building. A snorting exhalation of breath, followed by a wheezing growl. There was a loud *thud* as something hit the outside of the boathouse wall. Then two more impacts, a fist striking timber.

"Little pig, little pig, let me in. . . ."

Max cringed as the sound of claws scraping along wood accompanied the satyr's progress as he stalked down toward the front of the building. The wall squealed and rattled as the bladed fingers caught every panel.

"Who's trapped now, Max Helsing?"

Max looked back toward the door and spied the telltale trail of blood on the ground that had marked his passage. Cursing, he climbed out of the Pequawket kayak and looked around for a backup plan. The water was always an option, but how far would he get without the monster spotting him? His hands brushed across a rack of oars and twin-bladed paddles as his eyes shot up to the rafters. More boats were stored there, stowed away in the rickety building. It was too cramped. Too confined.

He heard footsteps on the jetty floor, saw the shadows of those hoofed feet appear through the crack of faint light at the base of the door. Black claws reached through the gap between door and frame as it creaked slowly open, loose chain rattling. The satyr stepped into the room, burned, half-blind, and bloodied, towering over Max as he looked in vain for an escape route.

"What a chase you gave me, Max Helsing, but the game is over."

"We could've made this work," said Max. "Bone Creek was big enough for all of you."

"Never," growled Gideon, taking a step toward the boy.

As its hoof struck the wooden floor, the building shook, dust showering down from the ceiling. That surprised Max.

The satyr, too. The monster looked at his big black cloven foot, back to the walls, and then to Max.

"Did I do that?"

Max didn't answer. He was too busy jabbing an oar beneath a great tower of canoes. He cranked down hard, dislodging the bottom one and sending the eight balanced on it toppling. They came down onto the satyr in rapid succession, striking Gideon repeatedly, sending him crashing heavily into the wall. Max heard the building groan with the impact, saw the whole structure shift to one side as it transformed from boathouse into lean-to. The groaning continued as a timber came free from the roof, thundering down to bounce off the satyr's shoulder and knock him to his knees. Gideon screamed as a second beam fell, glancing off a horn and splitting it.

A canoe tumbled from the rafters, bashing Max's back and sending him to the floor. More boats fell, the building roaring now as the walls and ceiling began to tear themselves apart. Max had landed beside the ancient handmade kayak. As the roof collapsed directly overhead, he reached across and took hold of the animal-skin boat, dragging it toward and over him. He was cocooned beneath it as the building tumbled down around him. The kayak's hull caved in as wood, metal, and boat rained down. Max winced, turning his face, holding his breath, expecting the cured hide to break at any moment. Somehow, it held together, shielding Max from the debris until all fell silent once more.

Max waited a moment, listening for something, anything,

a sign that the beast was there. He gave the boat a shove, heaving hard, wood and splintered fiberglass sliding off the crumpled kayak and clattering to one side. The air was thick with choking dust, the boathouse now transformed to a pile of timbers and wood chips. Max looked about in vain, his vision obscured by the mist, as he tried to get above it. Slowly, he rose, every muscle aching, until his head was above the fog. Jagged shafts of wood and kayak jutted up all around him, a field of broken boats and torn timber that he'd somehow lived through. He allowed himself a smile of astonished satisfaction.

It was rather premature.

He sensed the beast rise from the mist behind him. He felt Gideon's breath upon his neck, smelled his musky aroma, burned flesh, hair, and blood. Before he could move, the satyr's hand was around his neck.

"Ruined," Gideon whispered in his ear, his voice like crushed gravel. "Everything ruined. By you, boy. By you. Yours was going be a drawn-out death, away from here, in a dark place, far from the light. I was going to make it last. But time waits for no man or beast. You die now, Max Helsing. You shall—"

The satyr's voice was cut off suddenly, choked into silence. He released Max, who fell forward, bouncing off the ruins of the boathouse and turning around. The satyr was now the one being held from behind by the throat. A tall shape had appeared at Gideon's back, all thick dark fur and broad shoulders. Max knew immediately what it was: the

Sasquatch had returned to Bone Creek. That was what had struck the boathouse.

The bigfoot lifted Gideon off the ground. The goatman's legs kicked out wildly, hooves striking timber and kayak. Max saw the Sasquatch's eyes glowing bright, narrow slits that promised vengeance. Its knuckles cracked as they tightened around the satyr's throat. Gideon threw a hand back, scratching at the bigfoot's face, but the Sasquatch turned its head away, grabbing the satyr's straining arm and snapping it.

Gideon cried out, but his other arm was up, seizing the broken horn on his ravaged head. He yanked hard, the twisted black spike coming free with a wet rip. He spun it around in his hand and thrust it sharply behind his back.

The Sasquatch's cry caused birds to take flight up and down Bone Creek, and drove the creatures of the night back to their nests, caves, and burrows. The satyr twisted the horn, pushing it deeper into the stomach of the bigfoot. The giant beast of the forest released Gideon. It collapsed beside Max, groaning and heaving with pain. Max fell across the bigfoot's back, felt its warm fur against his face. Gideon weaved above them, a broken arm and missing horn now added to his long list of injuries, but he still managed to smile.

"They'll find your remains," said the satyr. "And those of your friends, who are cowering in the woods. They'll find your killer, the bigfoot. And they'll clean out any others, wherever they're hiding, and any foul fairy or cryptid that gets in their way. And I'll be watching over it all, the brave, heroic Gideon, the sole survivor of this night."

The devil raised the horn, an ax in an executioner's grasp, about to descend on the beaten boy from Gallows Hill.

"Bone Creek is mine!"

THIRTY-ONE

xxx

FRIENDS LIKE THESE

The satyr snarled as the curling black blade came down.

It never connected with Max, though.

The first arrow hit Gideon in the shoulder, causing him to drop his severed horn. The second struck the satyr in his chest, forcing air from his punctured lung. The third was left quivering in his throat, as the remaining eye on the side of his knobby head rolled in its socket.

The satyr collapsed slowly into the mist, turning and staggering on failing legs, like a ship going down in a storm. Then he was gone.

Max rose unsteadily from beside the wounded Sasquatch, and turned slowly toward the forest. A hulking figure coalesced in the fog, gradually taking shape. Abel Archer paced forward, prowling like a big cat. Another arrow was already nocked in his enormous bow, a murderous grin plastered across his face. *Okay*, thought Max. *I'll give him that one.*

Archer may have been the first to Max's aid, but he wasn't alone. There was a twinkling of lights in the forest at his back as he was soon joined by others. They were led by a swarm of will-o'-the-wisps, fluttering around their heads, illuminating their faces like angels. There was Syd, carrying an unmistakable long-handled ax in both hands. Wing danced about her excitedly. Boyle followed, Frank and Sissy side by side behind him. Jed appeared, with Kimble on his shoulder, the little man's fingers dancing across the barrels of his panpipes. "Holy moly," said Archer, slinging his longbow across his shoulder. "Is that really what I think it is? A bigfoot?"

"We prefer to call them Sasquatch," said Kimble, glaring at the big Brit as he strode through the mist and debris.

"Whatever. That'll do me."

Jed seized the young man by a massive bicep. "You can stop right there. You're not laying a finger on that Sasquatch."

Nose-to-nose, Jed and Archer missed what followed. The satyr rose out of the mist behind Max, roaring, his one good arm reaching for the exhausted monster hunter. There was a whooshing sound as something heavy sailed through the air, followed by a resounding *crack*. The Woodsman's Ax, Archer's favorite toy, was buried in the satyr's skull, splitting it like a ripe melon. Syd released her grip on the ax haft and let Gideon topple. He went down again, this time for good. Abel Archer shrugged.

"I'll take the satyr, then. That's worth just as much on the open market."

Syd reached a hand down to Max. He seized it tight, allowing his friend to haul him to his feet. The two hugged. Jed was next over, as Kimble hopped across to Syd's shoulder. She stood aside while the old man gave Max a squeeze that almost rearranged his vertebrae.

"You had me worried there for a while, knucklehead," he murmured quietly, his breath warm and comforting against Max's scalp.

"I can't believe you gate-crashed my vacation," said Max with a grin. "Soooo embarrassing." He turned to the others. "And you brought Wing, too? What were you thinking?"

"Trust me, he didn't come with my blessing." Jed scratched his head. "I have to admit, though, he was more than a little helpful. Kid's got skills. Got us a rookie monster hunter there, I reckon."

Max put a hand on Wing's shoulder. "Are you okay, Wing? This must have all been pretty traumatic, yeah?"

Wing's face was pale as Archer strode past them, bending to retrieve his ax from the slain satyr. "This . . . was . . . *epic*!"

Then Wing was off, yammering excitedly about all that he'd experienced and done on this most amazing of nights. Max felt something bang into his leg, almost bowling him over. Eightball was leaping up into his arms, giving him a great, slobbering lick. Max hugged the hellhound back, wiping the spittle off his face in the process.

"You haven't been giving him his dental sticks, have you?" asked Max.

"Why?" said Jed.

"His breath smells like brimstone," he said, placing the excited puppy back down. "And ass."

"Dental sticks are hard to come by in the wilds of Bone Creek."

Max turned to Boyle and the pair from Minnesota.

"Max," said Sissy. "What you and Syd did back there, for me, Frank, and Kenny here. Well . . . it was just so neat."

Max grinned.

"Think nothing of it. It's what we do."

"Think nothing of it?" Frank gasped. "You've got to be crazy. You guys are honest-to-goodness heroes. We can't thank you enough."

Max blushed and looked at Boyle. The bully seemed to have been injected with a triple shot of espresso.

"Helsing, I'm gonna level with you. I had you so wrong. You're one of the good guys. Scratch that—you're like a rock star, a freakin' superhero. What you did back there, it's just . . . just . . . unbelievable. Like, *mind-blowing*! I've got your back now, pal. Whatever you're doing, count me in. I owe you my life, buddy."

Max smiled. "Don't sweat it, Kenny."

Jed put an arm around the boy and led him to one side with Wing as Max was left with Syd and Kimble.

"Is it just me," whispered Max, "or has Boyle completely lost it?"

"Totally bananas," agreed Syd, watching the bully as he enthused with Jed and Wing animatedly. The pair from

Minnesota stood apart, hugging each other, more than a little shell-shocked. "Frank and Sissy, too. They seem all right now, but it's going hit them hard when it all comes back to them. The abduction? The imprisonment? The monster? They'll go crazy."

Max nodded. "And the whole New Best Friend thing, that can never work. This could be the end of everything that we're doing. The whole monster hunting thing, everything we've struggled to keep hidden from the norms, all my family's work for centuries—ruined by some well-meaning but big-mouthed reformed school bully blabbing my secrets to the world."

"What about the bigfoot?" asked Syd, looking across to where it lay in the mist, Jed already kneeling over its body.

"There must be something we can do," said Max, setting off toward the fallen giant. Kimble reached across from Syd's shoulder and seized the boy by his hoodie.

"You do *nothing*, Maxwell," said the little man. "Bone Creek will take care of its fallen."

Before Max could ask any questions, Kimble gave a nod toward the trees. Max turned, and his jaw dropped. They were no longer alone. Slowly, the forest around the camp came to life. To their right, a shape peeled away from the nearest tree, a great hairy arm swinging down to the figure's side. Another loomed forward from between the mist-shrouded pines, making no sound at all on those broad and mighty feet. A third emerged from around the boulders on the creek, pacing forward across the grass, its huge, sloping forehead bowed as it approached its fallen kin.

Max pulled Syd close in anticipation, as the other humans drew together. Jed retreated, hands raised peaceably, bumping into a stunned Abel Archer as he backed away. He dragged the Brit with him, back to the others, as their eyes searched the forest for more of the Sasquatches. The three figures bent down, lifting their brother between them. They held him lovingly, one big arm trailing limp to the ground. Their faces were lost in the darkness, but their eyes, golden amber, fixed upon Max. His breath caught in his chest. Then the trio turned, setting off toward the safety of their forest.

Max spied a tear rolling down Syd's cheek. She smiled and squeezed his hand.

"You did some real good here, Max Helsing," she said with a sniff.

Max didn't reply. He was watching the trio of norms, who stood staring at the bigfoot show, stunned into disbelief. Their lives would never be the same. Boyle turned around and caught Max looking. Max smiled and Boyle gave him a thumbs-up.

"Crapsacks," said Max.

"Not to worry, Max Helsing," said Kimble, from his vantage point on Syd's shoulder. He beckoned the two of them in close and ran his fingers across the reeds of his panpipes. "I may be able to help you with that."

THIRTY-TWO

xxx

HOMEWARD BOUND

The last of the bags were being loaded into the luggage compartments on the side of the bus by Mrs. Loomis, Mr. Mayhew, and Ms. Golden. Max, however, was keeping a firm hold on his messenger bag, which strained with oddly shaped contents. He ached all over thanks to the injuries he'd sustained the previous night, and although Mrs. Loomis had tended the worst of his wounds, a trip to the ER in Gallows Hill wouldn't go amiss. Principal Whedon was making himself as useful as possible to his colleagues, by chatting with the Greenwoods, the guesthouse owners. The school party had stayed there for only one night. The vacation week had been cut short by all the ghastly goings-on in Bone Creek. Jed stood a ways down the street beside his station wagon, speaking with Frank and Sissy. The woman glanced Max's way, giving him a big cheery wave, which Max returned.

"Well, Max," said Abel Archer, coming up from behind and clapping a shoulder-dislocating hand onto Max's back. "It's been emotional, chum."

"For you, perhaps. It's been exhausting for me."

He couldn't believe he still had to endure a four-hour road trip aboard a rickety school bus, accompanied by the shrieks of his schoolmates, all to the tune of Mrs. Loomis's awful radio station selections. There were fiery pits in the depths of the Undercity that were more appealing right now.

Archer straddled his Harley, the panniers loaded down with two enormous bundles covered with tarpaulin. A dark stain had spread on one of them, while the other seemed to be concealing the curved edge of an enormous goat horn.

"Is he . . . all there?" asked Max, pointing at the bloody packages.

"Most of him, all the bits I could find anyway, and those that I've got buyers for. The rest I fed to the bears."

Max shivered. "You got everything you need?" he asked, out of politeness more than anything. A trio of girls was hammering on the bus windows above, trying to catch Archer's attention, but the Brit ignored them. Instead, he looked down the street at Jed, then whispered to the younger boy.

"Remember, you know where I am. When you're done playing sidekick to that old fart, and you want to embark on some *real* monster hunting, you give me a call, *capisce*?"

"Don't break any speed limits on the way out of town, Archer."

"I'll see you around, chum," said the Brit, hoofing his kickstand as his bike growled into life. Then he was away, waving at the kids on the bus as he tore up the road and sped out of town.

"What a colossal buttmunch," muttered Max, as Mrs. Loomis marched past him into the bus.

"Language, young man."

"Sorry, Mrs. Loomis."

He set off toward Jed, passing Whedon coming the other way.

"No lollygagging, Helsing," said the principal, pointing at the passing boy. "I've got my eye on you."

Max shook his head. Great to know that his saving Whedon's bacon had brought about a thaw in their relationship. He may have been in pieces twenty-four hours earlier, but thanks to Jed and Max, the principal was back to his irritable and impatient best.

"Max," said Jed as the boy walked up to the old man and the young couple. "You've met Mr. Gunderson and Ms. Peterson already, I believe?"

"Sure," said Max. "At the general store the other day. Have you had a nice time in Bone Creek?"

"It's been neat!" Sissy grinned as Frank threw an arm around her shoulder.

"Beautiful part of the world," he added. "We must come back. You guys have a pleasant journey back to Boston, now."

The couple shook hands with Jed and set off up the road, the tin cups and plates clanking from the bottom of their backpacks. Thanks to Kimble, the Minnesotans were blissfully unaware of what they'd actually endured. Their memories had been rebuilt by fairy magic. Imprisonment in a dungeon had been replaced by skinny-dipping in the creek and camping under the stars. Max hoped the brownie charms remained in place for an eternity and then some.

When they were out of earshot, Max whispered to Jed. "About the deaths, Jed . . ."

"Don't worry. They caught the animal that killed Mr. Cooper, the reporter. It also killed poor Mr. Gideon as well: a big-ass timber wolf with black fur."

Max smiled as the old man continued.

"That should satisfy everyone's search for answers. Then the woods and mountains can return to normal, for the natural inhabitants . . . and Kimble's friends."

Wing sat in the front seat of Jed's station wagon, Eightball on his lap like a bloated black beach ball. Max made the sign to wind down the window, and the ten-year-old obliged.

"I meant to say," said Max, fishing around in his battered messenger bag. "I got you a souvenir." He pulled out the cracked base of a shattered snow globe and passed it through, dodging a lick from Eightball in the process.

"You shouldn't have," said Wing, nose curling in disgust as he spotted the flecks of gore that still stained its edge.

"It was all I could find in the store," said Max with a shrug. "However, I *did* manage to grab something a bit better last night." He reached back into the satchel and pulled out a large, curving parcel, wrapped up in ancient animal hide, the kind one might find on an antique kayak. "If your folks ask, just tell them it came from a ram, okay, Wing?"

The kid's eyes went like dinner plates as Eightball growled at the package.

"Epic!" he shouted, as he wound the window back up.

Max turned back to Jed. "You sure I can't ride back with you?"

"What do I look like? A taxi service? You came with your friends, you can head back with your friends."

"Fine," Max grumbled, staring at the big yellow bus. *Yellow.* It came back to him. "Jed," he called before the old man could get in his car. "Back at the hermit's shack, the suckers that Gideon sent there to kill me—one of them said something strange."

Jed arched a bushy eyebrow. "Yeah?"

"He said the King in Yellow was coming for me. I've heard that name before. The business with Udo Vendemeier last year; he was a high priest of the King in Yellow, right?"

Jed said the name quietly, as if uttering it might summon a storm or worse. "Hastur."

"Should I be worried?"

"Max." Jed sighed, opening the station wagon door. "You're a Van Helsing. You should *always* be worried."

Max nodded, not entirely pleased with the answer. "See you back at Helsing House."

"Not if I see you first," replied Jed, clambering into his car as Max climbed into the bus.

The kids of Gallows Hill jeered as he boarded, the last person to take his seat. He walked down the aisle, past a scowling Whedon who did the quick one-two with his fingers, pointing them at his own eyes and then Max. He passed JB, who looked up and smiled. Max was left wondering just how much JB was aware of the monstrous happenings in Gallows Hill and beyond. He plonked himself down next to Syd.

"I didn't see you screaming and blowing kisses at Boyband as he left," he said, relieved that Syd hadn't been drawn into the wave of Archermania that had swept through the female members of the bus. Even Mrs. Loomis had remarked upon what a handsome young man he was.

"I've never been one to follow the crowd," said Syd.

Max smiled.

She leaned close and whispered, "Besides, I said my good-byes to him earlier."

Max didn't smile.

He flinched as he felt a finger flick his earlobe. As he looked back at the seat behind, the freckled, grinning mug of Kenny Boyle loomed between the headrests.

"If it isn't Max *Smellsing*," he said, as Ripley and Shipley laughed hysterically from the rear seat of the bus. "Thought I got a whiff of something nasty."

"Your nose must be too near your ass, Kenny."

Max flinched again as the red-haired imbecile gave him a slap across the top of his head before lurching back to his sycophantic fan club, triumphant.

"Remind me again why we had Kimble erase Boyle's memory?" whispered Max. "The idea of that nugget being kept awake by night terrors for the rest of his livelong life is growing more appealing by the minute."

"Too late, Smellsing." Syd grinned as Mrs. Loomis gunned the bus engine. "The piper has piped; the deed is done."

"Well." Max yawned. "I am *beyond* wiped out. If I ever suggest we go on a nature vacation, you have my permission to punch me. Repeatedly." He rolled his bomber jacket up into a makeshift cushion and propped it against Syd's shoulder. "Mind if I take a nap?"

She let him settle, just as Mrs. Loomis cranked up the stereo and the bus pulled away, bouncing down the street.

"You can try, Max," she muttered, as Bone Creek rolled past beyond the dirty window. "You can try."

EPILOGUE

Marseille, France

The man in black looked hard into the dark liquid, watched it slosh around in swirling circles. As the motion slowed, his face stared back, pale as a ghost, rippling across the ever-changing surface. It could have been blood, that precious, powerful commodity that was the key to everything. His eyes remained fixed upon it as he felt the heat rise and inhaled the heady aroma. Placing both hands around the cup, he lifted it to his lips and took a long, savoring sip of his black coffee.

Brother Guillaume looked up from the drink and glanced about the truck stop café. He was the only customer at this late hour, perched on a stool at the counter. The café owner was banging around in the kitchen, washing pots at the end of a long busy day. A newspaper lay abandoned beside the cash register. Guillaume reached over and dragged it across the counter. He spun it around: *La Provence*, the local rag. It was dated April third. Had he really been traveling that long? The days had turned into weeks, had blurred into months. It had been a long, slow road from Buzau in Romania. Long and eventful.

The man in black let his eyes drift across the paper, skipping from one article to the next. A piece caught his eye: the ongoing police investigation into some deaths at a travelers' camp on the Swiss border, not far from Chamonix. It had been nice to pass by his hometown, albeit fleetingly. Guillaume smiled and pushed the paper away. It was good to be back in France, to see the words of his mother tongue all around him. He looked back at the grimy café interior. The bustling, beautiful heart of Marseille's old town was only ten miles away, yet Guillaume was stuck in a truck stop shack. Still, this was where he was needed. He couldn't leave Him alone, unprotected.

He threw the last of the hot coffee down his throat and let the cup clatter onto the counter. Dropping a couple of Euros into the tip saucer, he slipped out the café door, the bell signaling his departure. He passed an executive Range Rover with blacked-out windows parked outside the entrance. Beyond that, the parking lot was empty. A few big trucks and eighteen-wheelers had taken berths around the stop, their drivers already sleeping in their tiny, cramped cabs. Guillaume's Forzieri wing tips clicked against the tarmac as he marched through the darkness, his handmade Italian shoes one of many stylish indulgences. Suit from Savile Row, overcoat from Burberry, cuff links from Tiffany—fashion had always been a weakness of Guillaume's. Well, one of them, anyway.

He walked out to the edge of the truck parking lot, where there were no floodlights. The truck was exactly where he'd left it. He'd made sure it was utterly nondescript. Forgettable. As he neared the vehicle, he heard footsteps dash up from behind him. He turned just in time to see the butt of a gun strike him in the face. He went down, landing on all fours, as the three figures circled him.

"Your keys, man," said one of them, in a thick Marseille accent. "Hand them over. Now."

"You don't want the keys," said Guillaume, waving his hand, dismissing the request.

"Nice try," said another. "Hand over the keys, or my man here's going to use his gun again. Only this time he'll use it properly, you hear me?"

The thug got up in Guillaume's face. The man in black could smell the cigarettes and alcohol on the youth's breath. So, these three were the ones who had been lying in wait in the Range Rover. Guillaume fished the keys out of his overcoat and held them out, the leader of the trio snatching them from him and whooping.

"What's he got in the back?" asked the third man, hopping as he ran up to the truck, banging the side of it. The metal clanged. Guillaume smiled and dabbed the blood from his mouth.

"Open up. Let's see."

The ringleader fumbled with the keys and soon found

the one he was looking for. The thug with the gun grabbed Guillaume by the scruff of his neck, propelling him toward the rear of the truck.

"You're Italian mob, right?" said the gunman. "I can tell by the shoes. Whatever you think you can ship through Marseille, think again. This is *our* town. And this is where you pay your tax. You understand?"

Guillaume felt the muzzle of the gun at his temple. He nodded. The shutter rolled up at the back of the truck, and the first two thieves went straight in. The gunman kept his grip on Guillaume, standing on his tiptoes to look into the darkened rear of the vehicle. It was a big space, and dark.

"What's in there, man?" he asked.

"Some big box, Gabriel. Help me with this, Thierry."

There was a groaning, creaking noise within the darkness as the two youths struggled to lift the lid of the box. The man in black chuckled.

"What's so funny?"

There was a commotion within the truck, a scuffling, frantic noise. The vehicle shook, as if something struck one of the interior walls. A ripping, rending sound was followed by more thrashing.

"What the hell's going on, man?" asked Gabriel, alarm shrill in his voice as he craned his neck, trying to see through the gloom in the rear of the truck.

Guillaume moved fast.

His right arm looped, catching the thug's gun hand. He locked it in place as his left fist shot up, striking Gabriel's elbow and snapping it in one vicious punch. The young gangster screamed, dropping the firearm, which Guillaume caught in one fluid movement. It was now his turn to grab the gunman by the neck, forcing him back toward the rear of the rocking truck.

"What . . . what are you doing?" sobbed the youth. "You broke my arm!" All the while, he was trying to look behind him as he approached the darkened vehicle exterior.

"In you go," said Guillaume, pressing the muzzle against the thief's forehead.

The young man was crying as he clambered into the back of the truck, rolling onto his broken arm as he did so. He screamed.

"Hush, Gabriel," said the man in black, a finger on his lips as he kept the gun trained on him.

"Thierry? Christophe?" said the youth, turning slowly and squinting into the darkness. His breath steamed before his face, the air cold like a meat locker.

"Gabriel, as in the angel, yes?" said Guillaume, climbing up to take hold of the base of the shutter. He dragged it all the way down. "You may want to start praying, little angel."

The door clanged shut, and the vehicle began to shake once more. Guillaume looked at the handgun without interest before tossing it into the bushes at the side of the parking lot. He brushed himself off and returned to the rear of the vehicle. He checked his watch: one a.m. The ship would be sailing at six. Now was as good a time as any to head down to the freight terminal. He spied the blood dripping from the bottom of the shutter door, running off the metal to trickle down the license plate. Perhaps it was worth hosing the truck down first. He'd have to do that when he dumped the remains of the bodies. No need to attract unwanted attention at customs.

The noises had ceased in the truck. Guillaume picked up the keys where they'd been dropped on the tarmac and made his way to the cab. He settled into his seat, belted up, and gunned the engine. Immediately he was whispering the arcane words of the Unspeakable Oath, the secret language of the Brothers of the Endless Night. The darkness moved behind him, in the back of the truck, drawing nearer, Guillaume's flesh prickling with a chill, deathly cold. His Master was there at his shoulder, whispering through the grilled window that joined cab to rear. It didn't matter how many times he'd heard that voice—each occasion turned the priest's insides into knots.

"Brother Guillaume, do we near the French port?"

"We do, Master. We arrive at long last."

"Goooood," purred Hastur, the King in Yellow. *"Such a swift journey."*

To the Master, perhaps. Guillaume had been His chauffeur for four months, driving Him through the most inhospitable winter conditions Europe could throw at them. Not that the King in Yellow minded, stopping every short distance to feed and build His strength, to gorge on whatever

282 × CURTIS JOBLING

souls His humble servant could find for Him. Those months had dragged for Brother Guillaume, but they were the blinking of an eye to the God of Vampires.

"*Tell me, Brother Guillaume*," said Hastur. "*Will I be able to dine upon this . . . ship?*"

"There is a crew, Master," said Guillaume. "You may dine."

"*Excellent.*"

"I will meet you when you arrive in the New World, Master. All preparations are in place. Each and every eventuality has been covered by the Brotherhood. I will be waiting for you, Master. Fear not."

The laughter that resonated from the rear of the truck caused the entire vehicle to tremble on its chassis. Guillaume thought he might vomit.

"*Fear, child? I know of no such emotion! But Van Helsing will.*" Hastur chuckled. "*Van Helsing will.*"

ACKNOWLEDGMENTS

Thanks, as ever, to my wing-women—Emma Jobling for proofing and Kendra Levin for editing. I'd be lost without you two, and the book's all the better for your input, and that of copyeditors Janet Pascal and Abigail Powers. To Kate Renner and Jake Wyatt: another awesome, iconic Max cover—thanks, guys!

I should also probably tip my hat to the various books, films, and myths I indulged in as a child that instilled a love of monsters in me, specifically cryptids, or misplaced beasts. From *Arthur C. Clarke's Mysterious World* to *The Legend of Boggy Creek*, if it featured a gorilla-suited hominid, I was on it like a boss. So to every sasquatch, sea serpent, and sewer alligator out there—stay hidden and keep firing our imaginations.

Join Max on another adventure in . . .

PROLOGUE

xxx

THE WALDEN WOODS HORROR

The twigs snapped underfoot like skeletal fingers crushed before they could snatch and seize hold. The teenager's steps were hurried, kicking up wind-tossed leaves and weather-beaten branches as she swiftly climbed the slope. She glanced back occasionally, spying through the trees the neighborhood lights, twinkling into life at dusk. Her dorm backed up to the woodland's edge, her bedroom window overlooking the forest, this wild, wonderful world, right at her doorstep. His world.

Her eyes darted, searching the shadows on either side of the trail, checking to see that she was alone. He was a recluse for good reason; the folks who lived in this quiet corner of Lincoln, Massachusetts, were suspicious of strangers. Where better for him to hide away than up here, in the woods? She knew how he felt. She'd never fitted in, always the outsider, even in her own family. It wasn't easy being a Goth when one's younger sisters were preppy, pony-loving princesses. She'd imagined life might get easier once she got to college, but she remained a square peg in a round hole. Yet those misfit days were behind her now. That the two of them had found one another was a miracle. It filled her heart with hope that there was somebody out there for everybody, even the loneliest soul.

Stepping through the forest, the young woman emerged at her destination. She stopped for a moment, taking one last cautious peek back the way she'd come; nobody on her trail, nobody in pursuit. She turned about, toward her lover's home. The old mill loomed out of the darkness, its windows boarded, the stream rushing through its broken waterwheel. It looked sinister at twilight, but that didn't bother her.

It gave her a thrill, truth be told. Spooky things got the pulse racing, the blood pumping; they made her feel alive. A nighttime rendezvous in an abandoned timber mill? This was their secret place. She reached for the long black scarf about her neck, fingers twining through the material to brush her flesh. She would be in his arms again soon enough. She'd waited too long for his kiss.

"Lovely evening for a stroll!"

She looked up, startled to see a figure standing in the tree line at the top of the slope.

"Who . . . who's there?" she asked, squinting through the dim, dusky light. "Come out where I can see you. I'm not scared, you know."

He stepped out of the shadows. He was just a kid, a middle-schooler. His face was hidden within the hoodie cowl that poked out of his bomber jacket's collar. The scuffed leather had seen better days, as had the drainpipe jeans and battered Chuck Taylors. In his right hand, a yo-yo spun lazily up and down; he made it rise and fall with the deft skill of a seasoned slacker. Over his shoulder he carried a khaki satchel, the bag resting against his hip. Finally, the boy tugged the hood back, his grin emerging in the gloom.

"You should be."

MAX HELSING HAD HOPED HIS SMILE MIGHT PROVE disarming to the young woman in black. Unfortunately, accompanied by those words, it just came across as creepy. She gave him a sideways look, reaching a hand into her pocket. Perhaps a can of pepper spray in there? Or something worse? Not that Max was too bothered. Nothing could be as bad as last summer's Colorado job and the Case of the Cold Canyon Killer. The petrifying spitting venom of a dust dragon had turned his baseball cap into a bonnet of stone. That was his favorite hat, he recalled with a pang.

"Sorry," said Max, pocketing his yo-yo and raising his hands peaceably while stepping closer. "I didn't mean to freak you out. I promise, I'm totally harmless."

"That's close enough," she said, backing away in the direction of the ruined mill. "What are you doing here?"

Max made an embarrassed face. "Well, I was kind of hoping I could dissuade you from going in there."

He pointed at the dark building. She stole a glance, as if it might have transformed since the last time she looked.

"Why's that?" Her hand emerged from her pocket, clenching something solid and rectangular. It looked ominously like a gun. Max cringed; okay, so that could possibly rival the dust dragon.

"Haven't you heard? Legend says the old mill's haunted. Well, at least the locals do. They say it's cursed. That terrible things happen to anyone who enters. Some big bad juju went on here in the past."

"So?"

That wasn't the reply Max had hoped for. Usually the "big bad juju" line would put even the most numbskulled norm off. The fact that it hadn't only confirmed what he feared.

"So you're not scared easily? Cool. Maybe we can go in together?"

The woman eyed him suspiciously. "You shouldn't be here."

Max strolled toward the building, its double doors slightly ajar. He peered through the gap, the dark void impenetrable. A host of smells assailed his nostrils, none of which was pleasant. He was getting the musty aroma of mold and damp, a hint of rotten timber, and the sweet scent of decaying flesh; a heady bouquet indeed. This was the place, all right.

"I said you shouldn't be here," repeated the young woman.

Max looked back at her. She was in her late teens, no doubt a student from the university in nearby Waltham. A Goth, too, judging by her dark attire. He might have known; they were so often Goths. He spied the scarf bound around her throat. Hiding something? Before he proceeded any further, he needed to discover just how deeply she'd been glamoured.

"There's no harm in taking a look inside, is there?" he said finally, fishing a flashlight from his bag. "It's abandoned, isn't it?"

"It's not abandoned. Somebody lives here."

"Don't be silly. Nobody would *choose* to live in a wreck like this."

"My boyfriend does."

Max arched an eyebrow as he seized a door and tested it. It groaned, resisting his pull. "Boyfriend? Is he a hermit?"

"He just doesn't get along with people," said the student, her words both cautionary and concerned as she stepped suddenly toward him. "You really should leave."

"It doesn't look like he's in," said Max, before ducking between the doors into the gloom beyond.

While she called after him, he flicked his flashlight switch. A bright beam lanced through the pitch black, the atmosphere alive with a swirling sea of dust particles. Max gagged now, the woodland aromas no longer providing adequate cover for the stench. This was the lair, undoubtedly.

Behind him, the Goth girl struggled through the entrance, cursing the intruding twelve-year-old. Max ignored her objections, instead searching the chamber for signs of life. Or worse . . .

Exposed rafters were vaguely visible in the darkness overhead, the rest of the ceiling shrouded in shadows. A rusted saw was suspended from a wall bracket up high, while log chains hung like iron curtains against the boards. The odd hand tool remained pegged in place, covered in cobwebs after decades of neglect. Long-forgotten offcuts littered the dirty floor, wedges of rotten timber that crawled with spiders and slugs.

"When you say he doesn't get along with people, what do you mean exactly?"

"He doesn't like crowds. Can't say I blame him." She seized Max by the shoulder and spun him around. "I said you shouldn't be here, and I meant it."

Max now recognized the item in her hand, and was shocked to see it leveled at him. "Um . . . you appear to have a Taser pointed at me. What gives?"

"You shouldn't have come here," said the woman, snatching the flashlight from his hand. She glowered, gesturing for him to move deeper into the mill. "I gave you fair warning, but you didn't listen, stupid little jerk."

Max smiled sheepishly. "Seems we might've got off on the wrong foot," he said, attempting to step within reach of her. If he could get in close, there was a chance he could disarm her. Slim, but better than nothing. He'd hate to be at Taser-point when the master of the house finally woke up. The teenager shone the flashlight beam directly into his eyes.

"Back up, and don't try anything stupid. You're going nowhere."

Max quit trying to get close to her, his dazzled eyes now searching the earthen floor of the building. *Where are you?* he wondered, seeking a sign that would reveal the occupant's resting place. His present predicament confirmed the girl's mental state; she was in the monster's thrall, completely under its spell.

"The man-purse," she said. "Throw it over here, now."

Reluctantly, Max unhitched his messenger bag, regretting the fact that he hadn't tooled up before arriving at the mill. There was an old, homemade catapult in the bag, his earliest childhood weapon, which might have come in handy if he'd had the foresight to pack it in his pocket. The canvas satchel that now sailed through the air to land on the floor between them was his box of tricks.

"So this boyfriend of yours," said Max as he backed up into a wall, the tools that adorned it rattling overhead. "He doesn't sound like a people person. Is he a bit of a shut-in? Only comes out at night?"

"He only comes out for *me*. We have something wonderful. Special. Our love's timeless. You wouldn't understand."

"I think I would," Max muttered, eyes still flitting across the floor. Maggots squirmed blindly in the soil, trying to avoid the student's booted feet. Unless Max was very much mistaken, the earth there was stained dark. Dried blood, perhaps? Was she standing over the beast? Maybe it would burst from the ground at any moment, just like in the movies. He shuddered. It was rarely like in the movies.

He looked back to the young woman. A goofy, lovey-dovey expression had appeared on her pale face.

"You got indigestion, or has something tickled you?"

"You'll meet him soon. Then you'll understand the nature of our love. Maybe, right at the end, you'll realize what a fool you were."

"The end? Sounds a bit final."

"My love will be hungry when he wakes. He'll need to be sated." She placed the fist that held the flashlight against her chest, caught up in the Gothic drama, the beam illuminating her face from below as in a Halloween prank. Her scarf hung loose, revealing the punctured skin of her throat.

"He sounds like a real catch. I take it he's the silent type? Broody and moody? I bet he even sparkles . . ."

"He's intense," she said dreamily, before frowning as she caught Max smiling. "Ours is a unique love. He and I shall live forever. He'll make me his bride."

"They all promise that," muttered Max, searching in vain for a way out of the fix, still mindful of the Taser. He glanced up. The one weapon that might prove useful was the saw, and that was a good ten feet above his head, balanced against the wall at his back. How to reach it . . .

There, by his right foot; one of the chopped hunks of

wood. Max slowly began to crouch, extending his hand down his leg, straining his fingers to reach the block.

"Hands where I can see them!" the young woman hissed, causing Max to snap to attention, arms in the air like those of a puppet on a string. She glanced toward the boarded-up windows, Taser still trained on the boy. The light between the planks was pale blue, the sun's warm rays replaced by those of a chill moon. Her voice was a whisper.

"He rises."

Max's eyes were fixed upon the earth, expecting it to crumble and part as the creature rose from its pit. Instead, a shower of descending dust caused him to sneeze. The student raised the flashlight skyward, settling its focus upon the building's resident.

The figure hung upside down from one of the loftiest beams in the mill. Its hairless head was opalescent, pulsating as the flashlight's beam caressed it. Even from a distance, Max spied the twitching blue veins that carried corrupted blood through the monster's foul flesh. Its arms, originally folded about its torso in a frigid embrace, slowly extended from either side of its body, fingers flexing to reveal long yellow nails. Translucent wings connected its arms to its bony hips. Its gnarled feet trembled, crooked knuckles cracking as it prepared to disengage from the beam. It tipped its head, neck craning to look down upon Max and the teenage girl. Coal-black eyes blinked. Its nose was withered away to nothing, dark, slitted nostrils twitching as it sniffed at the air. A puckered mouth yawned open, revealing a maw of jagged teeth dominated by enlarged central incisors, each fully an inch in length.

The girl returned her gaze to Max at the precise moment his sneaker connected with the block at his feet. Those Saturday morning soccer games in elementary school hadn't been a waste of time after all. He went for a controlled pass with the inside of his shoe, surrendering the power of a penalty kick in favor of accuracy. His foot struck the piece of timber sweetly, propelling it at the student's head. There was a resounding *thunk* as the rotten wood hit her temple before she crashed to the floor in a crumpled heap, Taser and flashlight tumbling from her hands. He dived forward, snatching up the stun gun as the monster hit the ground.

Max jumped and turned in time to see the creature advancing on spindly legs. The flashlight rolled back and forth across the earth, its flickering beam flashing wildly around the mill. The creature's pale skin was stretched taut over every bone, granting it the appearance of a staggering cadaver. Its dead, hungry eyes bulged in their sockets, fixed upon the young adventurer, a dark tongue fluttering across those familiar, hideous teeth. Max checked the Taser in his hands.

"Fool," groaned the girl from where she lay slumped at the monster's feet. The abomination came to a halt, chuckling as it ran a grotesque hand affectionately through her dark hair. "You really think that can harm my love?"

"No," said Max, aiming the weapon overhead and firing it up the wall.

The two Taser probes whistled through the air, wires trailing, catching themselves on the old saw blade. In a fluid motion, the young monster hunter yanked the stun gun back like a fish on a line. The rusted tool tore free from its bracket, spinning dangerously through the air toward him. Max made a silent prayer as his hand shot out to catch it, hoping to maintain a full complement of fingers. He snatched it by the handle and brought it around in a scything arc toward the creature.

"But this should do the trick!"

The monster's black eyes went wide as the rusty saw blade tore a jagged path through its neck. The decapitated head tumbled, landing neatly in the girl's lap as she let loose a startled shriek. It was as if a switch had flipped in her head—with the glamour lifted, the effect of the spell ceased instantly. No longer the beast's consort, she was just a confused young woman cradling a hideous, stinking, slack-jawed skull.

"Vampires," said Max Helsing, with a shake of his head. He tossed the bloodied saw aside as the monster's corpse collapsed into the dirt. "Terrible boyfriend material."